# AWAKENING
## the lost woman

# Also by Anna Buckley

CAPTURING the lost woman
(book two of the lost woman trilogy)


FINDING the lost woman
(book three of the lost woman trilogy)

# AWAKENING

## the lost woman

(book one of the lost woman trilogy)

**august**
XXIX

# Anna Buckley

Published by august XXIX, an imprint of August Twentynine pty. ltd.
mail@august29.com.au

First published 2014.

1-1-1.01

National Library of Australia Cataloguing-in-Publication entry: (paperback)

Author: Buckley, Anna, author.

Title: Awakening the lost woman / Anna Buckley.

ISBN: 978 0 9924781 0 0 (paperback)

Series: Buckley, Anna. Lost woman ; no. 1.

Subjects: Women—Fiction, Erotic stories.

Dewey Number: A823.4

Dear Reader,

I hope you enjoy this book as much as I loved writing and researching it.

My life has been spent working in design but now I have a new interest – story telling.

Home is Melbourne Australia. I love to cook, eat and drink wine with friends. I like to travel but am equally happy exploring the streets of inner city Melbourne, where the book is largely set.

I dedicate this book to my husband who lovingly encouraged and supported me while I wrote.

Thank you to Mary Lou for being an unfaltering listener, Karlene for being the first reader, and most importantly to Karyn, my editor and life long friend, whose wise words and vision kept me on track.

Lastly I must warn you this book may not suit those who find graphic descriptions of sex and strong language offensive. But for the rest of you, happy reading,


Anna Buckley
mail@annabuckley.com


P.S.
to keep abreast of what I am doing, and for stories behind the books, visit my blog at annabuckley.com

# Contents

# Part 1

## The Funeral

Another tedious dinner. Tuning in and out of boring conversations, pretending to care.

Sitting beside me, his arm brushes my shoulder, the charge of an illicit touch. He talks to the stranger next to him, his voice, the sound of seduction. Beneath my dress he strokes my leg.

My body hungry.

'Follow me,' he whispers discretely.

A few moments, waiting, so as not to arouse suspicion.

Into the corridor, opening doors, peering into empty rooms, thrilled with the chase, searching. My longing grows.

Where could he be? I am frantic.

An open window. I lean forward, he grabs me from behind, slipping his hand into my dress, roughly teasing out a breast, his knee forcing my legs apart. My back arches, lower, I spread my legs wider, needing to feel him deeper, to fuck me to oblivion.


Where am I?

I feel my damp warm sex, then reach across an empty bed. No ruffled sheet warmed by a lover's body, no smell of sweat, of lust.

I am in my bed, alone, starved of affection, craving to be touched, to be desired, desperate for intimacy.

What would it be like to be made love to, to love passionately back? Who would want me?

A dream that taunts, inappropriately, this morning. My mind and body so disconnected.

A rude awakening to the day.


My eyes focus. I'm in our bedroom. A large oppressive dark green room, acanthus leaf wallpaper, elaborate ceiling rose, laboured carved fireplace. A mantle adorned with ostentatious ornamentation. His things, layers of his family's history.

Windows covered in rich velvet drapes blocking out the light. Is it sunny this morning?

Heavy furniture, an overstuffed chair, his pants neatly folded, still draped across the back. He liked things to be tidy, orderly.

A rococo gilt framed portrait of his ancestor. Her beady eyes and weak chinned ugliness scowling at me every morning.

'Fuck off and leave me alone, I've had enough,' I tell her.

Layer upon layer of stultifying decoration threatening to suffocate me. I never really belonged here. Why had I chosen to stay?


I drag myself out of bed, into the shower, aware of the need to wash away the heat of my arousal and begin this dreadful day.

The drab outfits hang in my dressing room.

What do I wear to my husband's funeral?

In front of me a range of uninspired garments, the type of shapeless clothing favoured by women of a certain age. A wardrobe of blandness, things to disappear in. Nothing to wear.

When do women begin to disappear? I had become one of those nobodies, careworn and numb. Of course it would be black. A straight skirt, a tailored shirt, opaque tights and low heeled pumps. I pull my longish, mousey brown hair into a low bun and spray the few stray wisps. No make-up, it would smudge, just a few eye drops to take away the red. Crying for what had been lost. The mirror, something usually avoided, reflects the face of someone I no longer recognise.

Why have I let this happen?

Who am I?

I am thirty nine, not old enough to be dressing like this and not old enough to be a widow.

From my second storey window I could see the silver Mercedes bearing the name of the funeral parlour, pulling up to the portico. The flower beds brilliant with colour, the vast lawns mowed, the hedges clipped, ancient trees towering over this well kept garden, orderly, managed. He liked it this way.

'Kate, the car is here, are you ready?'

'Yes, mum,' replied my precious, quiet, eighteen year old daughter.

'Come on darling, let's go and face this together,' I said, hugging her.

The drive was a quick one through Melbourne's leafy eastern suburbs. Stately Victorian mansions and Federation villas lining the roads. Hedges and gates keeping the undesirables out.

Throughout these suburbs were the prestigious private schools their children attended. Where appropriate alliances could be made, occasionally letting the new money in when the inheritances were diminishing.

We drove slowly through the grand entrance, along a tree lined drive, past manicured lawns surrounding the imposing old bluestone buildings. We stopped in front of the cathedral like chapel at his school. The car park was full.

They were all there inside the church. His old mates, their fathers, the wives, his clients, shocked and numb that Paul Brown, was dead at forty. Fate had played the same trick on Paul's father, Charles, who had also suffered a heart attack just thirteen years ago. They must have wondered at the injustice of so much loss for one family.

We made the long march down the aisle. I could feel Kate recoiling from such a public procession and reached for her hand. Eventually we arrived at the front pew and sat down next to Paul's mother, Margot Brown.

Margot knew how to dress for such an occasion. A smart black Chanel suit, pearls, elegant heels, a discreet amount of make-up on her regal face. Her hair fashionably grey, stylishly back combed. Cruella, Lucretia, they were the secret names I had given her.

She looked over at me coldly and I imagined she must be thinking that soon we could end this charade. But for now, we must play the roles of the stoic, but contained widow and grieving mother.

The priest presided over a solemn ceremony. His friends eulogised about their boyhood antics. Talking more about themselves than Paul, unable to find interesting things to say about this dull, quiet, man. No reminiscing with final favourite anthems, just standard hymns and when the Lord was finally My Shepherd, it was over.

Kate and I walked into the grand reception room of our Victorian mansion where they had gathered for the wake. All was ready. I would be on show, judged.

The house was immaculate, perfectly prepared. The heavy antique furniture had been polished. Flowers from the garden had been appropriately arranged.

The kitchen was ready with porcelain cups and saucers waiting to be filled by the women from Kate's school who had volunteered to help. Women whom I had met when I joined their committees, thinking I'd made a connection, when really I was just good at getting the hard work done.

'Chris, you're amazing, I don't know how you do it.'

I had spent most of yesterday cooking. Food was my sanctuary, what else was there to do?

Spread before me was a perfectly laid table groaning with plates of tiny sausage rolls, tartlets, dainty crustless sandwiches, small cakes. Finger food that was easily popped into the mouth, very neat, no mess, food they understood.

This is what I knew, working hard to be accepted, trying to be one of them, seeking their approval.


I headed into the crowd of people, ready to be subjected to their schadenfreude platitudes. A discrete squeeze, an insincere hug from the blonde bobbed women who knew their roles.

'Chris, we're so sorry.'

'You know we're here for you.'

'Please let us know if there is anything we can do to help.'

The 'we' referring to the non committal, collective group, not the 'I' of true care and affection. The men not knowing where to look, offering emotionless one word condolences. Words to a woman who wasn't one of them, none of them real friends.

Numb to it all, I wished to escape, felt like running, screaming outside, to get away from this stifling pretence. If only they knew what was really going on inside my head.

The day dragged on, then, after a polite amount of time had passed, the rooms began to empty. I wanted them to go so Kate and I could have the place to ourselves, retreat into quietness.

But it was not to be, the doorbell was ringing.

Who could be here this late? I wished everybody would just piss off and leave us alone.

The door burst open, startling the stragglers.

'Cara mia, Christina, darling.'

With arms outstretched racing towards me, she was here, my beautiful friend Lola. The crying, the intensity of her hug, the outpouring of grief. At last someone who understood.

'I came on the first flight available. I couldn't stand knowing you were alone. Are you ok? Where's Katie?'

A whirlwind of words and emotion.

'Thank God you're here,' I whispered.

When Lola finally let go I could see she had been followed by her family. They too embraced me and for the first time in days I felt safe, protected, loved. They went straight to the kitchen.

I had farewelled most of the mourners. Only Paul's closest friends remained, his best mate and business partner, Justin Darcy, his wife

Fiona and Justin's twin brother Adam. Justin and Fiona hovered obsequiously around Margot, the dowager. They knew it was their duty to remain, to wait till she was ready to be driven home. I longed for them to leave and wished they didn't feel a compunction to stay. Hopefully the arrival of the Italians would give them the excuse they needed to depart.

I was surprised to see Adam. He was rarely in Australia, spending most of his time overseas supervising his global empire. He had become a kind of Machiavellian hero amongst his old school friends. They envied him. For the seemingly endless supply of money and the rich man's toys it bought. For the beautiful women, parading on his arm, (and crudely fantasised about by these men in their sad wet dreams). But above all of this they admired him for his intuitive brilliance in business. I would overhear them talking about his latest acquisition. Of his ability to buy struggling companies, stripping their assets, selling them off and profiteering spectacularly. He had a fierce reputation. Mining companies, undervalued, purchased before the China boom, now worth billions. Even the G.F.C. had been kind to him, cheap property, cheap money, a massive buying spree in Europe and America had seen his wealth increase enormously. Cashed up and ready to invest in whatever the next boom would be, the money men watched his every move. People were in awe of his Midas touch. They were surprised he had achieved so much. His wealth far exceeded that of his father. Had he become his father? It took a certain kind of sociopath to be that good. It didn't surprise me at all.

Adam was ageing well. His tall, lean body exuded arrogance and power. His hair was peppered with grey, adding to his dark, brooding, good looks. He dressed immaculately, beautifully cut charcoal suit, dark shirt, tie, handmade shoes,  black rimmed glasses framing his chiselled face. He seemed cold and distant, he hadn't changed.


Adam looked down at Christina acknowledging her loss with a melancholic shaking of the head, unable to find the appropriate words. He knew the circumstances of their meeting and why she looked drawn, tired, but it was more than that. He barely recognised her. He hadn't seen her since the wedding eighteen years ago.

He remembered the time he'd dropped by her place in Brunswick. At how aroused he had been by her beauty and sense of style, by her. Where was that feisty young woman now? She looked lost, a vacant shell. What was the real story? He wanted to stay, to talk to her, alone.

'I'm sorry for your loss. Paul was a good man. Please let me know if I can help in any way. Here's my number.'


I was surprised by what seemed to be a sincere gesture of condolence. I couldn't imagine what would provoke me to ever ask for his help. He was one of them and I couldn't wait for them all to be out of my life.

He took my hand and shook it, then unexpectedly embraced me, his firm body and strong arms holding me for what seemed a bit too long.

'I mean it, Christina, don't hesitate to call,' he whispered, then left.


Justin was looking more than his forty years. Stooped, overweight frame, thinning hair, with the pasty complexion of a man who spent too much time indoors, conjuring up his next deal. Fiona looked harsh, hardened.

What would happen now that Paul was dead? With no son to take over, who would inherit the company? Would I be forced to do business with this ugly man and his scheming, undermining wife?

Adam had started the final exodus.

'Christina, I'm exhausted. Justin take me home,' Margot commanded and with that they were granted permission to depart.

I stood at the door being offered perfunctory kisses and then, thank God, they were gone. At last I could let my guard down, relax.


Desperate for a drink and a chance to talk to Lola, I returned to the kitchen. The mess had been cleared by the ladies. In its place a very different scene awaited. At the stove was Lola's papa, Massimo, stirring a pot of something that smelt delicious. Sitting around the broad marble bench, Gabriella, Lola's exquisitely beautiful mama, was snuggling Kate into her warm embrace. Raphael, her older brother, with an opened bottle of wine and a glass in his outstretched hand, offered me a drink.

'Thanks, you've got no idea how much I need this.'

They knew.

'Darling, I bet you've not eaten all day. Massimo has made a ragu. Here, eat,' said Gabriella, gesturing to her husband to hand out bowls filled with the food she knew I craved.

Not much was said. It felt so good just having this family around me. It was what I needed right now. The fridge was filled with the food they had lovingly prepared. They told me they would come over to check on us.

And when they could see the food and wine was doing its job, they understood it was time to leave.

We said our goodbyes at the car and I walked alone back down the driveway.

I was about to shut the front door when Raphael came running back.

'Christina.'

'What Raphael?' I replied, tired but curious.

He held my shoulders, looked me in the eye then kissed me, deeply, sexually charged.

He whispered huskily in my ear, 'I will help you, set you free.'

And with that he disappeared.

# The Realisation

I woke, my head cloudy, not so much with the events of the last few days, but trying to make sense of what Raphael had said. What had provoked this behaviour, so soon after the death of my husband?

Had Raphael Finestra propositioned me? He seemed to be inferring he would guide me, set me free. Had he seen through the charade? Or had I dreamt the whole scene? What was more perplexing was that Raphael had kissed me. He'd always seemed sexually ambiguous. Not gay, not straight, but filled with a lustiness that affected both men and women. He was ridiculously handsome, desired by many, yet strangely he'd chosen to kiss me.

Confused, I got up and walked towards the mirror. How could anyone behave that way, think that way about the woman whose reflection I saw? What's more, he was a man with whom I had only ever felt a brotherly connection, one I thought was reciprocated.

A steaming hot shower brought me back to reality. Raphael had exposed my fraudulence, the lie that my life had become. For the first time in eighteen years I was ready to confront the truth.

Eighteen years ago I had made a decision that I thought was right. Paul had loved me and I thought I could change, grow to love him. But it was not to be. In the end ours became a partnership where we seemed to care so little about each other, neither of us could be bothered leaving.

His death had released me.


I thought that managing the family home and pouring all my love upon our beautiful daughter, Kate, would be enough. Being the wife of Paul Brown had become a full time job. I was always being observed. They were all waiting, his mother, his friends, waiting for me to falter. So I played the role of 'good wife' to perfection, just to prove them wrong. I would not fail.

A quiet, subservient mouse who followed their rules strictly. This is who I'd become.

I had not always been this person.

# Dress ups

I grew up on an isolated small farm near a town called Greenhope, in the dry mallee scrub of western Victoria. My dad, Edward Maxwell, inherited the farm from his father and had returned to the land after failing to make it in the city. My mum Mary, met Dad at a dance in Melbourne and was so charmed that she followed him back.

Dad worked hard to keep the farm going from one year to the next, drought and debt always hovering in the background. Men like my father were burdened by their obligation to keep the family farm, not wanting to be the son who lost the battle. No money, no ponies, no rolling green fields, no rural idyll.

It was a hard, monotonous life. Dad didn't seem to fit, he was tall, gentle, quite handsome and had delicate 'piano playing' hands.

My birth, twelve years after they married, ended the longing of a couple who desired a child more than anything they knew. I was much adored. The love that engulfed me came from two people who felt they had been given a precious gift.

They were much older and had little in common with the other parents of the town. They cherished each other's company and lived very privately in their own quiet little world.

As a child I had a happy life. My fondest memory was of playing dress ups. My mother had been a fifties beauty. With a somewhat misguided notion of what country life was, she brought to the farm a large trunk filled with the ball gowns from her past. I would dress up, Dad would put on records, play the piano and we would all dance and sing along to old musicals.

'What do you want to be when you grow up, Christina?' they would ask.

'I want to go to the big city where I can make beautiful dresses for all the pretty ladies,' I replied.


For a brief moment we thought our luck had changed. A new road was to be built, bypassing Greenhope. The official said the road would pass right through the middle of our farm. The government would buy our land and my father could make a gracious exit from the life that had tied him down for so long.

A letter arrived.

They had made a 'mistake' they happily informed us. The road would pass in front of the house and we would be free to keep farming.

The road was noisy. They paid for metal shutters to cover the windows, to help block the unrelenting hum of traffic, the house became dark. We felt even more trapped.

I was curious about the city, fantasising about the land of Oz, where all that traffic was heading.


Nobody bothered to take the exit to Greenhope anymore. The next town, Smithfield, was only twenty miles away. The road went through its broad main street. That's where all the travellers stopped and the town thrived.

In Greenhope the shops closed, businesses failed and the people became more insular. No place for a dreamer like me.

The road and its destination became even more tantalising.

# The Student

I quite liked school when I first started, excited to explore a world beyond the farm. Greenhope Area School was in the middle of town and tried to meet the needs of all the kids in the surrounding districts. But this was a near impossible task. It was a small school with limited resources and a narrow range of subjects.

Lots of kids started, very few finished. The first exodus was at the end of year six when the wealthier families sent their kids to boarding school. This is when childhood friendships began to disintegrate, where we started to understand our status in life. At age fifteen another group would leave, the children of middle class families who had saved for the better education a private school could offer. At the same time the young apprentices and the sons of poorer farmers would begin their working lives and some girls began their unfortunate gamble with motherhood. By the end of year eleven, the 'nice' girls took up the much prized jobs in town, pharmacy assistant, doctor's receptionist, vet nurse. They were considered very suitable marriage material. Mothers of the town's good sons kept watch. By year twelve only a few kids remained. Girls who wanted to become teachers, clever boys who may join the armed services, become policemen or at a push enter university. And then there were people like me, the misfits, who no one really understood, let alone knew how to categorise. Where did I belong? I didn't play sport, didn't share their taste in music, dressed differently, was smart and longed to leave. I dreamed of the unbounded possibilities a life away from Greenhope might offer.

Every year new teachers would be sent to our school, an undesired country location. Time spent in Greenhope was considered penance. No one wanted to be posted here. To compensate, the teachers who came earned points and were rewarded by getting their choice of school when they returned to the city.

The yearly parade of new recruits was good for quiet speculation. Who would last, who would need to be transferred and who of the younger female primary school teachers might find a suitable husband? These educated women were valued. They were welcomed into the homes of the establishment families, the government wage came in handy during the lean years.

Some of the younger teachers would give me tantalising glimpses of the outside world, their dress, their travel stories, the food they ate and the music they played. Few would mix, they kept to themselves, most would return to Melbourne on the weekends. Inevitably I would feel cheated by their condescension, their patronising attitudes and their eventual desertion. None of the interesting ones stayed.

Occasionally we would be sent young student teachers who naively thought they could change the world, or Greenhope at least.

During the middle of year eleven, Ryan, or Mr. Summerland arrived. He was twenty two years old and in his final year at teachers' college. I was sixteen. He had long blond curly hair, wore an earring and a leather band around his wrist. He liked to surf and loved photography. The girls fell in love with him and the boys called him 'gay'. That was the term they gave to any male who dared to be different.

Mr Summerland came up with the idea of a photography camp to the seaside town of Lorne, directly south on the Great Ocean Road. He knew not many of us got the chance to go to the beach. And that is how a few parents, teachers and a ragtag group of students found themselves, hundreds of miles from home, camping in the caravan park on the foreshore of this picturesque seaside town.

The students cared little about photography. The camp was the perfect opportunity to get away from the heat and dust, to hang out with their mates. Holiday romances blossomed amongst the horny teenagers. Teachers and parents went to the pub most nights. Only Mr Summerland and I seemed to be interested in photographing or drawing the beach.

He knew the area well. His family had been coming to their holiday house here for years. When he could not tempt the other kids away from the trampolines, the shops, the main street action, we went to his favourite surfing spot alone. The remaining adults happy to be left to sleep off their hangovers. School trips were very different back then.

The beach was magnificent, not a soul in sight, clear bright blue winter light, damp salty air, the roar of the sea, my senses alive. I took my sketch pad, drew shells, found smooth rocks polished by the sea and picked up small pieces of driftwood that caught my eye. Occasionally I glanced up as he surfed. After some time he came back and sat next to me, looking at the drawings, seeing through my eyes what I'd discovered on the beach.

'Why do you get into that freezing cold water? You hardly catch any waves, I don't get it.'

He paused and looked out toward the ocean before he answered.

'I feel free when I'm out there. I like floating on my board, it gives me time to think. And when I do catch the perfect wave, I like the adrenalin rush. It makes me feel alive. It's quite addictive, you should try it.'

'Nah, I wouldn't like it. It's not my thing. I'd be hopeless. And anyway, we hardly ever get to the beach.'

'Fair enough. Well, what is it then that Christina Maxwell does to escape? What do you dream about? What makes you feel alive?'

I was too embarrassed to say. I had learnt not to talk about my ambitions beyond school. A conversation about such a fanciful idea would often result in unrelenting teasing. I had become conditioned to keep my mouth shut, only my parents supported my dream.

'Nothing really,' was my unconvincing reply.

'Bullshit! I don't believe you. You're not like the others. I've seen you spending your time in the art room, the library, armed with loads of books. What do you really do during that time?'

My heart skipped a beat. He'd said 'bullshit', he'd used a word not spoken between a teacher and a student. The informality felt strange and kind of exhilarating.

'Draw, sketch ideas. I want to go to Melbourne, to study clothes,' I clumsily babbled.

'Fashion design. How come?' he continued, smiling.

'Don't know, maybe it's a bit like what you said about surfing. I feel free when I design dresses, imagine a world where they might be worn. '

'Not many of the girls at school even think about a life beyond the town. What makes you so different?'

'My mother, she was from Melbourne originally. She has a trunk full of amazing clothes. We used them as dress ups when I was a kid. I liked how it made me feel when I transformed myself with her beautiful gowns. I don't really fit in here.'

He didn't laugh or mock me, but just sat there with an understanding look on his face. I liked that I'd found someone to talk to. I trusted him.

The next day it rained. Predator and Full Metal Jacket were screening at the Lorne cinema. This was a real treat for the kids of Greenhope. Our town had no movie theatre, not even a video store, so the offer of an afternoon at the movies was eagerly anticipated. Mr Summerland sensed my lack of enthusiasm and volunteered to take me to the local gallery.

Unfortunately it was closed and would not reopen until the summer crowds returned in December.

'Doesn't matter. We could go to my place, I think you'll be interested.'

It was a house like nothing I'd ever seen before. Two huge glass, concrete and steel rectangular boxes set into the cliff, suspended high above the ocean. Inside the main wing a wall of glass gave uninterrupted views of the vast stormy sky and the raging ocean below. It was a space filled with light and life. Even the furniture was unfamiliar, designed to fit the uncluttered space, minimalist, functional. So modern, so strange, more like a gallery than a house.

'Wow!' was all I could say.

It was so unlike the old, dark cottage I shared with my parents.

'It's pretty good, isn't it? My father's an architect. He built it in 1961 when he'd just graduated. His parents owned the land.'

I couldn't believe it was twenty six years old, nothing about it seemed old fashioned or dated.

It was truly majestic, sitting so defiantly in this wild landscape, letting in the light, the views, yet protecting us from the tempestuous weather outside.

'It's this house as much as the surf that keeps me coming back here,' he said proudly.

I could perfectly understand why.

The walls were adorned with photographs and art, all originals. I had no words to describe such luxury.

We spent a wonderful afternoon drawing, looking through art books, talking about the future.  He told me about his favourite streets, galleries and restaurants in Melbourne. Painted pictures in my mind of what I could expect. The lure of the city became even more tantalising. Mr Summerland had made it real. I was glad he had come to our town to tell me what my future could be like, that it was just around the corner and all I had to do was wait.


The end of the year was looming. The careers teacher felt obliged to take us to Melbourne and reluctantly the students followed. Most couldn't see the point. Their lives had already been planned. They didn't like Melbourne and couldn't understand why anyone would want to live there. Cities were foreign hostile places.

Mr Summerland's time at the school had finished. He would accompany us on the trip, but remain in Melbourne to finish his final exams. I dreaded the thought of what my final weeks at school would be like without him. Who would I talk to when he was gone? Who would understand?

We stayed in the gym of an inner city school, it was a swap. We felt like country hicks. The Melbourne kids were supposedly getting a taste of country life. I shuddered to think of the entertainment the locals would provide.

Mr Summerland took a group of us to Melbourne Uni. They made us wear our school uniform, I felt like a stupid kid, we all felt out of place.

The cafeteria was even more confounding, food I'd never eaten, people who looked different. He sensed our discomfort and ordered for us. People he knew came and chatted, he introduced us as his students and they dismissed us with casual disregard.

'Who was that woman with the piercings? Was she your girlfriend?' I asked, slightly wary of the cool woman who had just left us. I had become very possessive of our relationship.

'No, no, that's Zoe, we share a house,' and instantly my premature jealousy abated.

A day of visiting universities saw my fellow students restless with boredom, so the teachers decided a trip to the state sports centre the following day would be more entertaining. I groaned at the thought.

Mr Summerland volunteered to take a group to the National Gallery on Saint Kilda Road and once again I was the only participant. I could barely contain my enthusiasm.

He introduced me to paintings I'd only seen in books and took me to galleries filled with modern masters. My first Picasso, Kandinsky, I almost cried at the madness of what I saw and loved.

'I can't believe you have this reaction. Most people just don't get this type of art. They find it too confronting. They fear things they don't understand. It's usually the McCubbins and the turn of the century chocolate box shit that gets people worked up,' he said conspiratorially.

I liked his irreverence.

We had walked through all the galleries, seen the exhibitions and had no plans for the afternoon.

'I've got an idea.'

'What?'

'Do you want to see my old college, it's just down the road.'

'Sure,' and I followed him to the campus just a few hundred metres away.

He had studied at the Victorian School of Art.

'So why did you become a teacher?'

'My parents. They thought I needed something safer, knew how hard it would be to make a living as a painter. I'm doing my diploma now, training to be a teacher. I'm doing it at Melbourne Uni and live just around the corner in Carlton.'

'So why aren't you doing it here?'

'They don't offer it, it's just for art.'

'You mean that's all they do here? Art for the sheer hell of it, no strings attached?'

'Yeah, that's about it in a nutshell. Want to have a look around?'

He took me into the studios and I marvelled at such a place. Just as we were about to leave he bumped into one of his old lecturers, who asked if we'd like to join a drawing class. Without hesitation I nodded enthusiastically.

We positioned ourselves in front of two spare easels. I was wondering what the subject matter might be, when a tall man dressed in a robe walked into the room. The lecturer introduced the model and to my complete and utter horror the man let the robe drop. It was a life drawing class. I didn't know where to look. I had never seen a naked man before.

'You ok?' he said, sensing my extreme discomfort.

'Jesus Mr Summerland! What the hell am I supposed to do? Where do I start?'

'Ryan, call me Ryan, we're not in school now. Just watch what I do,' he said, smiling at my reaction.

I watched as Ryan started faintly sketching, mapping out a rough outline of the body, then slowly filling in the detail. I tried to follow suit, but couldn't concentrate. I kept being drawn to the model's penis, glancing then quickly looking away, embarrassed by my voyeurism. I decided to focus on the torso, the well defined muscles on the model's chest, but still my eyes wandered past his navel, to the dark curls of pubic hair, the soft penis dangling languidly from between his thighs.

I had lead such a sheltered life, no boyfriends, no clandestine sexual encounters, not even porn. The male body just wasn't something I had any experience of.

After a twenty minute pose, the model left and we walked around looking at each other's drawings. Ryan talked to me about what worked and I came back to my easel feeling a little more confident.

The next model was a woman and this brought some relief to the anxiety I had experienced. Ryan started drawing and once again I was unsure of where to start.

He moved to my blank sheet of paper and sketched a line roughly marking out the angle of the woman's body as she lay stretched languorously on the mattress on the floor.

He took my hand and directed the charcoal I was holding.

'Look how the parts of the body are connected in relationship to that central line I've just drawn.'

He was right and suddenly what he was saying made sense. I flipped over the pages on the easel and drew with more confidence, thrilled with each new sketch, eagerly awaiting the next pose.

I was brought quickly back to reality when the lecturer thanked the model and asked us to finish up. I didn't want this day to end.

I rolled up the paper and wondered what on earth the rest of the kids from school would make of the drawings, of what I had just seen and felt.

It was well after five and I was starving. We walked back into the city. Ryan grabbed my hand as we negotiated the trams and the traffic on busy Bourke Street. He didn't let go until we reached the restaurant. Valentino looked far too posh for me. Men in suits and well dressed women, trophy wives, were seated in this elegant Italian restaurant. Again everyone looked so different, their clothing defining them. I wished I could've worn something more appropriate. Jeans seemed far too casual in this sophisticated place. At least they hadn't made us wear our uniform today and perhaps I could get away with not looking like the awkward school kid I knew I really was.  Ryan ordered us a simple pasta dish and a glass of red wine. I felt so grown up. We chatted about the day and after a second glass of wine I confessed that I'd never seen a naked man before. He smiled and told me there always had to be a first time and he was sure it wouldn't be the last.

 I imagined what it would be like to have a boyfriend. Someone more sophisticated than the stupid immature boys at school and fantasised about the possibilities of what might happen when I eventually moved to Melbourne.

After Valentino we sat at the bar of a fifties looking diner, Pietro's, and I sipped my first espresso, nothing like the instant coffee I was accustomed to. Then a little way up the street to a book store called The Artists Library, where I marvelled at the gorgeous art books.

It was getting late, we were supposed to meet the rest of the group back at the school library. Dinner at McDonalds had been planned. What a come down. I felt melancholic, knowing that our amazing day was coming to an end.

'Why the sad face?'

'Going back to them, to Greenhope. It's alright for you. You teachers think it's ok to fill our heads with all these possibilities, but you get to stay here in Melbourne. It fucks with my head. The thought of being stuck back there for another year makes me want to end it right away,' I pleaded somewhat melodramatically.

He understood.

'Let me make a call.'

He walked up the road to the nearest phone booth, talking to a teacher perhaps, gesticulating, pleading my case? He returned smiling.

'No problems, told them I was taking you to a gallery, wouldn't finish till late. They said as long as I got you back before nine it would be ok.'

I clapped my hands with glee, thrilled that I wouldn't have to explain today to my fellow classmates, who by now would be eagerly awaiting their Big Macs.

'So what's the gallery?'

'Big new place near the university. A lecturer of mine is curating a new show of installation art. It opens tonight, thought you might be interested.'

'What's installation art?' I quizzed, completely unfamiliar with the term.

'Well, it's hard to describe. I guess you'd say it's not painting or sculpture, not art in the traditional sense. You'll understand when we get there.'

The high school where we were staying was near the university. I had spent the day in jeans and was pretty sure that a gallery opening required a change of dress. He waited outside as I changed.

'You look pretty,' he said.

I emerged, looking like Princess Diana, dressed more appropriately, or so I thought, for a gallery opening. I had made the dress myself, nothing like this could be bought in Greenhope.

'Actually, would you mind if we called past my place? I need to drop some of this stuff off,' he said, pointing to the roll of drawings he'd been carrying around all evening.

My heart skipped a beat. He was taking me home. The tram on Swanston Street took us just past Melbourne university. We got off and walked the few streets till we reached his house. It was a two storey terrace, paint peeling, weeds in the garden, threadbare couch out the front. Inside it was just as run down. The rooms were filled with clutter, shabby furniture, posters on the walls. It smelt of dirty dishes and stale cigarette smoke. We went to the kitchen and he handed me a beer.

'Welcome to my share house,' he said rather apologetically.

We drank and slowly a procession of scruffy, radical and not so friendly tenants walked through. I felt like the uncool, overdressed country girl that I was. I didn't know what to say to them, and sensing my discomfort, Ryan took me to his room. It was quite spartan, a mattress on the floor, a desk, a wardrobe with a missing door and books stacked on the floor. Sanctuary.

He gestured to the bed, the only place to sit, loaded a pipe and put on some music.

'Here, want some?'

I took the device and copied what he was doing. I had never smoked weed before. He hit me on the back as I coughed away the burning, suffocating smoke.

'You ok?'

'Yeah, I'll be fine,' I said, barely audible, between gasps.

'You haven't smoked before?' he said, half questioning, half pleading.

'There's a lot of things I've never done before,' I replied, smiling as the drug quickly began to take effect.

I don't know how long we sat there, silently, before there was a knock at the door.

It was Zoe, the girl from the cafeteria.

'Hey, what's up?'

'Just having a smoke before we go out. Want some?' said Ryan handing her the pipe.

'Thanks, where ya goin'?' she said, before inhaling deeply.

'Show at the uni gallery, wanna come?'

'Sure, what time?'

'About now,' he said, looking at his watch.

After a short walk we were back at the now familiar university campus and entering a big white gallery. The room was crowded with people, mostly wearing black, talking seriously amongst themselves, nodding knowingly at the art. I looked ridiculous in my preppy frock. My head was spinning from the effects of the drugs and I reached out and took Ryan's arm to steady myself.

'You ok?'

'Yeah, I'm fine, just a bit wobbly,' I said, inexplicably wanting to giggle, eyeing off the food being offered and thinking how hungry I'd become.

Zoe grinned.

We moved to the centre of the room where I got a closer look at what was being exhibited. I couldn't quite understand the meaning of the massive pile of coloured pencils randomly scattered like pick-up sticks on a white rubber mat. On the walls a video projection kept repeating a scene of a woman, naked, sitting then standing, up and down, up and down. Then in the centre of the room, a man, with a stuffed cat on his head, rode a bicycle around screaming out, 'THIS IS NOT ART'. The people clapped politely as he wheeled past.

They talked about the irony of the work.

Ryan was comfortable here. He understood their language and obviously thought I was now ok as he disengaged and walked towards the beautiful woman holding court in the centre of the room. He kissed her passionately. They were more than friends. I felt abandoned.

'What the fuck is this all about?' I mumbled, as I watched the incomprehensible circus unfold before me.

Never before in my entire life had I felt so out of place. I was bewildered, confused and suddenly very aware that this was not where I belonged. My schoolgirl fantasy had just been shattered. What kind of an idiot had I been? The drugs, the alcohol and the noisy, crowded room saw me run out the door like a frightened mouse, barely reaching the garden bed before I threw up.

'It's ok, don't cry, it's all been a bit too much,' said Zoe, rubbing my back, trying to comfort me.

I felt so embarrassed.

What a naive fool I was. Ryan Summerland was just my teacher, he already had a girlfriend. He took me to places to show me what was out there and all I could see now was they were not for me. I felt like a fraud, pretending all these years I was better than the people I grew up with, only to discover that the world I'd dreamt about was more foreign than I could comprehend. It didn't include simple country girls like me with no understanding of art or clothes or food or people.

Zoe took me back to the school in her beaten up old car.

'This your first big trip to the city?'

'Pretty much.'

'Where are you from?'

'Greenhope.'

'Past Smithfield?'

'Yeah, you been there?'

'Driven past, lived further away near the border.'

'Wish I was back there now. I hate being here!' I mumbled petulantly.

'What do you want to do?'

'Don't really know. Thought I wanted to move to Melbourne.'

'Listen Christina, Melbourne is a really amazing place. It's still yours to find. You seem like a nice kid. Don't let what happened tonight fuck with your dreams.'

# The Last Year

But it had. The kids I'd gone to Melbourne with started to bully me, tease me about the things I had chosen to do when we were in the city. They couldn't understand the attraction of the life I'd been given the briefest glimpse into. Of the trip to the big city, they remembered sport, stadiums, junk food and taking the piss out of all that was strange, foreign. Most of them were glad to return home to what they knew. I remembered something different.

When they started to call me the freak, I decided I'd had enough, didn't want to be different. My dreams of a life beyond Greenhope had been tainted. I was broken and decided it would be easier if I fitted in.

So the remainder of my time at high school was a blur of mindless conformity. I went to the football games, played the perfect debutante, got drunk on Saturday nights, gossiped with all the scary girls and shut up about the things that had always driven me.

My parents saw the changes, too. I rejected their oddities. Couldn't stand it when Dad tried to cheer me up with his old records. Didn't want Mum to remind me of the beautiful gowns in the dress up box.

What I did find was boys, whose graceless affections I tried to convince myself could be love. Or perhaps it was just that they had cars. I could escape with them to out of the way places where awkward gropings inevitably led to a clumsy excuse for sex. My virginity was lost somewhere along those back roads. In fact I didn't really know who could claim that prize because it was so ill defined. Sex was an obligation to the girls of my tribe. It was not magical. My amateur partners didn't know how to give me pleasure and quite frankly all I cared about was that they didn't come inside me. I wasn't stupid enough to desire the baby that made the lives of some girls complete.

And when the year was over my ambiguity continued. It had become too easy to do nothing.

'Why not just give it a try?' my mother begged, when we received word that I'd been accepted to study fashion design at the Melbourne Institute of Technology.

She couldn't understand why I had changed. All she knew was that life was too short to live with regret.

# Dreams Reawakened

It didn't take much. That first week at uni reignited my passion. We were shown videos of couture shows, documentaries about fashion icons. We got to touch and feel the clothes created by past students and were taken to the costume department of the Sate Theatre Company. For the first time in my life I got to be with people who unquestionably loved the same things as me. I was no longer different and said a silent thank you to my beautiful mother, who so wisely knew where I really belonged.

And as much as my parents loved me, would miss me terribly, they were happy I had escaped. Perhaps to find the life they had failed to discover. I felt ashamed of the terrible way I had treated them during that last year.

It scared me to think how close I'd come to a life of teen pregnancy, unfulfilled dreams and shattered hopes that so many of my peers quietly accepted.

In the city I felt alive. I could be me.

My parents had little money, so I quickly found a part time job with a clothing manufacturer.

'JD Dresses' was situated in a large, old, red brick building in an inner northern suburb. Brunswick was a blue collar, new immigrant place with warehouses, factories and workers cottages. It was considered a bit rough and it would take a few more years before it would become a Brooklyn-like hipster hangout.

I started working in the design department. When I say design, it was more just reworking the same old skirts, pants and shirts. A slight change in cut, colour or pattern. Our market was middle aged women.

Sometimes I looked at the garments and wondered who wore these bland clothes? Had they given up on themselves, their looks? Had fashion become an irrelevance?

Ok, I couldn't stand seeing mothers dressing like their teenage daughters, but had wondered why some women were content to disappear into this world of drab nothingness.

I wanted to dress people in clothes that worked, transformed them, made them feel great, confident.

Good design was not about fashion, it was about making things just right for the individual.

Most of my colleagues had been with the company for a long time. They were 'job for life', 'work your way up' type of people. All but one.

Lola Finestra was a vivacious young woman working in the marketing department. We clicked immediately.

Her father owned a large furniture store catering to the tastes of the Greek and Italian immigrants. He was well known for the TV ads he fronted.

I couldn't understand why she was working here. She explained that although her father wanted her and her brother to take over the business, he wanted them both to get some real life experience first.

We shared our dreams with the idealism of youth. She wanted to take her family business in a new direction and I wanted to design the perfect dress.

We vowed to never settle for mediocrity. To always be there for each other.

We joked about how we would change the world and what wicked old women we would become.

# Sydney Road Flat

I had been boarding with a woman who took in country students. We didn't 'click'. I hated the long commute to and from the dreary outer suburbs, so it was with some relief that I found the one room flat above an old shop front near JD. It was cheap, near work and just a short tram ride to uni.

The entrance was right on busy Sydney Road. The small plaque set into the decorative facade said 1880. After climbing the narrow staircase I opened the door onto one large room. An ornate plaster rose decorated the ten foot ceiling. Two tall, grand, windows, facing the street, lit the room. Against the back wall was a rudimentary kitchen with an old enamel gas stove and a sink cupboard. A small bathroom was tucked into the corner, barely hidden by a rickety old screen. Despite it being filthy with nicotine stained walls and pigeon shit piled below the windows, I could see what it could become. I couldn't wait to move in and make it mine.

I knew it would take a bit to make it liveable, but I wasn't afraid of hard work. The Easter break was coming up and the maintenance guy from JD said I could borrow any of his tools.

Dad would have none of it, he and Mum were coming. He loaded the ute with all he thought was needed and they turned up ready to help with the transformation.

'Bit of work to do here, love,' said Dad, master of the obvious.

By Sunday afternoon, dirty and exhausted, we were finally finished, it was beautiful.

The late afternoon sun shone through the windows illuminating the newly painted white space. After ripping up the filthy carpet, I had discovered pristine floorboards that only needed mopping and some polish. After removing years of grease, the stove was restored to its original pale green enamel. The sink gleamed from a thorough scouring and the white kitchen cupboard was relined with fresh paper. In the bathroom the toilet and claw foot bath just needed a scrub and again the same beautiful boards were exposed when I pulled up the peeling linoleum.

From gigantic, raw cotton painter's drop sheets, Mum had made curtains to cover the windows. Dad attached a rail to the ceiling and hung a second curtain to replace the bathroom screen. I could imagine pulling back these giant ten foot drapes, luxuriating in the decadence of taking a bath in this big sun filled white room.

We were all starving and I wanted them to try some of the food I'd discovered on this vibrant street.

Sydney Road was home to a vast array of middle eastern shops. The street was teeming with life. Burqua clad women buying exotic looking food, men sitting outside cafes smoking hookahs, families gathering to share delicious flatbreads at the Lebanese bakeries. Even grandfathers carried boxes of sweet pastries, gift wrapped to bring to the homes of friends.

What would my parents be feeling in this alien environment?

I took them into my favourite bakery and waited in the queue to buy the manoushe, Lebanese pizza.

'Tina, darling, lovely to see you. What can I get you today?'

'Hi Fatima, this is my mum and dad, Mary and Edward. They've never had manoushe before, could you put together a selection for them to try?'

'Welcome, you here to help fix up that old place across the road?' she enquired as she worked.

'Nice to meet you, Fatima. Yes, we've come down from the country, Greenhope,' Dad replied awkwardly.

'Your daughter, she works very hard, you must be proud? I always look after her when she comes in. Take a seat. I'll bring the pizza when they're ready.'

We sat down. They didn't know where to look, how to be in this strange, exotic place.

'I think you will like this,' said Fatima, as plate after plate of the strange pastries arrived. Tentatively Dad took a bite, he smiled.

'Not bad,' he said and pleased at his approval, we hungrily wolfed down the delicious meal.

We all relaxed, the food having worked it's magic.


Mum and Dad needed to get back to the farm and so after long hugs, I said goodbye.

'Miss you darling, love you,' called Mum, waving out the window.

I returned to my beautiful flat, tumbled onto the mattress on the floor and slept soundly.


Over the next few weeks I added some furniture. The first piece was the most important, a large, old cutting table found in the junk pile at work. I sanded the timber top and varnished its wooden surface. This huge industrial dinosaur fitted perfectly in the room. It became the permanent home to my sewing machine. The frame underneath stored the bolts of cloth I'd collected, sturdy old faux crocodile suitcases held just about everything else. Hard rubbish scavenging provided more pieces of other people's discarded furniture. I wasn't a hoarder and took just enough. I didn't want to clutter my big elegant room.

Like my table, JD was also a dinosaur, still cutting, making and distributing its clothing from the Brunswick factory. I wondered how much longer they would survive? China's sleeping dragon was beginning to rouse.

# Meeting Paul

My life for the next three years was pretty much work and study. Any spare time was spent designing and making my own creations. And when I gave myself the odd weekend off, I usually caught the train home to see Mum and Dad.

Like a lot of country students, I felt divided, one person, two places. A loyalty to my parents,  to help them on the farm and a desire to create a new life in the city. Few friends in the city, few friends at home.

Sometimes this could be a very lonely life.


The design department realised many of their students, whilst almost gifted in their creativity, had absolutely no business skills. Towards the end of the final term, our lecturers paired us up with students from the Accounting faculty. The aim was to see if both groups could learn something from each other and come up with a business plan to suit the young designers.

Paul Brown was paired with me.

At first it was really uncomfortable. We were worlds apart. He found it incomprehensible that someone could imagine earning a living from something that in his eyes was a frivolous hobby. I couldn't understand how he could commit to a life working with columns of numbers, to such unmitigated tediousness and boredom.

We had almost nothing in common.

He was raised in the affluent suburb of Toorak. His family owned a small but trusted accountancy firm and had been rewarded handsomely for looking after the wealth of some of the city's richest citizens. Worlds away from my family's life of struggle. Paul attended an elite private boarding school and had a close network of friends around him. I went to a country high school where only a few of us completed year twelve and moved to a city full of strangers. He lived at home where everything was provided, including a generous allowance. I rented a room above an old shop and worked part time, giving me just enough money to survive.

There seemed to be one thing that we shared. We were both only children whose parents wanted the very best for their one precious child. This was our bond.

Funnily enough, I quite enjoyed our business project and learnt some fundamental principles that could one day help me set up my own fashion label. As for Paul, I think he just found me amusing with my eccentric clothes and opinions, an escape from his overbearing friends and regimented life.

When we weren't working on the project, we would often meet up with his mates at the uni bar, and although they were not my friends, it was good to get out and socialise. I had become a bit of a recluse.

Justin and Adam Darcy were twins. Justin was Paul's best friend. They had been at the same school and did everything together, including studying accounting. Unlike Paul, Justin was an untrustworthy schemer, who had the charm of a used car salesman. He seemed to have a bullying control over Paul and when he'd almost pushed the boundaries too far, redeemed himself with a 'just joking maaate!', followed by an overly demonstrative punch and bear hug.

Adam Darcy was studying architecture. He was tall, handsome, with dark hair and looked nothing like his unattractive brother. It was hard to believe they were twins.

Adam was insufferably arrogant. So at odds with Paul's bland, but nice boy persona and Justin's thuggishness. His contemptuous self importance infuriated me.

Justin and Adam were always together. Adam was smarter than these people, often even contradicted their opinions. I wondered why he bothered to hang around them? Perhaps I just didn't understand that tribal mentality.

Their father, Graham Darcy, was the property developer responsible for tearing down much of the beautiful, gold rush era architecture of inner city Melbourne. He replaced it with ugly multi-storey office blocks, built cheaply and quickly, making him extremely rich.

Paul used to say that Adam was studying architecture just to piss Graham off. Graham thought architects were a nuisance, whose artsy fartsy intellectualism got in the way of a profitable job. He preferred the services of draftsmen and engineers who did what he wanted, efficiently, cheaply and without question.

Graham's was the kind of new money the old money welcomed, simply because there was so much of it. Graham enjoyed showing off his wealth. Marquee at the polo, mansion in Brighton, fast cars with personalised plates, holiday homes in exotic locations and an ego big enough to require a new wife every few years. He could always be seen with some bimbo on his arm in the social pages of the city's down market tabloid. These unions all eventually produced children, guaranteeing the mothers some financial security.

The lone female of Paul's tribe, Fiona Snelling, was a slim, fair haired woman who confidently wore the uniform of the upper class. Faded jeans, crisp white shirt with a pale cashmere cardigan, flat leather designer shoes and pearl earrings. Fiona was studying Arts, a course favoured by these women who were just killing time, waiting for their trust funds to mature and their carefully matched husbands to arrive.

Her family were western districts farmers whose property was the size of a small European nation. My farm life of hard work and struggle knew no comparison to Fiona's world of horses, grand houses, boarding school and overseas holidays.

Fiona was a nasty piece of work. Barely acknowledging me with a thin lipped smile, just tolerating the person she most certainly considered beneath her. She knew her place, allowing the boys to continue their boarding school antics like a sexy, dominant, house mother with a whip.

Like all good dynastic pairings, Fiona, the prized bitch, had chosen the top dog, Justin. When they married, she would get the money and he would get the status.


'Pauly, mate, you and the little lady gonna save the world by floating her frock company on the stock exchange?' said Justin.

Paul responded with a one fingered salute, smirk on his face.

I found these experiences quite intimidating, with their 'in' jokes and blokey camaraderie. A subtle kind of bullying that let me know I wasn't one of them.

I often wondered why I kept going back for more? Did I want to prove that I was just as good as them?

Maybe it was my own vanity, wanting to be able to tell the people back home that I had lots of friends in this fabulous new life. Perhaps it was simply that I envied what they had. I wanted them to like me, so that

I could feel what it was like to be part of their close knit gang, to be included.

In truth, I really didn't know where I fitted. I think I just wanted to belong.

That said, I was no retiring wallflower and often challenged their 'born to rule' opinions.

Naively, I thought I could win them over with my clever banter and witty repartee and have them embrace me as their new chum. I wasn't going to let their smart assed, brattish behaviours defeat me.

On one particular night I sat down right next to Adam, determined to get him to speak to me, to break his haughty silence. I wanted to push his buttons, get a reaction. Or just maybe I was attracted to this controlled, elusive man?

I had become sick of them talking about themselves, of a life so clearly mapped out ahead of them, of a world that so obviously excluded me.

There was an election coming up and they thought the conservative government would win. They needed to be back in control. I couldn't stand their self righteousness and tried to join in, maybe ruffle their feathers a bit.

'So do you really think much will change with a new government? Do you think politicians have that much control? The things that affect change are subtle. Politicians react to a situation, they don't create the mood. Are you aware of the subversive power we designers have? We can affect the mood, the environment, the comfort of the people around us. Fuck the politicians, imagine how we could change the world if we designers were in control,' I said, tongue in cheek.

He looked up, surprised I was sitting next to him and almost offended that I had spoken.

'Designers? Change the world? You can't be serious? Fashion is about frivolity, discarded from one year to the next. St Vinnie's is overflowing with that special dress, so special it's dumped as soon as some new bit of superfluous crap comes along,' he spat.

For a brief moment I was taken aback by his vicious retort, then I felt my blood boil and snapped back.

'Bullshit! When women began wearing miniskirts in the sixties, they were saying much more about their place, their sexuality, their freedom. It wasn't just about what they'd chosen to wear that day.'

'That's just one example. Are you seriously telling me every chick in a short skirt had a political agenda? I think they were just advertising for a husband or a fuck. No intention of changing the world. You're reading far too much into it,' he paused for a moment before continuing his attack.

'When a building is erected, it's there for all to see, to be commented on. It must be enduring, stand the test of time. I can't believe you're so naive to think that a dress has the same power as a building!' he said leaning closer, moving into my space, emphasising his contempt.

'Yeah, like the shitty high rises in Collingwood or the office blocks your father builds, the ones that feed your trust funds. Suicide towers, ugly enough to want to kill yourself, high enough to ensure death. Yeah, you're right, they do affect change. Not just for the poor bastards who live in them, but also for the innocent bystander who has to live with the blight on the landscape. No choice about that fucking building, good or not. No wonder you architects are so bloody arrogant, you need to be to protect yourselves from the shit flung at you by the people who feel pissed off at what you impose!' I snapped back.

Adam was surprised at her fiery attack, furious she had connected him with his father. No caring, sharing hippie bullshit from the girl Paul had been hanging around. She was typical of the 'alternative' crowd. Studying some useless subject and by the look of what she was wearing, designing shit that no one in their right mind would ever wear.

Who the fuck did she think she was?

'More beer anyone?' said Paul, trying to change the subject.

They were subtle in their taunting and, as usual, the night ended with them drunkenly reminiscing about school days. Talking about the things they did together on weekends, reaffirming their place in this exclusive little club. Pushing me further away.

I grabbed my beer, drank till the glass was empty and walked out.

That night I came to my senses. This would be the last time I would bother to go to the bar with them.


Paul and I were still working on our project together. Away from his friends, he was a really nice guy. I was aware he liked me, but he wasn't my type. Did I even know what 'my type' was? He seemed disappointed that I no longer went out with him to the bar after lectures, so I told him of my feelings toward his friends. How I thought they didn't like me intruding, how uncomfortable I felt around them.

He dismissed my insecurities and told me I had nothing to worry about.

'Give 'em time Chris, they'll come round.'

I didn't have the heart to tell him I hoped I would never see any of them again.

It was getting close to exam time. I had an hour to kill between lectures and decided to head to the bar. Not because I needed a drink at 2 pm, but because the space was almost empty. Much quieter than the library full of students desperately cramming for exams. I sat in one of the booths that lined the edge of the room, took out my notebook and began to write. My peace was interrupted by the familiar sound of Justin Darcy's voice.

'Too early for a beer, ladies?' I heard him say.

I slouched into the seat, hoping they couldn't see me.

The 'ladies' were his usual entourage. I could hear Fiona and Adam. I knew Paul was away that day, he had an appointment with his father. I remembered being shocked that a son would have to book a time to catch up with his father.

Justin returned with the drinks.

'Here's to our last day of freedom before exams!'

They clinked glasses and a temporary silence ensued as they downed the beer.

'Where's Paul?' asked Fiona.

'Probably still sniffing around that little bitch, pretending to do some sort of assignment together,' sneered Justin.

'Thank fucking Christ he doesn't bring her to the bar anymore. Wanted to tell her to shut the fuck up after that rant she gave,' he added.

'Gave you a fair serve, Adam. Who the fuck does she think she is?' said Fiona.

'Pauly should watch out. Bet she wouldn't mind getting a slice of that action. He'd better make sure he keeps his dick in check or there'll be trouble. Girls like her are just looking for an opportunity to freeload on nice guys like him. She'd be pregnant, with her hand out for cash in no time,' snorted Justin.

'Don't think I'd let her get away with it. If she screws with any of you boys I'd let her know just how misguided she was. She's not one of us and never will be. She'd regret it for the rest of her life. I'd make her pay,' snapped Fiona.

'Trouble is, Paul's so desperate I don't think he can see it. It's been ages since he's had a good fuck,' said Justin.

They all laughed. It was Adam who spoke next.

'I think you've got it all wrong. You don't give Paul enough credit. Just let him have some fun. He needs something to play with before his old man locks him into that tenth floor office.'

'Anyway, people like her despise people like us. They're just not self starters. They have some morally superior, left wing ideal that money is distasteful. She'll never make a living out of her bullshit dress thing. She'll probably pick up some job in the arts bureaucracy, sucking off the taxpayers tit, living with some cuckolded dickhead she meets at the community garden,' he said, finishing his rant.

I was seething. Fiona and Justin's comments were so predictable. What hurt most was what Adam had said. To be so easily dismissed, with contemptuous disregard for all that mattered to me. As if I was some completely disposable commodity, something for them to play with on their rise to the top. Adam Darcy was the most despicable of them all.

# Christina finds the Italians

Finally it was over, my exams were done, portfolio submitted and now I just had to wait for my results. I wasn't really worried, my lecturers had quietly informed me that my designs were some of the best they had seen in a long while. In the meantime, with rent to find, bills to pay, I headed straight into full time work at JD. It would be great to see more of Lola.

Lola could not believe I had no celebrations planned to mark the end of my student days, so we agreed to meet at my flat after work. She would bring something to drink, maybe we would go out somewhere.

'God Christina, I love coming to your place. I envy you. I wish I had the freedom to live on my own, but it's not the Italian way! My father would have a fit if he knew what really went on when I came to stay!'

I smiled. She often told her parents she was staying with me. What she didn't tell them was that I wasn't even in Melbourne when she came to visit. I let her use my place when I was back home in Greenhope. I was her alibi when she dated the inappropriate men who would never meet with her father's approval. On those weekends spent back at home, I helped my parents, was the good daughter. And Lola spent some weekends at my flat being the very opposite.

She was carrying a bottle, so I grabbed two glasses while she popped the cork.

'Mmm, what's this?' I asked, after taking a sip of the sparkling wine.

'Prosecco, my favourite. Everybody thinks we Italians drink only that disgustingly sweet Spumante,' she replied, taking another sip.

'But this, I think, can be as good as any French champagne.'

'I don't know the first thing about wine. How did you learn?'

'Ah, at the family table. We've always had wine. Dad would give us small sips when we were little. As we got older we were allowed a bit more and Dad would describe the wine, telling us why it suited the food we were eating. You should come to our home this Sunday, meet my parents, experience one of our Sunday feasts.'

I hadn't planned on doing anything this weekend. I wasn't going home and now that the pressure of uni was over, I had a bit more free time.

'Love to, can I bring anything?'

'No, nothing, in fact I'm sure you'll be leaving with enough food to fill your fridge. My mother wonders how you survive on your own, no mama to cook for you.'

We talked for a while, ate some manoush and finished the bottle, too tired to go out.

'See you at twelve Sunday. I'll pick you up,' said Lola, as she headed out the door.

It was a perfect late spring morning. What to wear? I looked in the mirror, young punk, spiky hair streaked with a garish purple. An image quite at odds with the elegant, sixties inspired dresses I was designing. This was not an appropriate look for a lunch with a traditional Italian family and it was not the look for a young woman wanting to be taken seriously by the fashion world. I ran to the pharmacy down the road and bought a bottle of hair dye, dark chocolate brown, my natural colour. Tamed, I would wear it up, a French twist.

I looked through the rack of dresses I had been working on, having recently been inspired by some of the outfits a young Jackie Kennedy had worn. I chose a little white linen shift, no sleeves, fitted, cut above the knee, a subtle black trim around the hem and sleeves. Teamed with a pair of espadrilles it would look very La Dolce Vita, perfect for an Italian lunch.

Beep! Beep! Lola was here, I ran down the stairs.

'Mamma mia! What the hell? Where is Christina?' she exclaimed, as she circled me on the pavement.

'You look amazing!'

We jumped in her car, a stylish aqua blue Carmen Ghia. She glanced at me with a big grin as we drove off. I smiled back, happy she approved of the transformation. Feeling very confident with my new self.

I had preconceived ideas about what I would see. I imagined a grand faux palazzo in one of Melbourne's newer outlying suburbs, but was surprised when we headed in the direction of Kew, a short drive out of the city, up Studley Park Road. We arrived at a large block hidden by a tall hedge. As we drove through the gate I was struck by what I saw in front of me. An understated elegant sixties modernist villa, white sandstone walls, massive glass windows. Set magnificently into a steep cliff, overlooking the Yarra River below. This was so not what I had expected.

We pulled up and were greeted by Lola's parents.

'Mama, Papa, this is Christina.'

'Buon giorno, Christina, I'm Massimo, welcome to our home.'

I recognised him from the ads, a big man, short grey hair, generous girth, warm smiling face, two kisses, one on each cheek.

'This is my wife, Gabriella.'

'Christina, lovely to finally meet you. Please, come in.'

I saw a small, exotic, gypsy like woman. Not at all what I expected. She was wearing a loose fitting, asymmetrical charcoal top over leggings, bare feet, a single strand of large orange beads her only adornment.

I couldn't help myself, 'I love what you're wearing.'

'Asa Saito, a young Japanese designer I saw in Sydney,' she took my hand and led me inside.

We entered a large, gallery like room, white walls hung with modern paintings. A lurid Howard Arkley picture of a clichéd suburban house stood out immediately. Lola had told me Gabriella owned a gallery on Gertrude Street. She must have been one of the first people to recognise the value of some of Australia's emerging modern painters. I looked at the walls and was amazed by her foresight. All these painters were now represented in Australia's top galleries.

We walked through the glass doors to a stone terrace. Verdant gardens rolled down the river valley, gum trees framed the view. This sanctuary only ten minutes from the city.

We sat under a vine twisted pergola. A large wooden table was laid simply and stylishly with cutlery, big white plates, crisp linen napkins, water and wine glasses, set for five. Lola looked at me and the empty space.

'My brother,' she cocked an eyebrow and with a wry grin said, 'He's always late.'

Massimo offered me some olives, plump, salty morsels, slick with oil, and a glass of red wine.

'Some Aglianico, a wine native to my region, Basilicata, in Southern Italy.'

'I've never heard of Basilicata,' I replied politely.

'It was a very poor area. Carlo Levi wrote about it in his book, 'Christ Stopped at Eboli'. I left to escape the poverty.'

'We built this house using a white sandstone that reminded Massimo of the cave houses of his home town of Matera,' said Gabriella.

'True, my darling, but that is where the comparison ends. This,' he gestured expansively at the house, 'is the work of my beautiful wife. You know she studied architecture in Milano, before she ran away to Australia and seduced a brute like me,' he said proudly.

'Please, Massimo, enough, I never practised,' she responded coyly.

'The land was cheap when we bought it. Market gardens used to grow on the flats near the river, close to the city, planted long before trucks and refrigeration. The land became too small to cope with the demands of a growing, hungry city. No one thought it would be possible to tame the bush and build on the steep river slopes. And it goes without saying that no insurer would cover housing built on the floodplains. People thought we were mad building on these cliffs. Only my wife saw how beautiful a house in this setting could be. And now we have the last laugh. Everyone wants to live here. Those real estate agents in the High Street are always trying to convince me to sell up and subdivide the land. But I tell them, this land is for my grandchildren, there is enough room for all my family to live here.'

I could well imagine Massimo being king of his own little realm. I wondered what Lola thought?

We were interrupted.

'Ciao, ciao, Mama, Papa, Lola'

'Raphael, come sit down next to my friend, Christina.'

'Ah, Christina. At last we meet.'

Raphael reached for my hand, pulling me gently to my feet and kissed me twice, one cheek then the next.

'Is this your secret friend? Why haven't we met before?'

'Because I was keeping her away from you, my mischievous big brother!' she replied playfully.

Christina could see why. Raphael was gorgeous, dark olive skin, mystifyingly blue eyes and tousled light brown hair. He wore a loose white shirt, jeans hanging just so from his hips. This man could be trouble or.... fun?

'You work with my sister, what do you do?'

'I'm in the design department.'

'And this dress, is it one of yours?'

'Yes, actually'

He stepped back, still holding my hand, slowly looking me up and down, 'Bellisima'

'Raphael, enough, sit down, we must eat!' said Gabriella, as they brought out platters of delicious antipasti.

Pickled artichoke, eggplant, red, green and yellow capsicum. Salad of arugula, mesclun and radicchio. Cured meats, salamis, porchetta and a rustic loaf of bread.

'This food is delicious,' I said, as more and more was handed to me.

'Thank you, Christina, I do most of it myself. I am still just a peasant at heart. It is my hobby, what I do to relax. I hope to do more when the children take over the business.'

'When do you think that might be?' I asked.

'Very soon. My son, Raphael goes to Italy next week to oversee the buying and production of a new range of contemporary furniture. Lola will follow as it nears completion. You see, Christina, my old customers are a dying breed. We have big plans to open a new emporio next to my wife's gallery on Gertrude street. The young people of today don't want that fussy old furniture and my children don't want to sell it,' he said wistfully.

We finished the day with fruit from his trees and like Lola said, I returned home, generously laden with gifts from their garden and pantry. I was slightly saddened knowing my friend would soon be leaving and that my connection to this day, this family, was only fleeting.

# Help from a Friend

By the time I returned to work after Christmas, Lola had gone.

Not that I had spent much time with her anyway. My range of little La Dolce Vita dresses had been selling well to a number of small boutiques in Carlton and Fitzroy and this growing business was taking up all my spare time. My bosses at JD had allowed me to have them made at work and had charged very little. By late January this arrangement was no longer simply about the machinists making a few extra dresses at the end of the day. I knew I had to commit to larger orders and wondered how I would fund this development. Paul would know.

'Hi Paul, Christina here, how you going?'

'Chris, how the hell are you? Made your first million yet?' he responded enthusiastically.

'Ha ha, if only. Actually, I need some advice. Do you think we could get together?'

We had arranged to meet at the Hot Cat on Brunswick street. I was running a bit late and arrived to find Paul wearing a business suit, sitting at a table in this retro fifties cafe. Surrounded by black clad, bohemian types he looked uncomfortable.

'Chris Maxwell,' he stood, smiling.

'Paul, sorry I'm late. Have you ordered? Cappuccino from memory,' I asked.

'And the usual espresso for you, Christina?' asked the barista.

'Thanks, Tony, that'd be great,' I replied.

That was the Chris he remembered.

He'd missed that confident enthusiasm. He loved how her presence had always thrown his mates. She didn't play their games, flaunted the rules, was free to be herself.

He noticed she had changed. Gone was the crazy hair and clothes, she looked different, older, more grown up. She was more beautiful.

She sat down next to him, his body responding immediately to the electricity created when their legs accidentally touched.

'So Paul, look at you in your suit. You look like a proper accountant,' she grinned.

Is this how she saw him? Did she have any idea of how she made him feel?

She spent the next few minutes telling him of her plans to expand her design business, but he found it hard to concentrate. He knew if he offered to help, he would at least get to see her again.

Time flew, he needed to get back to work. Being the boss's son didn't let him off the hook. He had more to prove, not only to his father, but also to his colleagues. He needed to show he would be a worthy heir.

As he walked back to the office, Paul wondered whether there was any real future in her plan, but he admired her guts at wanting to give it a go. Their lives were so different. She had the liberty to explore a whole new world without constraint. His life was mapped out before him. There was no risk, but also no freedom.

He knew if he lent her the start-up money, she would have to continue to see him. It would be a kind of informal partnership and honestly she probably didn't need that much. They agreed to meet the following night at her place to work on a business plan. She lived in a dilapidated old room, in a part of town he would not normally have ventured into. She seemed to thrive on its edgy eclecticism. He didn't know if he could live this life of uncertainty, but he loved living vicariously through someone who did. He couldn't wait to spend more time with her.

Paul was great. I loved the way he took the emotion out of my schemes and was able to give me clear, considered advice. He made me realise I would need to have some money to take the next step. To commit and pay for bigger production runs, to become a real client of JDs. Also to have the stock more readily available to meet the ever increasing demand of the shops.

Paul said he would lend me the money, I thanked him for his generous offer and told him I'd like some time to think about it. I'd always been so independent and was slightly reluctant to mix our friendship with business.

We worked solidly every night for a week, papers spread out on the cutting bench, ordering manoush from Fatima.

'Well, Paul, I think we should call it a night. My brain is fried and anyway we need to look fresh tomorrow.'

'Oh yeah, I'd completely forgotten. Your mum and dad coming?'

'They wouldn't miss it for anything, I'm the first to get a degree in our family. They're a bit nervous. They've never attended a graduation before. What about yours?'

'Yeah, they'll be there, but under sufferance. Dad doesn't understand why he has to sit through the whole long drawn out process. The Chancellor is a friend of his and I'm sure he thinks a private dinner would be more in order.'

We both said goodbye. Paul leant forward and clumsily kissed my head.

I slept soundly knowing a clearer picture of my future was beginning to form.


They were late, it was not like Mum and Dad, they always liked to have plenty of time up their sleeve. I'd expected them to be here at least an hour ago. The radio was on, there were reports of a collision, train crash. A creeping fear started to come over me. There was a knock at the door. It was the police, they had bad news. My parents were dead. The world I had known came crashing down around me. Lola was in Italy. I called Paul, I had no one else.

When someone you love dies, you join a club you don't want to be a member of. You observe everyone around you, walking the street, laughing with friends, going about their business, all so normal. But your life has been turned upside down. You feel anger at their indifference. You retreat under a shroud of sorrow.

I'd always prided myself in my ability to be independent. Now I had no choice. I felt angry at my abandonment. As if I'd never been someone's child. Lost without the two beautiful people I loved more than anyone in the world. Who would I call to share in good news? The kind of thing only a parent cared about. Who would care? The word orphan was such a simple word used to describe such a complex state of being. For the first time in my life I was deeply and truly alone. Nothing seemed to fill the black hole of despair.

Paul was a comfort. He came back home to help with the funeral, talked to the bank, the accountant, the lawyer. Sorted out all the stuff I didn't know how to handle and supported me when the bank put the farm up for sale. He did what he was good at. I said my final farewell to Greenhope.

He called frequently, suggested I get out of bed, said work would be good and generally was a dear friend and decent human being. Some days the grief and loneliness was all consuming. The future blurred, what was the point in eating, working, living?

Paul had worried he would lose his beautiful, bright, effervescent friend. He kept ringing, visiting, trying to coax her out of the suffocating grief.

It had been a month and it hit me. This was it, I was alone, they weren't coming back. It shook me. I had to do something. Paul had been calling often, but tonight when he rang and suggested we go out, just dinner, get out of the house, I said 'Yes'. It was a start.

# Dinner

There is something magical about the process of transformation that we as women are allowed to make.

I decided to see this as a ritual toward healing.

First I flung open the curtains and windows and allowed the light and warm summer air to come flooding back into my apartment. I had neglected the space and cleaned it till it shone. I filled the bath, pulled back the drapes and submerged myself in the water.

I chose a little black dress, cut just above the knee, modest, except for the low back. A little make-up, some eye liner, mascara and dark red lips. My hair, now a long dark brown bob, dried and combed straight. Black, high heeled strappy sandals and the transformation was complete. A sense of control, the first step toward a new normality.

Adam was heading over to Brunswick to look at some property, a big old factory, ripe for redevelopment. He felt that this part of Melbourne was undervalued. His mate, Paul, had mentioned he was going to Sydney Road to meet up with a friend. Adam volunteered to drive him. They arrived and Paul knocked on the door. She opened it.

'Chris, do you remember my friend, Adam?' asked Paul, as they both entered the room.

'Adam, how are you?' she said coldly.

He barely recognised her. She was exquisite. He looked around the room, all white, simply but tastefully furnished. A Harcourt chaise, a Featherston Contour chair, a low slung Scandinavian sideboard, two

Clement Meadmore stools. How did she know about this furniture? Where had that naive, wild girl gone? Who had she become? Who was this sophisticated woman standing before him?

As she turned to walk into the room, he saw the cut of the backless dress, the power of understatement, he felt his cock stir.

He wanted to stay, be with her, find out more, but knowing Paul had already made a claim, he politely refused the invitation to join them.


I was surprised to see Adam standing at my door. I should have known that reconnecting with Paul would inevitably mean bumping into some of his obnoxious friends. Strangely I was a little thrown by Adam's presence. He seemed different. Something about his whole demeanour had changed. He looked more sophisticated, much less standoffish. Maybe it was because he was not with his brother? I was almost disappointed when he said he would not be joining us. He seemed to have no interest in staying.


Paul had booked a restaurant on Lygon Street, a large, bustling, Italian eatery. It was the type favoured by busloads of tourists wanting the 'authentic' Italian experience. Checked tablecloths, Chianti bottles and modern day frescoes of old Italy adorned the walls. We were shown to our table by a heavily accented, handsome, Italian maitre d'. The clichés continued. Dean Martin was singing 'That's Amore' and Paul bought me a rose from the rather sad woman wandering past the tables. He was trying hard, but it was not the sophisticated Valentino on Bourke Street, where I had almost succumbed to a different type of charm just a few years ago.

I felt overdressed, but was rewarded by the attention I received from the flirtatious Italian waiters.

The food, the noise, the people were just what I needed and despite my initial reservations, the night was fun. The wine helped.


We couldn't find a cab, so we stumbled across to Sydney Road and caught a tram.

We had both had too much to drink.

'Come on, Pauly, you can crash at my place. You'll never get a taxi from here,' I said drunkenly.

Paul took the sofa and mumbled 'goodnight'. During the night I was aware of him tossing and turning. The chaise was not a comfortable place to sleep. He was keeping me awake.

' Jesus Paul, why don't you just get in to my bed and go to sleep? I've got work tomorrow,' I called out to him.

He got into bed and tentatively tried to spoon me. The closeness was kind of comforting and I was not really surprised when, after some time, I felt his erection pressing against me. I had been turned on by the attention of the waiters and had shamelessly flirted with them all night. It left me with a lingering arousal. I had a sexual hunger that needed satisfying. He began to touch me, I didn't reject his advances. What could happen? This was the nineties. Surely two mature adults could handle a bit of casual, consensual sex? This was not an unfamiliar situation, he was not my first. We faced each other, fully aware of what was about to occur. We were both naked and, in the darkness,  he moved on top of me, smothering me with his sloppy kisses. He entered me clumsily and started pumping, panting, grunting. And it was done. Another unsatisfying fuck. He rolled over and I pretended to sleep.

Thank God that was quick. The idea of him grinding away, trying to come, would have been more than my body, or mind could endure. I lay still, not wanting to wake him, not wanting to suggest we be more intimate. Eventually the alcohol did its job, Paul was snoring and I finally got to sleep.

The next morning I woke, head pounding. I got up to look for some aspirin, some cold water, anything to kill this pain. I sat at the bench and saw his note, 'Darling Chris, had to get to work, didn't want to wake you, best night, love Paul x.'

God, what had I done? It was coming back to me. I had let him stay, I had let him fuck me. It was wrong. I had sensed Paul wanted more than just friendship and I'd let my guard down. He was kind and gentle and it would hurt to tell him the truth, that I did not feel the same way about him, as he felt about me. Why did I let this happen? Had my grief made me vulnerable? I looked at the time, shit, work! I raced around to get dressed and ran out the door. I'd call him tonight.

# Just like all the Rest

I thought I'd escaped that life.

But there I was, just like girls I'd gone to school with, pregnant, unemployed and alone.

I was exhausted. I couldn't do it on my own anymore. I thought I was resourceful enough to manage, that I would be ok. In my grand plan I would keep the baby. I had lost my parents, she would be the family I so desperately needed. I would continue working while I grew my business. Paul would remain my silent partner and keep his distance. Or at least that was my plan.

This was not the reality. JD closed down. They couldn't compete with the cheap imported clothing now flooding the Australian market. The building they had leased for the last thirty years got sold and the rent went through the roof. They couldn't afford to relocate, so they just stopped. All their workers lost their jobs, including me. Depriving me not only of an income, but also the resources to continue to produce my range of dresses.

Constant nausea saw me hospitalised with dehydration and I was behind in rent.

Even though Paul had been upset by my rejection of his love, we had maintained a friendship. When he pleaded at my bedside, 'Chris, it doesn't have to be this hard? Let me look after you. I love you. I've loved you since the first time we met. Will you marry me?'

I took the coward's way out and, defeated, said...... 'Yes.'

And so began the lie.


We had a small, quiet ceremony in the grounds of Paul's family home. His mother Margot's coldness a clear indication of her disapproval. And why not? I was hardly the girl deemed good enough for her only child.

She had groomed him for more than this, more than me. She could barely hide her disdain. She had sent him to the right schools, introduced him to many well connected young women.

Justin made the usual inappropriate best man's speech, Fiona smiled condescendingly and Adam looked at me, cynically. I felt humiliated. So much of what they'd predicted had come true. I could just imagine what they were thinking.

Pregnant and tired, I was glad the day was finally over. There would be no honeymoon, Paul was too busy at work. He had arranged for us to at least get away for the weekend.

On the way to his family's holiday house in Portsea, Paul looked over at me lovingly, squeezed my leg and warmly smiled, 'Hi, Mrs. Brown.'

I smiled back. Christina Maxwell had become Chris Brown. I had chosen him, his name, and it was at that moment I fully committed to us and this new life. I would not let him down. He was a good man and he deserved to be treated with respect. Someday, I hoped, I would learn to love him.

Kathryn Mary Brown was born in late November, I had just turned twenty one and at last had someone to truly love.

Paul and I lived in a new Neo Georgian duplex near his parents' house in wealthy Toorak. It was in a development just finished by Justin's father who sold it to us at 'mate's rates', or so Paul said. Charles had helped out with the deposit.

'Better than wasting your money on rent and anyway, it will be a while before you inherit the house, son,' I remembered him saying.

Our new home was the display model and came furnished.

'Chris, it's all done. You won't have to bring any of that junk from your old place,' I remember him declaring proudly, upon viewing our new home for the first time.

I said goodbye to my dream and all that was left of my past.


Margot and Charles' Toorak home was a grand, ornate Victorian mansion built by Paul's great, great grandfather, Herbert Brown. He had made a fortune brokering land deals during the gold rush. It became Brown and Sons when Paul's great grandfather, Duncan, joined the firm, so beginning the long line of Browns who would continue the business.

For Paul it was a life he always knew would be his, groomed for it since birth. For me it was a completely foreign world.

I had been stripped bare and was someone I no longer recognised.

Every day I tried to observe their rules, mimic the behaviour that would make them accept me as one of them.

Margot dictated the way in which this life should be lived, she was the matriarch. We would often be summoned up to the big house, where she would instruct me via Paul.

'Paul, you will set up an account for Christina at... ' and then the name of the firm, the business, the school, the practice, the institution would be mentioned. No guiding hand of a gentle mother in law, just statements of fact that I was to follow.

'Paul have you organised a babysitter for...?' and again the events would be listed that we were expected to attend with her.

Even my precious Kate was treated with the same coldness, maybe because she was not a son or perhaps because she was my daughter?

I remember one day in particular when Paul and I were both required to sign some legal documents in the city. Our regular babysitter was unavailable. Margot was at home and agreed, begrudgingly, to take Kate. She was not the kind of grandmother who warmed to children. It was lunchtime and I had placed Kate in the front room on her ruggy, with a bowl of apple slices, to watch the Wiggles. No sooner had Kate settled, than Margot said, 'We do not eat on the carpet!' And proceeded to pick her up, repositioning the ruggy in the doorway entrance, outside the room.

'She can watch the television from here!'

My heart broke as my poor little girl sat alone, in the vast corridor, happily eating the apple, singing along to the familiar tunes, completely oblivious to the coldness of her grandmother. Paul had been raised by a nanny, perhaps this was all Margot knew?


A year later, Charles died of a heart attack. He had just turned fifty. We were all shocked.

I wondered whether Paul, at twenty eight, was ready to take on the burden of heading the practice?

According to their contrived and somewhat archaic law of primogeniture, it was now Paul's turn to move into the mansion, the family home. Thankfully Margot had no desire to live with us and she quickly decamped to the sprawling Portsea house. She timed her visits for when I was out, but I always knew when she'd been. A vase shifted, a chair returned to its rightful place, reminding me of how things should be, keeping watch. She kept a townhouse in the city, where she could attend to her many charities, animals mainly, benevolent Margot.

I saw her rarely, it suited us both.


It was a few years after Charles' death that Paul decided to take Justin on as a business partner. He claimed Justin would bring fresh ideas, a more entrepreneurial approach to the firm. Justin had convinced Paul that the company was too old fashioned, that there was a world of opportunity waiting for them to conquer. Justin said they should be giving more investment advice, that money could be made with each transaction. China, India, South East Asia were booming. Infrastructure projects were a licence to print money in these rapidly expanding economies. And after a short time he proved the conservative old partners wrong. Their new approach worked and the business grew.

Paul changed. I saw very little of him. He became even more consumed with work and when he wasn't in the office, he was with Justin. Football watched in their corporate box, golf games with potential clients, late nights out with associates.

As practice manager, Fiona was always present. She had taken up this position not long after Justin had been made a partner. Her family connections brought in even more clients. Paul was always telling me what a brilliant job she was doing. I'm sure she just liked the control.

# Perhaps I could make it Better

Over time, things settled down. I had accepted my life, it became more familiar, easier. Sex had never been great, still more of that same unsatisfying pumping and grunting. And eventually, as Paul's hours away from home grew, our couplings all but disappeared. And honestly, while I had a small child, lack of sleep and a burdensome house to manage, it didn't really matter. But once Kate started school and I had more time, I decided to do something about it. Sex had always been about Paul, a quick fuck, roll over and go to sleep.

I noticed he'd also become less interested and just assumed that it was because he too, was tired.

I had been looking through some old trunks in the attic, when I found what looked like a stash of elegant old nightgowns. A new bride's trousseau of exotic silks and satins, from a more glamorous era, perhaps the thirties? I held them up against my body and saw they would fit. Underneath the silks was a pile of books, including Henry Miller's 'Tropic of Cancer' and some old albums. As I turned the pages I realised these were not family photos, but page after page of pornography. Grainy old prints showing men and women in various states of undress, smiling for the camera as they stiffly fucked.

Who had been the owner of this intriguing collection? Was she just another bored housewife like me? I began to turn the pages and something inside me awakened. I felt desire. It had never occurred to me to demand something for myself. Was it because I did not see Paul as a lover, only as a friend?

It was a Friday night, no work on Saturday. A sleepover for Kate meant we would be alone. I would make tonight special.

Carefully I washed the nightgowns and chose one to wear. I looked in the mirror and felt pleased with the way it draped smoothly over my body. I felt sexy.

Everything was ready, champagne on ice, hot scented bath, candlelit bedroom, new sheets.

I waited… and waited.

He came blustering in, it was after midnight.

'Sorry I'm late. Justin had organised drinks for some new clients.'

'What's all this, power blackout?' he said, as he entered the bedroom to change out of his suit.

The bath had gone cold, I had drunk the champagne and the flickering candles had all but gone out, the beautiful gown wrinkled and crushed.

I couldn't be mad. It wasn't his fault, he didn't know of my plans. I had spent the time waiting, reading the book, pouring over the erotic photographs, aroused and still hungry for sex. He took off his clothes and headed for the shower. I stopped him, 'What?' he said, looking at me, puzzled, as I dropped the straps of my gown, letting it slip to the floor. I stood before him completely naked. I had never initiated sex before, but knew intuitively to pull him toward me. His penis twitched, we stumbled onto the bed. He entered me immediately, face down, head in the pillow, grunting, a staccato jigging and he came. He rolled over. I lay rigid as he began to snore. Nothing had changed and I put the notion of sexual fulfilment to the back of my mind. I decided to forget the trunk in the attic, the secret stash of another unsatisfied wife, married into this line of impotent men.

I got up, went to the kitchen and gorged myself to try and find satiation.

The food worked.

# Escape Money

I had become involved with various committees at Kate's school. It gave me something to do, especially on the days the housekeeper came.

It was good to meet people other than Paul's friends and business associates.

Talking to some of these women, mothers, I discovered that many of them had part time jobs. Perhaps they were bored like me? Surely none of them needed the money?

'Why do you work?' I enquired of one woman.

'Escape money,' she replied.

She was not alone. I heard this response frequently. They were all squirreling away small amounts of cash, giving them some financial independence, just in case they needed it. It was like I was being allowed into a secret world of women's business.

It reminded me of just how dependent upon Paul I had become.

That night I broached the subject with Paul and mentioned I was thinking about getting a job, now that Kate was at school. After all, even Fiona, Justin's wife, was working. She had become the practice manager. She was good at keeping these men and their clients in line. Paul was always telling me what a good job she was doing. She had no children.

'I work bloody hard so that no wife of mine will ever have to work!' he snapped back.

Conversation over. I needed a different approach.

Since taking over the firm, Paul often complained that running the household was almost as time consuming as running the business. It was an exaggeration borne out of exhaustion and an inference that he questioned what I did all day. He worked long hours, spent most of his free time entertaining clients and had very little left for us.

And there was my answer. I would manage the household in its entirety. We agreed on what the weekly expenses were and he arranged for the money to be deposited automatically into an account every fortnight. I decided any money saved would be mine, my 'escape money'.

First I fired the cleaner. I never knew what to do when the woman came over and had always thought I could do a better job.

Then I sacked the gardener. It was time for him to go. Watching him pull his cock as he pored over a collection of dog eared porn magazines added insult to injury. It disturbed me that sometimes I lingered far too long in the upstairs bedroom where I had a bird's eye view of the greenhouse, and through broken panes could see his frantic tugging. It was such a cliché, young gardener as lover. Luckily he was too stupid to be attractive. He was no Oliver Mellors and I was no Constance.

None of the things I paid him to do was beyond my reach. I grew up on a farm, familiar with hard work.

Then I taught myself to cook. I would no longer get the caterers in every time we entertained.

I stopped visiting the expensive gourmet supermarket where his mother had always shopped.

I found a new skill in urban hunting and gathering. Finding the cheapest butcher. Shopping at the markets at the close of day, when the stall holders were keen to get rid of produce, pickling and bottling the excess.

I taught myself to bake bread and saved by not buying the organic artisan loaves that Paul requested. My friends loved the bread so much, I would bake extra loaves to sell to them.

I even dusted off my old sewing machine and began making costumes for the kids. Fairies and tutus churned out at a ridiculous rate. The committee women and school mums thought I was clever and they happily paid. The industriousness that was so much part of my farm life was coming back and I loved it.

The cash I withdrew and the money I made began to pile up. I needed a safe place to store it, somewhere no one would look. The dress up box in the attic would be perfect. It was all I had taken from the farm. Everything else had been sold off by the bank to cover the debt that had accumulated over the years.

Paul was proud of the way I managed the house. I was a good accountant's wife. He trusted me.

He had no idea.

I knew how to make it work.

# Farewell

Over the years this marriage of ours, that was never based on love, slowly faded.

Paul still worked hard and now spent almost no time at home.

Occasionally, I would have vague pangs of desire and approach him in bed, but he showed no interest. Sometimes I would try to arouse him with my hand, but his flaccid cock never responded.

My satisfaction came from cooking and eating. At least he loved my food, grunting his approval as he ate.

We both started to put on weight.

His snoring kept me awake, so most nights I slept in another room. He didn't complain.

We barely spoke, not out of hatred or spite, but because we had nothing to say to each other.

I thought about losing weight, but couldn't do it. Food was the only thing that gave me pleasure.

Paul took up bike riding and lost the weight. He was home even less.

He rarely saw Kate.

Our lives had become separate, we only shared a house.

I didn't care. At least I had my beautiful daughter. And my escape money. Although I was almost fearful of what it might mean, if I actually needed to use it.

I grew to accept my life.

Eventually Kate finished school and moved to Canberra to study law at ANU. She had been an easy child. A deep thinker about to start a life of her own. She had been my reason for trying to make this marriage work. What next?

I was 39, young compared to most of the parents at Kate's school. People had often said I was lucky to be a young mum, that I would have my whole life ahead of me once my daughter had left home. Ah yes, so lucky, all the time in the world, but to do what? How would I fill this empty nest?

Kate was due home for the weekend. She had only gone to Canberra for a short visit, for orientation, the uni year hadn't even started. She'd been absent for just a week, yet the days without her already felt so desolate. Life in this big house, with these people, with Paul, seemed so aimless. I looked forward to the distraction her return promised.

I was still cooking, cleaning and gardening, but found myself becoming increasingly hostile towards this overbearing house with its dark rooms, antique furniture, massive garden and all it represented. I longed for something, something so distant I had forgotten what it might be.

Kate's plane was due to arrive late afternoon. She was coming home for the weekend. Eager to be on time, I told Paul we needed to leave for the airport at four. He told me he wanted to go for a quick ride first.

He never came back.

Anna Buckley

# Part 2

## Today it Begins

Raphael phoned and told me to keep Thursday free. This was easy. Kate was back in Canberra and my time was my own. No one to cook for, to care for. Not even Margot had bothered to remain. A postcard from London said she was staying with a cousin, away from the sadness and reminders of the son she'd lost. Margot in mourning showed at least some emotion. I couldn't imagine what it would be like to lose a child. It was hard enough that Kate was away in Canberra, but at least I knew she wasn't gone forever.

I presumed Justin and Fiona were continuing to run the business. Justin had made a brief visit not long after the funeral. He was his usual sleazy self, leering at me, saying he'd always felt there was something more than just friendship between us. Was this the reason for his visit? To proposition me? He had tried this periodically throughout my marriage. His lack of respect for me was not surprising, but the complete disregard for Paul showed what a truly nasty piece of work this creep really was. Perhaps he thought that because I got pregnant so young I was an easy lay, there for the taking. My stomach churned at the thought of him. What did he really want?

He wanted to help. He'd suggested I sell up, get out of this rambling old mansion. The land was worth a fortune, buy something smaller, reinvest the money in the business. He claimed to be on the brink of something big and wanted me to be a part of it. Kate and I would be set up for life. I politely refused. Justin was about as trustworthy as a shark in a small tank. Paul had been a conservative man and I was waiting to hear from his lawyers about the will, insurance, investments. Paul would have made sure we'd be provided for. These things just took time.

That was a month ago. I hadn't heard from him since, but knew we would eventually have to meet, talk about the future, the company. I dreaded this day, but knew it would be soon as my allowance was no longer being paid. Was this Justin's retaliation for my lack of enthusiasm regarding his investment advice? The upkeep of the house, the bills, the funeral costs were eating up what little I still had in our joint account.


The weeks spent on my own gave me much time for reflection. One shocking reality became clear. All this indulgent martyrdom had been of my own doing. I could easily have taken up designing clothes, resumed my own business from home, possibly even have asked for Paul's help. After all he had been so supportive when I first started out. But instead I chose differently. The anger at my own idiocy and self absorbed victimhood began to rattle. I'd spent eighteen years trying to prove myself to people who didn't care. Never really investing my time or my mind in anything but this self imposed exile. What an idiot!

And now, almost completely unencumbered, with no ambition, and a crushing lack of confidence, I had absolutely no idea of what the hell to do next.

I was bored beyond belief and looked forward to getting out of the house. It was amazing how much time I'd spent fucking around, cooking, cleaning, gardening. Busy every day when there seemed to be a reason for such endeavours. Now I'd lost interest. Why bother, who would notice, who was there to please?

Lunch with Raphael was just the thing I needed.

In the weeks since Paul's death, as they had promised, the Finestra family kept watch with visits and food. Raphael had dropped by, but at no stage did he even hint at what he'd done or the remarks he'd made on the night of the funeral. Perhaps he'd had one too many glasses of wine or maybe he'd forgotten? Perhaps he'd chosen not to remember? It was a little uncomfortable. At least our lunch date, away from my house, a change of scene, might resolve the situation.

The taxi dropped me off at Cantina, a wine bar on Gertrude Street, Fitzroy. Three streets defined the suburb, Brunswick, Smith and Gertrude.  I can't remember the last time I was in this area. Paul had always felt intimidated by its mix of inner city graffiti grunge, housing commission flats, converted factories and expensively renovated real estate. He couldn't understand why anyone would ever spend such ridiculous sums of money buying terrace houses in this former slum. Looking around me today I got a sense of why. The place buzzed with activity, felt alive, beckoning the visitors to its streets, to come explore.

My enthusiasm was short lived. I felt anxious, out of place, waiting for him to arrive. Alone in an unfamiliar, dark, narrow room, surrounded by racks of wine bottles, the smell of espressos and food. I imagined small bars like this hidden in the back streets of Rome. The room was filled with the smartly dressed arts crowd, huddled around small tables, in quiet conversation, looking comfortable, blending in.

He walked in, his beauty lighting up the room. He saw me, smiled, the laughter lines familiar and comforting, putting me at ease.

After the funeral he'd left me with a proposition, 'to set me free'. Is this what today would be about? I was too scared to ask.

'Christina bella, ciao, ciao,' he greeted me, the usual kisses, gesturing 'two' to the waiter.

'Today I have arranged for you to be pampered.'

The wine arrived with a plate of antipasti. The staff knew him, knew what to bring.

'Pampering? Mmm...delicious, what's this?' I responded quizzically as I sipped.

'Lacryma Christi del Vesuvio, the Tears of Christ.'

An intriguing name. I liked the taste of the rich, almost smoky, red wine.

'I've arranged for you to be looked after at some of my favourite places along the street. I won't be with you, but my friends will know what to do.'

I was vaguely curious, but a little disappointed Raphael would not be involved. Obviously he had forgotten about his comment to me. He evidently felt sorry for me, my drab clothing out of place in this chic little cafe. I was a pathetic looking creature, to be pitied, not desired.

He looked at his watch.

'Time to go.'

We finished the wine and food, he took my hand and lead me out the door.

Gertrude Street was magical. Leafy cedar trees softening the streetscape, people sitting outdoors, animatedly chatting, drinking coffee. Noisy trams rattled past old Victorian shop front terraces. These emporiums of a bygone era, now being filled with a new breed of trader revitalising this formerly down at heel street. Hip restaurants, galleries, artists supplies, funky boutiques, vinyl record stores, modern tattoo parlours and bookshops. A young crowd dressed in a mix of vintage and eclectic fashion. It felt edgy, youthful, forbidden.

He walked me to the first stop, a designer boutique.

'Raphael, darling, this must be Christina.'

We were warmly greeted by a stylish, middle aged woman, wearing Iris Apfel glasses, a black fitted tunic, sharp geometric bob to match.

'Christina, this is Vivienne. She makes these beautiful dresses and you can choose any one of them.'

'But Raphael...I don't need anything new. I'm not sure.... I....'

'Shh, enough, you will have to trust me. Remember what I said, you have come here because I think you are now ready to be set free. This is my treat, my rules. By being here you have agreed to start. I must go now. No more objections.'

My heart began to race. Fear and trepidation hit me. He had not forgotten. How exactly was he going to set me free?

'Vivienne, could you please make sure you organise a cab for Christina when you finish. She rarely ventures across to this side of town, we don't want her getting lost,' he said cheekily.

What was he thinking? My disappointment was overwhelming, he was buying me a new dress! Did he honestly think it was as simple as a frock and a cab ride home?

And with that he left.

I didn't know what to do. Luckily Vivienne stepped in.

'Christina, don't worry. I have some things in mind. Why don't you get undressed? I have locked the door, we will not be interrupted.'

Bloody mirrors, I looked terrible. Vivienne sensed my fear and draped a large swathe of cloth over the mirror, completely covering it.

'We won't be needing this. Let's just start.'

Without the mirror she'd made it easier. I tried on about six different dresses. None of them felt right, not what I had been accustomed to wearing. They were all figure hugging. I was not familiar with the closeness.

'Perfect! I can see which one works best for you. It will need a little alteration and be ready later this afternoon.'

'Now shoes, I need to get an idea of size.'

And like Cinderella I tried on a number of pairs before we found the right fit.

'Excellent, I will ring my friend Carmen. She'll have just the perfect thing, a heel I think?'

I had stopped wearing heels. Paul had always made disparaging comments. He didn't like to look short next to me.

She handed me a soft white bathrobe and a pair of slippers.

'Put these on,' she said and ushered me through a door at the back of the room.

I looked around, wondering where on earth she was sending me.

'Christina, over here,' beckoned a voice down the alleyway, behind the shops.

I walked, tentatively, along the cobblestones and through another back door, wondering what was coming next.

'Can't have you walking down Gertrude Street in your dressing gown! Welcome, I'm Claire.'

I had entered a pristine white spa room, a massage table in the centre. Claire pointed to a frosted glass cubicle and asked me to take a shower.

'It will help you relax, soften your skin. Take your time.'

When I had finished, she directed me to the massage table. I lay on my back, pillow under my head.

'Have you been waxed before?'

I could hardly tell her that I had no need to remove hair, that I had no one to see my naked body.

I just answered no. It was easier.

She began with my legs. The first strips pulled off elicited a startling, though strangely invigorating sting. After my armpits, she tidied up my eyebrows, no over plucking just a subtle reinstatement of an elegant arch.

'Now Christina, let's neaten your bikini line.'

'Relax, bend your knee and let your leg fall to the side.'

This encounter with a complete stranger was the closest I had come to intimacy in many years.

'Christina, I've finished now. Mark will be in shortly for your massage. Take off your gown, lay on your tummy and I'll cover you with a towel.'

I was aware of the lights dimming, the faint scent of sandalwood, quiet strains of music playing indistinctly in the background.

'Hi, Christina. I'm Mark.'

I felt the warm drizzle of oil as he started at my feet and began to move his way up my legs. He massaged my thighs, my backside, the oil seeping into the most intimate parts of my body. He didn't speak. It felt good and I fantasised about what this encounter could become. For the next hour I floated in a dream like state. He finished and cocooned me in a soft cotton blanket.

'Christina, wake up,' someone gently whispered. I looked up, Claire had come back into the room.

'Hi, you were fast asleep, it's time for another shower. I've hung up a fresh gown.'

Again I let the hot water run all over me, my body smooth, tingling with the new sensation of touch.

Claire took me to another room, a beauty salon, again with mirrors covered.

First a young woman washed my hair, her expert fingers massaging my scalp. I then sat in the chair where the hairdresser said, 'Ah Christina, I know exactly what I will do. You just need a little colour, something to put a bit of body back into your hair. How about a rich chocolate brown?'

'Perfect,' I replied.

As he worked, another girl gave me a manicure and pedicure and when they were both done, Mel came in to do my make-up.

Just as she was finishing, Vivienne reappeared carrying a garment bag.

'How's our gorgeous girl going?'

'Ready for you, I think, Viv,' said Claire, who had overseen the entire process.

She took me back into the spa room where I would at least have some privacy.

'Vivienne, I don't have any underwear!' I realised, slightly panicked.

'You don't need it. The dress comes with the bra already fitted into the bodice and no one needs a pantie line showing,' winking mischievously as she explained.

I opened the bag and removed an elegant black dress, scooped neck, long sleeves, low cut back, fitting snugly below the knee. Hair luxuriantly brushing the tops of my shoulders. Towering black heels made all the proportions just right.

The team had gathered. They smiled, all nodding proudly.

They positioned me in front of the mirror and before I could prepare myself the drape had fallen.

I couldn't believe it. I didn't recognise the woman I saw. The more I looked, the more I stood tall, enjoying the new found confidence this was giving me. It was as if a dear friend was returning, more Nigella than Audrey. We had a lot of catching up to do.

# Raphael

I heard a quiet clapping and turned to see Raphael smiling, nodding with approval. I was so pleased he was here.

'Christina, I hardly recognise you. Are you happy, what do you think?'

I could barely contain my delight, 'I feel amazing.'

'Well then, come. I've finished for the day and have an icy cold bottle of Prosecco waiting at my place.'

We both thanked all the people in the room.

'It's cold, here take my coat.' He took me by the arm and we stepped out onto the street.

What was it about this process of transformation? It was as if I was emitting an aura. I caught the admiring stares of men and smiled back, confident.

Raphael lived above their store, a converted warehouse on Gertrude Street. I had never been there before.

Over the years I had tried to keep in touch with the Finestra family. When Lola was back in Australia, we still tried to catch up over the occasional Sunday lunch. Paul had always been uncomfortable, speaking loudly to Massimo, in that way Australians do to anyone with an accent, as if they are deaf. It had been easier to stay at home.

We arrived in front of the store. I could see the designer furniture, brightly lit, displayed as room settings in the large emporium. It was a stylish world of sleek modern minimalism, as if from the pages of some exclusive interior design magazine. We passed the main entrance and went down an alley beside the building. A huge, black door with a large orange enamel 7A, screamed 'here we are'. We went up a flight of concrete stairs, to a landing and another door.

'Come in,' he said, holding the door as I stepped into his private world. He took the coat.

Raphael was an interior designer. His stunning apartment taking up the entire second floor of the converted warehouse.

Large industrial steel windows encased this massive space. I could just make out the spectacular view of the city as daylight faded. Sheer charcoal drapes sensually softened the harsh lines of this former factory. Before me a sleek, down lit kitchen with a long bench dividing the space from the expansive lounge room, where two elongated sofas sat just perfectly. To one side of this vast galleria a refectory table surrounded by a dozen Philippe Starck chairs.

Against the opposite wall a king sized bed, white linen, a charcoal throw at the foot. As my eyes adjusted to the dim lighting I could see the shower. A stainless steel head hidden in the ceiling with dark tiles defining the space. A single pane of glass to contain any splashes. No walls. Exposed.

I was awestruck by this cavernous room's brooding sexiness.

Without speaking, Raphael walked ahead of me. He placed his jacket over the back of the couch and kicked off his shoes. Barefoot he turned, staring intensely and without taking his eyes off me, slowly began to unbutton his shirt. It fell to the floor. A seductive strip tease. His body was magnificent. I wanted to touch it.

What was happening?

Today's slow build had been like a subtle seduction. A day of foreplay readying me for what was presenting itself.

He reached out, pulling me against his chest. My dulled libido aroused. The hibernation of my soul gently being coaxed awake. I offered no resistance.

My heart raced, my body burned as his hands cradled my face. His lips brushed mine. I loved the silence. He turned me around and slowly unzipped the dress, nudging it off my shoulders. It fell to the ground. I was naked. He lifted my hair from the nape of my neck, kissed, then gently nibbled at the sensitive skin. He held me from behind, his arms encasing me, skin on skin. We stood still, I felt safe. His hand moved down my arm, until our fingers interlocked. I felt drugged with touch. He guided me towards the bed. I covered myself with the sheet, closed my eyes. The faint sound of clothing being removed, falling. He lay down. I could smell his presence, his earthy masculinity, the scent of a man. Slowly he peeled the sheet back, I felt no shame or embarrassment. I was aware of his hand delicately trailing over my body, my breast, taking his time. Retracing over a nipple, a deft pinch, the nipple hardening, coming alive, my sex smouldering. His firm mouth teased mine, delicately sucking and biting. I thought I would die at the sheer pleasure this elicited. I had never been touched like this before. He moved down my body, fingers combing through the hair on my pubis. His hand continued and, with one finger, two fingers, three, gently opened my cunt, teasing me, circling my clitoris, taking his time to explore this part of my body with real tenderness. I groaned with pent up desire.

'Bella Christina, you are magnificent,' he whispered.

If only he understood just how much how my body had ached for this.

His weight shifted, he was on top. His rigid hardness nudging the place his hands had so masterfully awakened. I spread my legs, desperate for him to enter. Slowly I felt myself opened by his thick, hard cock. He paused, allowing my body to adjust, letting me feel every part of us slowly connecting. Our bodies warm,  skin touching, melding together. I began to feel him move, a subtle shift, filling me, against my clitoris. Rhythm building slowly, whispering sweet nothings, telling me I was beautiful, lingering inside me, preparing me for the first real fuck of my life. And then he began, heavier, faster, I wrapped my legs around his back with a sense of urgency, pulling him closer, needing him to be deeper. We rocked more desperately together until panting, I felt the explosion of my first orgasm. He kept moving as the energy of its force continued. I trembled to the core of my being. Desire had been unleashed. He groaned and kissed my mouth fully. I felt him come. My whole body tingled ecstatically. And I relished with satiated calmness the dying sparks of electricity that had charged every nerve ending, every fibre of my being. I had never experienced this before, this tantalising wanton lust. I felt so alive. He held me tightly until slowly our bodies quieted. We lay there spent, still.

The room was dark. I became aware of the twinkling lights of the city illuminated before me. He turned on the bedside lamp. I could see his smile, those sexy laugh lines cheekily crinkling as he asked, 'Are you hungry?'

I nodded.

He got out of bed. I heard him piss. He returned with a gown, 'Something for you to wear?'

Of course he had a women's bathrobe. I was not naive enough to think the beautiful Raphael lived the life of a monk. In fact I felt a deep affection for this man, but not infatuation. I had known him for too long. I had no desire to change our wonderfully familiar relationship and perhaps he was just a bit too pretty for my liking.

I stepped out of bed, needing to piss as well. I noticed the used condom on the floor.

'A considerate and responsible lover,' I said to him as I picked it up and headed for the bathroom. He laughed, I smiled.

I caught sight of my reflection and for the first time in many years did not recoil. I was going to have to get used to this new woman. I think I could like her.

I returned to find him in the kitchen wearing the briefest boxers. His lean hard body was magnificent. I observed the concave line of muscle where his hips met his legs, the profile of his penis clearly visible, as he turned to greet me.

I pulled up a stool and he placed a champagne flute in front of me, 'Prosecco?'

'Oh yes, please,' and he poured.

I watched him cook. I had never seen a man this comfortable in a kitchen before, so comfortable in his own skin.

'What's on the menu?' I asked.

'Nothing grand, just some pasta with pork and fennel sausage, some chilli, garlic, a little olive oil.'

'Not only do you fuck me, but you feed me as well. A true renaissance man!'

'At your service,' he replied, launching into a high camp bow.

Within a few minutes it was ready and I wolfed it down hungrily. I had barely eaten all day, had completely forgotten about food.

'Thank you, Raphael, for this extraordinary day. It was truly one of the best of my life.'

'And Christina, to you,' he said, toasting me with his glass.

'I have to admit I was a bit nervous about today. I remembered what you'd said on the day of the funeral. But when you left me at Vivienne's, I thought that would be it and was somewhat relieved. I don't think I could've completely relaxed if I'd known what you had in mind. What your real intentions for today were.'

'I kept my promise. I am a man of my word. Do you feel set free?'

My smile gave him his answer.

When we'd finished the meal, he invited me back to his bed. I could have stayed, but decided it was the right time to go. I didn't want this night to end with the awkwardness of not knowing when to leave a lover's bed.

I dressed, he called a cab.

On the way home, I thought about this extraordinary day. The stunning view, the beautiful interior, the magical street. Of sex, of touch, of desire. I'd been awakened. I knew I had to get out of that claustrophobic house, get out of that suffocating world. I was ready for an adventure.

# Goodbye House

I woke the next morning to the sound of someone knocking at my door, banging loudly. I grabbed the dress, it was the nearest thing, pulled it on and ran down the stairs.

'Mrs. Christina Brown?'

'Yes, that's me.'

'I represent Smith Blackburn Receivers and am here to inform you that this house is part of the assets of Brown and Sons Accountants. I have been instructed to escort you off the property. You have thirty minutes to vacate. You may pack a bag of personal belongings.'

So this is how it was to be, no procrastination. I was being forced, kicked out, dumped on the street. Left with no car, no house, nothing. I grabbed a bag and tossed in a few essentials. Suddenly something caught my eye. I looked out the window. The press had arrived, cameras, news vans, reporters. Someone must have tipped them off.

Don't we love to see the mighty fall! When the death of your husband commands a half page obituary in the newspaper, the collapse of his company is equally newsworthy. Sometimes Melbourne could be a very small bitchy town.

I rang Lola. Thank God she was in the country. She came immediately.

We sped off to the Finestra house. Massimo was waiting at the gate, ready to keep out the leeches who had followed.


My lawyer called and was able to shed some light on what had just happened.

It appeared that over the last few years Brown and Sons had been investing heavily in infrastructure projects in Cambodia. It was recently reported the construction company facilitating many of these projects was withdrawing. This caused a negative run on investments, many of them having been made on the advice of Justin Darcy.

This crisis of confidence lead to the loss of many of Brown's clients, who preferred to take their business to companies that could be trusted.

With Paul Brown dead, no sons to follow and Justin Darcy at the helm, it seemed the company, Brown and Sons, could no longer be relied on. It had only taken a month. There was nothing left.

I remembered Paul talking about wanting to change the will? Had he, too, thought the investments were too risky?

I asked about ownership of the house. To my surprise, Paul had put the title of the house in Kate's name. This was news to me. The lawyer told me the legality of the will was being questioned and so the house would remain with the receiver until it was sorted out.

All the accounts had been frozen, no superannuation had been paid, even the insurance policies had lapsed. It seemed that the company's problems had been going on for a lot longer than I thought. Perhaps Fiona had not been the brilliant practice manager Paul had so often raved about.

How had this happened? Paul had been such a stickler for the rules. He always played it safe. What had changed?

'Our house is your house,' said Massimo.

'Take as much time as you need. I will ring around, get some advice.'

'Thank you, Massimo, Gabriella.'

I was shocked by the speed of change and knew Kate needed to be contacted. When I tried to dial her number the phone was already dead.

'Would you mind if I used your phone? It appears that my mobile has been cut off as well. I need to ring Kate.'

Eventually I was able to contact her. I warned her about the media coverage and assured her that we would be fine. I gave her my new contact details and told her she had to be strong. I had been able to speak to the Dean of the residential college where Kate was living. He said Kate's fees had all been paid upfront and that she would have accommodation until the completion of her studies. She would still need a living allowance, but apart from that she would be fine for now.

It was still a puzzle? Fees, board, tuition covered, exactly as I would expect from Paul, but absolutely nothing left for me. Fiona probably had something to do with my excommunication. I remembered what she had said all those years ago. Was this the way she 'would make me pay'?

'Knock, knock. It's me,' said Lola.

Gabriella had taken me to the guest wing of the house. It was quiet, private and after a wine with lunch, I had fallen asleep.

'Come in.'

Lola sat on my bed.

'Just thought I'd come and see you were ok. Did you get some rest?'

'Thanks, the wine helped.'

'Christina, I'm having real trouble comprehending how Paul could behave in such a way. It's so out of character?'

'I know, me too.'

'What are you going to do?'

'Look Lola, it's not as bad as you think. Do you remember when I brought that old chest of mine around to your place after the fire scare?'

'Yes, the one with your mum's old ball gowns in it?'

'Well, as much as I needed to keep the dresses safe, the chest holds something else.'

95

It was about a year ago. Some wiring in the old house was faulty, there had been a small fire in the laundry, nothing major. But it made me think, 'What would I save?' and of course I suddenly realised all that cash I'd been hoarding could easily have gone up in smoke. Massimo said, that years ago they'd built a fire shelter after a long hot summer had put their house at risk. Luckily they'd never had to use it, but it had become like a vault for all their important papers, some valuables and the precious mementos accumulated over time. He let me put my chest in the shelter.

'What's in there?'

'If you could just grab the key, I'll show you.'

We retrieved the chest and lugged it back to the bedroom. First I took out the photos, my parents, baby Kate, Kate growing up. Then I removed layer after layer of my mother's dresses until I reached what I had been looking for.

'Fuck, Christina, where did you get this from?' said Lola in amazement. I told her the story.

'How much is in there?'

'I don't know, I've never counted it. Let's see.'

I tipped the contents out and we began to count.'

'Jesus Christ! That's almost one hundred and twenty thousand dollars.'

'Yep, that'd be about right. I've been doing this for twelve years and I knew I was saving about ten thousand a year.'

'You cheeky minx. I had no idea you were such a wicked woman. Imagine how much interest you could have earned if you'd put it in the bank!'

'Yeah and imagine how excited the receivers would've been if they'd gotten their fat little fingers on that lot as well.'

We both looked at each other, grinning like naughty school girls.

'And speaking of wickedness, I couldn't help but notice what you had on when I picked you up this morning. Your hair, the traces of make-up. You had an air of 'Sprezzatura' as we Italians say, a kind of artful carelessness about you?'

I was worried about how much I could tell her, fearing that she would be possessive of her brother. They were very close. I would tell her about Raphael's treat, just the makeover nothing more, but Lola was not fooled.

'Christina Brown, you're not telling me everything. I know my brother very well. Are you seriously saying he turned you into a princess then sent you home in a pumpkin?'

'Well...' and without giving too much detail I revealed what had happened next.

Wide eyed and slightly shocked she eventually spoke,

'Wow, this is not what I expected to hear. How do you feel? You know my brother is a bit of a Casanova. He has broken many hearts.'

'Lola, I love your brother, but I'm not in love with him. What he did for me was very special. He broke the spell or should I say the curse. He set me free.'

I knew I had never been able to fool Lola about my sham of a marriage. She had been a good friend who tolerated my charade, aware of a life half lived. Choosing not to remind me of the vows we had made as young women. And today she seemed to delight in the events of the last twenty four hours.

Looking slightly relieved, she then said, 'You know what this calls for?' we looked at each other and said together, 'Prosecco!' We both laughed.

'Cheers, Lola Finestra.'

'Welcome back, Christina... Maxwell'

# What she Really Saw

Even though I had loved my 'Raphael day', it had taken a lot of effort. I could now look in the mirror and actually see myself. I loved the new woman Raphael had awakened. What I didn't like was that I had gotten fat. I still could not go into any dress shop and just grab something off the racks. Women my shape had to choose from the dull plus size section. I hadn't weighed myself for years, but my clothes told the truth.

I had been good at covering it up. No one really knew how big I had become, not even me. People were too polite to say. I guess everyone was getting bigger and the sight of someone extremely overweight was no longer that unusual. I needed to know what was normal and so I began to do some research.

I found that if I calculated my body mass index or BMI, I would at least know where to start. I had bought myself a laptop, was connected to the internet and so began my research. I found a site where I only had to enter my weight and height and the computer would automatically calculate my BMI. I read that a figure of between 18 and 25 is 'normal', up to 30, 'overweight', above 30, 'obese'. I entered my numbers and there it was, 31. It was official, I was not cuddly, not voluptuous, but obese.

As confronting as this was, at least I had something to work with. I had 30 kilos to lose to reach a normal weight. I would turn 40 in November and was determined to lose it before then. This would be my goal. I had eight months.

This time I wanted it to be different. Like most women, I had tried to diet before. For the first few days I would attack the diet with vigour and like most women, the regime was unsustainable and before long my old habits would return.

The other complication was that food had been the only way Paul and I had connected. It was one of the things I excelled at, cooking. It gave me a sense of self worth. Unfortunately, I was equally as good at eating. Food comforted me when I was down.

I had been in a relationship where I was no longer touched or desired. I had stopped looking in the mirror, accountable to no one. And there was the answer, I would be accountable to the mirror, to me.

I decided that once a week I would photograph myself, same bra, same underwear, nothing else. By being honest with myself, I would stand a chance. Today was as good as any to start. The mirror was not going to get any kinder.

Click, first shot, print the photo, paste it into a diary. Day one, zero kilos lost.

Food was the next problem. I simply ate too much. I thought that staying with the Finestras would make the problem worse, but it didn't. Both Gabriella and Lola weren't fat, so I started to observe what they ate. Breakfast was often an egg, some spinach, sometimes bacon, sometimes fruit. Lunch was usually a big salad, all picked fresh from the garden, perhaps some tuna, or a small piece of chicken, leftover from the meal last night. Dinner a ragu, some meat, lots of cooked vegetables and a small glass of wine. Good food, just a lot less.

I asked Gabriella about this and she said, 'Christina, we are not peasants, we do not work in the fields all day.'

'But what about the Sunday lunches?'

'They are a special time, for friends and family, not for every day. We would become the size of houses if we always ate like that. What's more, my darling, I like to look good naked. I don't want Massimo to wander,' she said with a twinkle in her eye.

I could do this, just a little bit less on my plate and lots more of the fresh stuff from the garden.

But the food would not be enough. I would have to exercise and that would be the hard part. I hated exercise. I'd done the research and saw that a gym was not for me. I didn't want to sign up for a year and have the money debited from my account. I didn't have an account and honestly, the thought of fronting up to a gym, wearing some frightful outfit was as enticing as having a tooth pulled.

It did dawn on me, however, that since losing the car, I had begun to walk everywhere. Some days a simple errand could take two hours. Even an early morning walk along the river front and back up the cliff meant an hour of exercise. This for now would be enough. At least it was a start.

Week one was over, photo morning, but first the dreaded scales. I couldn't believe it, four kilos in one week and it hadn't been that hard. I printed the photo, stuck it in next to the first one. Could I see just a slight difference?

I had also been keeping a daily diary, writing about the dramatic changes in my life in the last few weeks and it had helped.

I continued with this for a month, more weight gone, ten kilos in fact. The photos didn't lie. I could now see a change. I felt a new confidence.

What didn't change was the hounding by the press. Every time there was new information about the collapse of Brown and Son, the reporters would be at the gate. Cameras intruding as soon as I left the safety of the Finestra compound.

# Lola Queen of Marketing

I was writing in my diary when Lola came in.

'I hear you had another bad day. Papa told me they were out the front early this morning.'

'Yeah, I wish they'd just piss off and leave your family and me alone.'

'What's this?' she said, looking at the pictures.

I showed her the diary, the photos. Her face lit up.

'Christina, I have an idea.'

'Why don't you tell the truth, your own story. The press write any bit of gossip they can find. Why don't you write it first?'

'I don't understand?'

'It's here, this diary. You should start a blog.'

'But who would be interested? It's just a way for me keep myself accountable, to help me lose the weight. And to record the craziness of the last few months.'

'Oh please, Christina, look at them camped by the gates. Someone must be interested or they wouldn't be there!'

'But it's more than that, these photographs, your story. Most women struggle with their body image, their weight, their relationships. The women's magazines are full of the 'before and after' pictures.'

She had a point.

Lola then outlined her idea.

She told me that first I should give an interview to someone I trusted.

'But why would I want to do that?'

'Because we need to tell the world about your blog. You give them your story and mention the blog at the end. A mass circulation magazine will alert more people to your site than just the few friends on your contact list.'

'And let's face it, Christina, you need to earn a living. You've seen how the lawyers' fees are eating up your nest egg and that's a fight that could go on for years.'

'People think they know who you are and they attack you because they think you're some privileged rich bitch. What these diaries show is that you are just like everyone else.'

Lola's marketing genius went into overdrive. Firstly she got her I.T. guy to set up the blog, with a subscription facility, so that I could interact with my readers and automatically send them new posts. Then Lola started to ring her media contacts, only to discover a bidding war for my story had already begun.

'You won't believe it. I've got Jane Smith from 'Your Weekend' magazine, very credible, very up market. The gutter press will have a field day, pissed off that they didn't get in first.'

A week later the story came out. Within minutes the traffic to my blog began to build. I would give my story to no one else, although it didn't stop the tabloid TV programs from doing one of their shitty exposés. I didn't care, the traffic just increased. I had the last laugh.

Initially negative comments on the blog were biting, but slowly the focus changed. It was no longer the 'fall of the empire story' that interested people. The weekly photo, the truthful insights about how we feel as wives, lovers, workers, mothers kept people coming back for more.

At the end of the second month I added two new categories to the blog. Firstly, a page where my readers could post their own 'before and after' photos and stories. Then a section called 'Escape Money', where women could share their money saving secrets.

My readers loved it, responding with great enthusiasm. I had hit a nerve and the traffic grew exponentially.

# Real Estate Agent

I had loved living with the Finestras, but did not want to strain our relationship by outstaying my welcome. I needed somewhere to live.

I had made some money from selling my story, but the lawyers always had their hands out for more. I wasn't destitute but had no idea when or if I would ever have a regular income. I couldn't afford to buy a house but I did have enough money to rent something modest.

I walked up the road to the High Street where I had noticed a few real estate agencies.

'Can I help you?' said the receptionist.

'Ah yes, I was wondering...'

'It's ok, Debbie, I've got this. Mrs Brown, welcome.'

The real estate agent had recognised me. He was on the ball. He welcomed me into his office, I sat down.

He was tallish, overly tanned, middle aged, his hair slickly gelled. He was well dressed in the kind of suit you would expect a real estate agent to wear. He looked fit, probably good at sport once, but perhaps just a bit too much time in the gym? His body screamed of a man desperately fighting off the threat of middle age.

'Greg Hunt,' he shook my hand and gestured towards the seat.

'Chris Brown.'

'Now Mrs Brown, what can we do for you today?'

'I was just looking in your window, saw a couple of properties. Thinking about finding a place of my own.'

It was then that I decided to have some fun. He had obviously read the papers and knew who I was, but he didn't have to know everything. I was curious to see what he thought I might need.

'In fact, I was just about to step out for lunch. Would you care to join me?'

He obviously thought I had a secret stash of money somewhere, a client worth having. I was sure I wouldn't be getting the lunch treatment if he knew I was only looking for a humble flat to rent. What the hell, I needed some lunch and I needed to get out of the house.

'We can take my car.'

We got into his black Porsche and with the slight squeal of tyres, raced up the road. Real estate must pay well or perhaps men like him borrowed heavily to pretend it did?

He pulled into the car park of a newly renovated hotel. I couldn't help but notice the room to my left as we entered the foyer. Sad people, heads down, feeding poker machines with their hard earned cash. Dreaming the next big win would be theirs.

'Table, Greg?' said the overly familiar waitress.

She led us into the bright, airy dining room. The modern decor, long bar, linen covered tables surreptitiously masking this business's real intent.

We sat down.

'Have you been here before, Mrs Brown?'

'Oh please, Chris. No, I haven't. In fact I've never even played the Pokies. It's all a bit new to me.'

'What, you've never put a coin into one of those evil little bandits?'

'Come with me.'

I followed him into the gaming room.

'Here's the deal. I'll buy you lunch, but if you win, you can buy the drinks.'

He handed me a gold coin and directed me to put it in the slot.

I put the coin in, the machine whirred to life and within seconds the bells and whistles were ringing. I'd won fifty dollars. I grinned, it was a bit of idiotic fun.

'I think your luck is changing, Mrs Brown....ah Chris. You owe me a drink.'

We went back to the table. He recommended the steak, the waitress brought the wine list.

I looked, 'The Barossa Shiraz, thanks.'

'You know your wines?'

'I have some friends who have been attempting to educate my palate.'

We talked about property and he inferred he knew what I might like. I was curious to see just what that might be.

I was enjoying this, flirting ever so slightly, he responding. I quite liked playing this game, the wine helped.

Lunch finished. 'After you,' he gestured, as we headed toward his flashy car.

'Mrs Brown,' he said, opening the door for me, grinning as I climbed into the car.

'Thank you, Mr Hunt.'

We sped off, heading further away from the city, to the suburbs, not quite the direction I had anticipated.

'I've never driven in a Porsche before.'

'Well then, I bet you've never done this either,' he said, as he flicked a switch and the roof began to fold back. I looked at him, grinning like a schoolgirl.

'Hold on, you'll need these,' he said, handing me a spare pair of sunglasses from the console.

He turned abruptly, leaving the street and entered the freeway. He planted his foot to the floor. I grabbed his leg to steady myself and squealed with delight, hair trailing behind me, wind in my face.

Before long we had arrived, pulling into the driveway of a brand spanking new McMansion.

'You're gonna love this little baby!' he said, in a smug proprietorial tone.

Embarrassingly my hand was still firmly gripping his leg. I had completely forgotten about it. I looked down. Was that what I thought it was, just beginning to nudge the seam of his trousers? I quickly released my hand, trying to focus on the house.

Past the columns, through double glass doors, ornately etched with what looked like a pair of swans, we entered the entrance hall of this very ugly new house.

'This, Mrs Brown, is a palace fit for a queen.'

The inspection had begun. It was hideous, too much marble, too much brass, too many chandeliers. Did I look like this type of client?

We went upstairs and he pointed out all the obvious features of a house I had absolutely no desire to live in. One massive master suite, a faux Juliette balcony facing the road. At the rear three tiny bedrooms, small windows overlooking a tennis court occupying most of the back yard. Obviously tennis proficiency was more important than a decent sized garden for the children who might occupy this house.

A kitchen with every brand name appliance, two ovens and a fridge full of TV dinners telling me that only a microwave was needed.

Strangely enough, I was voyeuristically enthralled by this ostentatious show of wealth.

'If you think that's impressive, wait till you get a look at this.'

We were downstairs again, heading outside, past the pool and to a separate building.

'This is where the fun happens.'

We had entered a massive games room, huge pool table, gigantic flat screen TV on one wall, bar, complete with filled dispenser bottles. Man cave, signed and framed sporting memorabilia decorating the walls.

'Integrated sound system,' he said and pointed the remote.

The room filled with the sound of heavy metal, he strums his air guitar, I cringe at the noise.

'And just in case the party gets too rowdy, we have this.'

He took me through a door at the back of the room and into a giant bedroom. A spa bath in one corner and what looked like a large round bed covered in faux fur completed the picture.

'What the hell?' I asked.

'It's a waterbed.'

'A waterbed? I didn't think those things still existed? I've never been on one.'

'Mrs Brown, what have you been doing all your life?' he said in mock horror.

If only he knew how pertinent that question actually was.

'Go on, sit on it, try it,' he said, patting the surface.

Hesitantly I moved forward and sat down. I swayed involuntarily as the water moved beneath me.

'Not like that, Mrs Brown.'

And with that he landed heavily, causing a waterbed tsunami to almost throw me to the floor. I started to giggle and decided to play.

I kicked my shoes off and stood up.

'You call that a wave, Mr Hunt?' and proceeded to launch myself into the air. It was on! We both started to jump like naughty school kids, bouncing on a trampoline, seeing who could topple the other over, shrieking with laughter. Another bounce, we collided, and suddenly I found myself underneath him, the wave action rocking our bodies together.

Laughing, staring at each other, the movement started to slow, and as I was just catching my breath, he kissed me hungrily. Wine diminished my guard. Two could play at this game and I responded greedily.

As we continued to move together, I could feel his hardening penis being pushed against my thigh. Frantically he reached up under my top and roughly grabbed a breast, pulling it from my bra. My hand shot down the front of his pants, unzipping him. I grabbed his long, stiff cock. This was fun and I was ready.

'Wait,' he panted and dashed to the en suite. I quickly yanked off my panties. I was burning up, my sex swollen with an unabashed carnality. He returned and rolled the condom on with urgency. I spread my legs and he thrust into me. I felt an animal like response and gyrated hard against his taught pelvis, creating the friction my clitoris demanded. Sensing this, he grabbed my arse and ground more desperately into me, moving wildly with the force of the waves. The harder he drove, the closer I came, till eventually I reached orgasm. I continued moving as it began to falter and was able to come, ever so proficiently, again. I had command of my body and was surprised at how easily I had been able to make it respond to my demands. He had not yet finished. When I looked to one side I caught him staring at himself in the mirror of the wardrobe, 'Oh yeah, baby,' he groaned, as he narcissistically watched himself perform, riding me, quickening the pace until I felt the throbbing of his ejaculation.

The music stopped.

He collapsed on me, the waves slowing, both spent. I had enjoyed this satisfying, selfish fucking, no pretence of love.

His phone rang.

'Shit, right, yeah. I'm onto it, thanks!' he hung up.

'Gotta go baby. Completely forgot about a contract signing.'

We both hurriedly tidied up. I found my underwear and thought how neatly condoms solved the sperm running down the leg problem.

All we could do was look at each other with conspiratorial smirks as we drove home. We were nearly there when I started to wonder, how did he know where to find the condoms? Did he know the house that well? Was it his?

He dropped me off in the car park behind his office.

'Be in touch,' he yelled and the door slammed behind him.

'I don't think so,' I said to myself.

It was fun, but he had no idea and didn't have my number. He wasn't the agent for me.


The most sensible thing to do was look for a place in the area where I wanted to live. Anywhere around Gertrude Street, Fitzroy.

I wanted a small place, no garden, two bedrooms for when Kate came home.

Fitzroy, formerly an inner city slum, was now a much sought after place to live. Rows of once neglected terrace houses, now stood proudly renovated. During the sixties and seventies some of the larger houses had been demolished and small blocks of flats built. Such an apartment would be more suitable for me.

What I found was perfect. Built in the late sixties, my flat was on the top floor of a double storey block. It was big, the rooms generous, built at a time before developers squeezed as many tiny boxes onto a site as possible. There were two double bedrooms, a large open plan kitchen and living room. A sliding glass door opened onto a balcony overlooking a small park,  giving me the views to the city beyond. Rooms were lit with large windows, sunlight streaming in through the thick white metal Venetian blinds.

It reminded me of 'Dexter's' place. I used to watch a lot of TV once. Television, sadly, had been my window to the world.

I didn't want to over commit myself financially, the lawyers' fees were costing me a fortune. An hour of their time was more than I had been able to stash away in one month.  Fighting to keep the house was making a massive dent on the savings in the trunk.

However, I wasn't completely broke and could afford to rent this modest flat. Eventually though, I knew I would have to get serious about earning some real money.


Moving was simple, just me and my clothes. I loved this unfettered freedom, no large house to clean, no big garden to maintain.

The Finestras had offered to give me the basics, but I had politely declined. I wanted to make this little apartment mine and quite liked the idea of starting from scratch. I had done this once before and remembered the great pleasure I'd got from creating something from nothing.

Smith Street, less chic than Gertrude, was a bustling utilitarian strip with a supermarket and more practical mix of shops and people. Standing tall, just one street away from the inner city 'renovators' delights', were the housing commission towers. Here new immigrants were given refuge, before they made their escape to more gentle homes in the suburbs. The towers were also sanctuary for those whose lives were bleaker, without ambition. The odd junkie begging, concocting stories, asking for small change. A mix of people who inhabited this suburb long before it became desirable. A combination of comfort and confrontation.

I liked the idea of wandering along the strip, looking for things to furnish the flat.

There were a few retro furniture stores that sold the modernist fifties and sixties pieces I liked. I was blown away by the cost. I remembered picking up the beautiful pieces for my first flat from the streets on hard rubbish day for free. Those same items now commanded high prices. Thank God the apartment was small. It was just me and I didn't need very much.

I wondered what had happened to the things I'd left behind in my Sydney Road flat? I had been too sick to care and Paul had done the clean up. I remembered what a kind man he had once been. I felt sad at what our married life became.

After a few days my flat was liveable. A cool, uncluttered minimalist interior, furnished with just the right pieces, a few modernist collectables, along with some contemporary items so as not to make the place too museum like.

I stood back to admire the space. The light streamed in. It was mine. I felt intensely satisfied, and for the first time in many years, independent.

# The Meeting

The letter said that we were to meet in the city offices of the receivers. I hadn't seen Justin Darcy since his annoying visit not long after the funeral. All communication since had been done through our lawyers. This was truly a meeting I was loathe to attend, with people I despised more than anyone else on this planet. Unfortunately I had no choice and hoped that we could sort something out to tidy up this unholy mess. To hopefully put this behind me, so I would finally be rid of them and completely free to move on with my new life.

The plush foyer told me that the winding up of companies could be a very lucrative thing.

Fiona and Justin were already waiting when I arrived. They were seated on a grey suede couch, looking a little awkward in my presence. I broke the ice and said 'Hello.'

Initially we were all very cordial, Fiona responding by asking how I was, her insincerity barely masked.

I knew not to trust her, many times in the past I'd fallen prey to her bitchiness.

Like the time I had tried to cook for new clients at a dinner Paul was hosting. I served pork, Fiona conveniently forgetting to tell me that most of the guests were Jewish. She saved the day by calling her caterer. Justin and Paul marvelled at her resourcefulness. She failed to mention that I had shown her the menu long before the night of the dinner.

Or the time she was holding a charity event and said that a ticket would cost $1500. Paul had approved, pleased that I might get to meet a few more women. What Fiona hadn't told me was the $1500 bought an entire table for ten. I sat alone, humiliated, not understanding how these particular ladies did lunch.

Or the Cup Day garden party where I wore a pretty little floral dress and hat. I was proud that I'd got the sewing machine out, made something unique, only to find all the other ladies wearing black. They had donated the cost of their outfits to a favourite charity and dressed plainly to highlight their sacrifice. The hostess had wondered how I had got it wrong. Fiona had given me the invitation.

Enough of these undermining incidents at the beginning of my marriage, led me to withdraw from socialising with Justin and Fiona. Paul had stopped pushing it and seemed to be happy to let me slip into the background. Fiona had very cleverly stripped me of any self confidence I had left and had certainly known how to make me pay.

Remembering things like that now just fuelled me with a new strength, a drive to not sit back and take all the shit they dished out to me. And it wasn't just remembering those past events which helped, I was also reminded just how powerful transforming oneself, dressing to convey a state of mind, could be. It was something that day with Raphael had helped me understand. I remembered how confidently I'd stepped out onto the pavement after that spectacular makeover Raphael had masterminded.

I had very carefully selected my clothing for today's showdown. A fitted suit, carefully tailored to sit perfectly. A heel to elevate me and a top cut low enough to show I was a woman but not so revealing to imply I could be bought. No more drab nothing outfits, no more drab nothing woman.

The receptionist took a call,

'Yes, sir. I'll send them in.'

I walked into the board room. The chatter stopped. Some men stood, I took the seat at the head of the table. I was ready.

The receiver, a nasty little balding man with a scratchy attempt at a hair transplant, tried to explain that if I were to agree to the sale of the house, then all the debt would be cleared. This way the company could continue to operate and all my financial problems would go away.

I really couldn't give a damn about the business or the dark old mansion, but the house was rightfully Kate's. It was the last decent legacy of her father's life. Paul had changed the will and it was for her I would continue to fight. If I let Justin Darcy win, the sale of the house would cover all the remaining debts of the company, effectively letting him off the hook. But it had been Justin's financial recklessness that had gotten the company into the mess. Why should my daughter have to pay?

They nodded knowingly, for if the sale went ahead they would all be paid handsomely and for some odd reason it was I who was covering the total cost of Justin Darcy's fuck ups. The property was worth about eight million. It was the only saleable asset the company, or Justin Darcy, thought they could lay claim to.

It was interesting that the house had not been sold already. Apart from my signature on the papers, something was stopping them from seizing it. I called their bluff.

'But it's not yours to sell. The will most definitely states that it belongs to my daughter.'

'Well, it's not quite that simple,' responded Justin's lawyer, as he pushed a sheet of paper towards me.

I glanced over it and got the general gist. In what looked like a very amateurish pact, written more like a schoolboy pledge than a legal document, it said that both Paul and Justin would use their personal assets as collateral for a loan taken out to expand the business.

Why didn't my lawyer speak out? Although the document was signed, there were no witnesses. Anyone could have forged Paul's signature. For all I knew, it could've been completely fabricated.

'This document isn't worth the paper it's written on,' I responded.

'That's what you may think Mrs Brown. But the date clearly shows it was written after your husband's will, superseding it, rendering the will null and void,' chipped in Justin's lawyer, smirking like the cat that got the cream.

'You're telling me that this made up piece of shit has some validity?' I scoffed.

'We're sorry you are so dismissive, but my client knows this was written and signed in good faith and I'm sorry to say, we are now taking legal steps to have the matter heard in court.'

He pushed more papers in front of me and I could plainly see I was now being sued for breach of contract. The legal nightmare just got turned up a notch.

My lawyer asked that we be excused. He tried to explain that they had a case and maybe I should consider selling. Telling me this fight could go on for months and if we lost, the costs against me would be huge. I read between the lines and knew he was worried about whether he would get paid. I started to wonder just whose side he was on. We returned to the meeting.

'Unfortunately my client does not wish to sell. Regrettably we will see you in court.'

The room was silent. They seemed surprised I hadn't fallen for their little ploy. I wasn't that naive.

I could see Justin's face reddening, his jaw twitching. He looked like he was about to explode.

'You fucking gold digging cunt! I put everything I owned into that company, so did my wife, while you sat at home on your fat lazy ass doing nothing!' he spat.

Hooray, the real Justin Darcy had finally returned.

'And now that the money's gone, I'm sure you're on the lookout for some new soft headed fuckwit. Don't think I haven't noticed what you look like these days, you little cock tease.'

'Mr Darcy that kind of language will not be tolerated in this room!' said Mr Baldy, trying to assert some form of authority.

'Shut the fuck up, dickhead. I've sold everything I owned to try to clear the debt and still you bastards want more!'

The meeting disintegrated into a slanging match between the two men and when finally some peace had been restored, Mr Baldy handed my lawyer another set of papers.

It appeared that I was now being sued by the receivers as well. Without the house, they would earn nothing for their trouble.

I didn't want this, but absolutely refused to be intimidated or bullied by them. They were not going to win without a fight.

As I waited for a cab, Justin came up behind me.

'Well, well, little lady. If you think you can win this, then you're more stupid than I thought. Don't you know who my brother is? He would do anything to protect his family. Fund any legal battle. He's someone you really don't want to go up against. He'll bleed you dry till you have no choice but to sell!'

A cab pulled up. I got in and slammed the door before Justin could continue his rant.

Bring it on dickhead, I'm not that same weak little wife anymore.


I talked to Massimo about what had happened, how I felt unsupported by my lawyer. He agreed, also pissed off at my lawyer's inability to fight, to defend me, to do the job I was paying him obscene amounts of money for. Massimo thought I had a good case, but knew it would take a different kind of lawyer to win. The following day I met with his lawyers. A new young partner, they assured me, would be perfect for my case. Ruth Steinbeck loved a challenge, loved tackling the 'old boys' and relished a fight. She was very keen for us to win. I liked her and more importantly trusted her. She wasn't one of them.

The playing field was starting to level.

# The Blog becomes my Job

The blog was becoming a full time job.

Mondays were always busy. Still my weigh in day, photographing myself and then uploading the images. Then there were my readers' 'Before and After' shots to be included. By the end of the day I usually struggled to finish replying to the many comments this subject generated.

Tuesday was 'Escape Money' day. This page was growing just as quickly as the weight loss column. Women were very keen to tell the world about their money saving ideas and secret stashes. It was morphing into a kind of 'home economics' section, not unlike the columns once seen in women's magazines. The readers just couldn't get enough of it.

On Wednesdays I had introduced a new section on relationships. I would often pose questions like, 'How do you keep your marriage interesting?' or 'When is it time to leave?' One week I asked 'How do you get back on the dating bandwagon?' and was so swamped with interesting stories that I realised this would become Thursday's page.

Very quickly my little blog was growing and I was slowly allowing selective advertising. I would only choose advertisers whose products I would use myself. It also occurred to me that there were many of my followers offering services, small businesses, things to sell, that my readers would find useful. Selling the pram, home baking, sewing classes, all generating interest. Not unlike the back page of the school newsletter. To these women I gave another page and charged a small fee.

Within a few short months I had created my own magazine. It was generating some money and the readership was growing. Every time a new story about the Brown scandal appeared, more readers came on board.

The legal bills continued to pile up and my little nest egg was disappearing at an alarming rate. I realised the blog would need to start earning me more than a bit of pocket money. It needed to generate a proper income.

Surprisingly none of it daunted me. The more demanding my life got, the more driven I became. Every chance to earn, I took. The more subscribers and hits to the site, the more I was able to charge the advertisers. Slowly but surely my finances were starting to grow. At long last I was able to see a more secure financial future for myself.

The job brought many pleasant surprises and occasionally I got to enjoy the fruits of my labour. Tickets to shows, product samples, restaurant meals, even weekends away in 5 star resorts. If I liked them, I would mention them.

The biggest surprise was when I was asked to speak at a conference on the changing face of women's media. I had no real idea of the impact my blog was having. I didn't have anything to compare it with. I didn't even know what a healthy readership was. The conference organisers would pay me a small fee and I would talk for a few minutes, then contribute to a panel discussion.

The day arrived, I was sick with nerves. I went to the registration desk and told the clerk my name. She told me to wait, someone would be along soon.

'Hi, you must be Chris. Welcome, I'm June.'

'You've been generating a lot of interest. When we advertised that you were speaking, our enquiries spiked and the bookings started rolling in. You have a lot of fans.'

'Really? I had no idea?'

June led me to the side of the stage and I waited nervously as she introduced each of the speakers, before we walked on.

I felt like the odd one out. The other panellists were an academic, a journalist and an author, all clever women who had strong opinions and much more experience at public speaking than me.

I could barely digest what was being said, I was so nervous. I kept thinking, speak about what you know, don't try to be too clever. Suddenly June directed me to stand.

'Our next speaker is blogger, Chris Brown.'

Polite, restrained applause.

My heart was pounding so hard my name tag was pulsating with each beat.

'Thanks, June.'

I walked to the podium, put my notes down and started to speak.

'Before the sudden death of my husband, I was a quiet, stay at home mum. I hadn't been involved with his business at all and was completely unprepared for the attention the company's collapse attracted. What was more shocking was the media storm which followed. My private life became public property, rumour became fact, cameras followed me. Things would settle for a short time until some new aspect of the case was revealed and it would all be back on the front pages again. I lost my privacy, had no voice.'

'It also had a big impact on my daughter. Fortunately, she was not living in Melbourne at the time and didn't witness the day to day hounding and the physical intrusions. But it still affected her. Friends would call, wondering about some new bit of gossip. It was up to me to set the record straight, calm her down and comfort her. The portrayals of our family were so untrue. I had to fight back, tell my side of the story.'

I started a diary. Writing helped me focus. There were so many unknowns. How would I survive financially? Where would I live, what could I do? And most importantly, who had I become? I realised that to help me confront these issues, I had to be honest with myself. I started by looking in the mirror and like many women, didn't like what I saw. Where had that fiery young woman gone? Who was the fat, middle aged person staring back at me, accepting of a life half lived?'

I continued with the rest of the story, not a cough, not a shuffle, the audience transfixed.

'The beauty of my blog is that it has given not just me, but many women the chance to tell their stories, sharing our common insecurities, but more importantly our strengths. Once upon a time all our information was vetted by a handful of men, media moguls who controlled what we read, what we saw, what we heard. It's different now. Electronic media allows women to more easily become publishers, editors and writers and speak to a much wider audience. All with the click of a button.'

I had nearly finished when I realised I had not used my notes, that the words had just come tumbling out. The audience was enthralled. I loved it. I felt empowered.

'So to all you women out there who think you have lost your voice, lost sight of who you are, stop waiting, take back control. You never know, you just might have something to say.'

'Thank you.'

The audience applauded loudly, the adrenalin was pumping, I could barely contain my excitement.

Time flew by with eager and enthusiastic questions from the audience. When the formalities were over, many women came up to thank me, avid fans who looked forward to each day's posting.

I was on such a high when I left and rang Lola, who was in Italy, to tell her of the day's success.

When I got off the phone it hit me, I was on my own, all these fans, but nobody to celebrate with.

I got back to my sweet little apartment, poured myself a wine and wondered what I would do about this situation.

# Sitting around Home will get you Nowhere

How stupid. Here I was, an adult, living within a short distance of some of the hippest bars in Melbourne, sitting at home alone, with nobody to share my excitement. I could do whatever I liked. I would go out.

I thought of ringing Raphael, but that just seemed a bit too needy. I would have to be brave. Many of the women had given me clues about how to do this on the blog. I guess now I would have to put their advice into practice.

I put on a favourite dress, heels, grabbed a bag and walked out the door.

There were so many places to choose from, but I just didn't have the courage to walk into a bar. Something more familiar might be easier.

A little further along Gertrude Street I noticed that 'Food Fiction Fact' was open. I stepped inside the book store. People were huddled closely together in this confined, overcrowded space. An email during the week told me Franco Stefano was launching his new Italian cook book. Not too intimidating, this could be quite interesting. We were waiting for him to speak, when suddenly, jostled by the crowd, I felt something cold and wet running down my back. I turned around.

'Oh God, I'm so sorry.'

He had a familiar face.

'You seem to have spilled your drink,' I said, looking up and seeing a wildly attractive, yet familiar, tall man.

That was it, the face, he was one of those chefs who often made guest appearances on cooking shows. I was instantly reminded of how much time, in my past life, I'd spent watching food programs on TV.

'Are you ok? Can I get you anything?' he asked, in a charming Scottish accent.

'I'll be fine, but I wouldn't mind a drink and looks like you might need one, too.'

'No problems, don't move.'

Luckily the dress was black, the stain unnoticeable.

He returned, handing me a glass of wine.

'Thanks.'

As the speeches were being made, the crowd edged in, trying to get closer, fighting for a view. We were being squeezed together.

'Sorry,' he mouthed, as we were pushed against one another.

I looked back in mock despair.

He made no attempt to move, to step out of my space. I didn't mind. The closeness of his body, felt good.

Eventually the formalities were over and the crowd started to thin.

I turned, expecting to see him behind me, but he had gone. I guess I had completely misinterpreted his actions. It was time to go. Pleased I had ventured out on my own and, with a slightly more confident step, headed out the door, back down the street.

'Hey, hey, wait!'

I looked behind, it was him, running to catch up, something in his hand.

'Here, I got this for you, my apologies for the spilling incident.'

He handed me Franco's book.

'I was getting it signed. Franco's a mate.'

I looked inside, 'To the beautiful stranger' it read, followed by a signature.

'It was the least I could do.'

'Why thank you, what a lovely gesture. Have you eaten?' I replied, with a new found bravado.

'No, got anything in mind?'

'How about San Sebastian, they do great Tapas.'

'Lead on.'


As usual San Sebastian, only a few doors down, was packed. We squeezed past the tables of satisfied looking diners and found two stools at the bar.

I grabbed the wine list and ordered two glasses of Tempranillo. We both watched silently as the barman poured.

'Now, that's a lot better than a book launch red and much better here than down your back! James, James McLaughlin or Jimmy, as my friends call me,' he said, introducing himself.

'Tina Maxwell. Pleased to meet you Jaa... Jimmy. Cheers,' clinking glasses.

The anonymity of my maiden name suited me for tonight.

We both looked at the menu.

'How about we let the lads here bring us the best from the kitchen? They seem to know what they're doing,' he said, in that very sexy accent, sweeping his untamed hair away from his face, as he handed back the menu.

'Brilliant idea. You know sometimes I can't be bothered thinking about food and just wish it would magically appear.'

'Me, too.'

Almost instantly a small dish of the tiniest olives arrived.

'So Jimmy, you say you know Franco. What's the connection?'

'He gave me work when I first arrived in Australia from Scotland, I'm a chef.'

'And where do you work?'

'I own a little place in Sydney. 'Jimmy's', in Bondi.'

I had heard of it, read the gushing reviews.

'So what brings you to Melbourne?'

'Some guys here want me to open a place. They're chucking shitloads of money at me to say yes.'

'Investors? You must be pretty good?'

'I dunno. Some people say I can cook, but I'm not really sure if I want to expand. It will mean more time out of the kitchen, less cooking, away from the thing I love doing the most.'

'And what about you, Tina? A gorgeous woman out alone on a Wednesday night?'

'Well, funny you should ask. I gave a talk at a conference today. The adrenaline was pumping and I felt a bit caged sitting at home, so I decided to go for a walk. See what the street had to offer.'

'I know what you mean. I feel like that after service most nights, but I go home to an empty house. A chef's life fucks up relationships. That's my excuse, what's yours?'

This was the first time I would have to tell someone about my newly single status and I wasn't sure how Jimmy would take to hearing I was in fact a widow. I would try.

'Actually, my husband died a few months ago,' I replied, pulling no punches, hoping it wasn't too alarming.

'Jesus, Tina, I'm sorry. You look too young to be a widow. What the fuck happened?'

'Please, don't apologise. I don't want you to feel awkward. His death was sudden. He died of a heart attack. I'm just getting used to doing stuff on my own.'

'Do you get lonely?'

I was struck by the poignancy of the question.

'We weren't in love. We'd grown apart. But it was still a shock. It turned my world upside down. Everything I knew changed. And yes, I am alone, but strangely I don't feel lonely. And particularly not tonight, sitting here with you, Mr Jimmy McLaughlin.' I finished on a lighter, more flirtatious note to retrieve the mood the night had begun so charmingly with.

He smiled and picked up his glass.

'And here's cheers to both of us. Alone, but not lonely, sitting here together, on a cold Melbourne night,' he said, initiating a second toast.

I clinked glasses with him and smiled, thinking what a lovely night this was becoming. The food continued, delicious morsels of exquisite Spanish fare. Jimmy was funny and charming. What was it about that accent that was so seductive? We talked about food, something we had in common and the night passed quickly. I didn't want it to end.

The restaurant was emptying and the waiters were beginning to pack up.

'Well, Tina, I think the staff are trying to tell us something. What would you say to a little night cap back at my place? I'm staying at a hotel just off Brunswick Street.'

'Mmm, as long as your intentions are pure, Mr McLaughlin?'

'Very pure, Ms Maxwell, come with me.'

He grabbed my hand and we went back out onto the street.


We headed west along Gertrude, then right on Brunswick. The street was buzzing with people, going to bars, listening to live music, parading. I felt that I was a part of it, that it was beckoning me to shake things up, come out and play.

'I love this street. We don't have anything like it in Sydney.'

I smiled back at him, nodding knowingly.

He felt the buzz, too.

We stopped off at Anastasias, a vodka bar, looked through their list of cocktails and ordered the opium and rose. It felt so easy, being here, sipping the drinks, fitting in.

I couldn't believe, such a short time ago, I would have been sitting at home, doing nothing, waiting for Paul.

It was exhilarating to be with this man who had gained a reputation for being a fiery tempered Scott. I remember reading about him being sacked from one job after his staff refused to work with him.

He was recognised by people as we bar hopped, people in the hospitality industry winding down after a hard night's work.

I was surprised when we abruptly stopped.

'This is where I'm staying.'

I looked around to see the foyer of a very sleek hotel.

'I think I mentioned a night cap. Wanna come up?'

Well, at least it was a slightly more sophisticated request than the 'coffee' cliché. I wondered whether this was a good idea.

I remembered my lonely flat.

'Sure Jimmy, why not!' I replied, not yet ready for the adventure to end.

The elevator took us to the top floor. He swiped his card and the door opened to the penthouse suite.

'Wow, Jimmy, you must be doing alright. I had no idea places like this existed around here, very LA, very Hollywood chic.'

'It's owned by those investors I was talking about. They're paying. Sit down, make yourself at home.'

I sat down on a sleek black leather divan and kicked my heels off, stretching my feet out over the white shag pile rug. Jimmy pointed the remote and blue flames ignited in the recessed fireplace along the far wall.

'Magic!' I said.

'Check this out,' he said, grinning like a kid with a new toy.

Again he pointed the remote and the curtains parted, revealing a panoramic view of the city.

'Gorgeous, I love this place!' I responded.

'Now about that nightcap? What do you fancy?'

'Good question, Mr McLaughlin, what are you offering?'

'Come and have a look,' he said, holding the fridge door open.

I got up, wandered over, nudged him out the way and peered inside.

'Mmm, what do we have here?'

After a few seconds I closed the door, deliberately, and turned to face him, knowing exactly what I wanted.

'What I want is you!' and with that I pushed him against the bench, laced my fingers through his hair and pulled his mouth towards mine.

He responded greedily, his strong arms gathering me closer. My heart pounding, I lusted after this wild Scotsman and was keen to be the aggressor. I reached for the top button of his shirt and easily slipped off the first button, then a second, a third, the fourth giving me access to his broad strong chest. I guided him backwards onto the divan, hitched up my dress, sat astride and continued to kiss him, sucking, pulling at his lips. He saw that I wore no underwear, closed his eyes and groaned. I moved my mouth to his nipples, repeating the sucking, biting, licking them erect. His cock stiffened. I felt its hardness as I sat astride, my cleft encasing him. I gently started to rock, increasing the pleasant sensation this was giving me. Although reluctant to stop, I paused to unzip him, I needed him to be inside me, filling me up. I reached for my bag and took out the condom I had thrown in. His cock was huge. I rose to accommodate him and slid back down against his immense, engorged manhood, aware of the slight, but tantalising pain as I stretched to contain him. I rocked, tilting my pelvis hard against his haired pubis, opening up my clitoris, delighting in the friction this created. His hands squeezed my ass harder down onto him, building the rhythm, stealthily grinding with me, slowly at first, aware as I arched my back, that we both were close to climax. We played this game for a while until I could hold back no longer. I began to ride him quicker, harder, faster, demanding release until finally reaching that almost otherworldly sensation as my body found its way to a most satisfying climax. I collapsed onto him panting. We stayed like this until I could feel our heartbeats slowing, his cock gently softening. We lay there motionless in silent recovery.

After a time I sat up, looked at him, brushed his hair from his face and smiled. He smiled back.

I said nothing as he undid the buttons at the front of my dress. Deftly he removed all my clothing and lay back admiring my new nakedness. I tilted my hips, he withdrew, then pulled me into his arms and we lay there facing one another.

'Come to bed,' he whispered.

And before I could reply, he picked me up and carried me tenderly to the bedroom. I watched as he took off his clothes, turned off the lights and climbed in next to me. Naked, he held me against him, skin on skin, a warm intimacy. Together we fell asleep.

At dawn I quietly left, I would remain his 'beautiful stranger'.

# The Book

The sun was rising, I felt exhilarated. The relatively short walk home was not as solitary as I'd expected. I noticed others returning from their own late night adventures. A woman with bare feet, her heels dangling from one hand. A couple stopping to kiss, he hopeful, perhaps, of an invitation to her bed. A lone man, swaggering, maybe a less successful night out. And me, smiling at the memory of my night with James.

Wide awake when I returned home, too excited to sleep, I decided to check my emails. Almost all were from women who had attended the talk yesterday, offering support and warm wishes, until I scrolled down to the last email.

*'Hi Chris, I have been following your blog for some time and attended the conference, specifically to hear you speak. My name is Karen Jones and I am the lifestyle editor at Carlton House Books. I would like to arrange a time to meet with you and discuss an idea of mine.'*

This was one of the largest publishing companies in Australia. After a coffee and some consideration, I emailed her back. She promptly replied. It was six in the morning. Wow! When did this woman sleep?

We arranged to meet the following day at a wine bar on Brunswick Street.

I wanted to dance around the room.  And I did!

Karen Jones looked the part, smartly dressed, short black hair, glasses, large bag tucked to one side. She stood up and proffered a hand.

'Chris, Karen Jones.'

'Hi Karen, nice to meet you,' I responded somewhat clumsily.

'Please, sit down. I have taken the liberty of ordering the house platter. What would you like to drink?'

'Just a mineral water,' I replied, wanting to keep a clear head.

'It was great to hear your presentation. I've been following you since that first article directed me to your blog. I've loved the way you've been able to tell so many women's personal stories by opening up about yourself. All my colleagues in the office love reading your new postings. We always talk about them.'

'Thanks, it's been very cathartic for me. I'm surprised a woman like you would be remotely interested.'

'Don't underestimate what women like me want. We all want better bodies, relationships, financial freedom. Your blog taps into this at such a raw level, in a way that gossip magazines try, but fail.'

'They do it by exposing the rich and famous, delivering a kind of schadenfreude that appeals to the bitch in all of us. What you do is make it real, empowering women, showing the frailties we all share, giving us some hope to affect change.'

'I'll get straight to the point. I think there are a few books that could be developed, with ongoing editions. Is this something you're interested in?'

'I'm not sure? I think so? What exactly do you have in mind?'

She discussed the format, a kind of 'home journal, agony aunt' with pictures and new updated editions depending on the subject matter.

'The first book would most definitely be about your body transformation and the stories, the photos your readers posted. How changing the way you felt about your body changed the way you responded to life.'

She pulled out a folder.

'I have a proposal and a contract I would like you to look over.'

The food arrived and despite having no appetite, I slowly raised my fork and began to eat, resisting an overwhelming urge to touch the folder that lay beside me, screaming to be opened. Deep breath, calm down. Play it cool, keep your cards close.

We continued our lunch, talked about the readers whose pictures she had been most shocked by, the dating stories she'd laughed at. Karen revealed she was single and sometimes wondered if she had forgotten to have a life. She wanted to find more balance, sometimes wished she'd done things differently. I remembered her early morning email.

'But you've achieved so much. You're one of the most respected editors in the business.'

'Yeah and I've given up so much to get there. Sometimes, when I walk into my apartment at night, with no one to share the events of my day with, I wonder if it's really been worth it.'

I was shocked by her candour. On the surface she seemed to be so together. I was surprised at her vulnerability. Perhaps we did share many of the same insecurities, weren't so different?

She looked at her watch. Time to go.

'It's been great meeting you. Let me know what you think after you've read through the contract. Here's my card, call me if there's anything you're not sure about.'

We shook hands and said our farewells.

I rang Lola. Blurted out my good news and wondered if she knew of anyone who could look over the contract, someone who knew something about publishing.

'Ring Papa, he's got lots of contacts.'


'Ciao bella, come va?'

'Good, good and you both?' I said.

I had asked Massimo to look over my contract and he had given it to Adele Fraser. Adele, now retired, was once a powerhouse in Australian publishing and they had met through Gabriella, at the gallery.

Adele had marked a few minor changes, but had commented they must really want me, as their offer had been exceptionally generous.

Not only would there be Australian editions, but they had decided this type of book would sell exceptionally well in America, especially since many of my blog readers were from the United States. They would use a staff writer to adapt the content to this market. They had seen the obvious franchise opportunities a book like this offered, a 'Chris Brown Stripped Bare' guide to everything.

They would also pay for someone of my own choosing to help with the blog, knowing how easily the goose that lays the golden egg could be lost, if I got too overwhelmed with the increased workload.

I had seen the content of many a favourite blog diminish once the book deal had been signed. One food blogger had become so pissed off by the negative comments of some of the more vitriolic trolls, that on the eve of her book's publication, she had posted a highly emotional rant, alienating her readers. The pages of comments she usually received after her recipes had been posted, were reduced to nothing. Now she only got an occasional response when freebies were being offered. The commercial value of her blog plummeted.

Karen certainly knew what she was doing, knew how to keep her authors on track. She had thought of everything and I was more than happy to sign.

'Prosecco anyone?'

I turned to see Raphael coming from the kitchen carrying a bottle and champagne flutes.

'I think we have something to celebrate!'

'To your continuing success,' said Raphael, clinking glasses and winking at me with a knowing grin.

Just quietly I thought of what a rollicking good fuck I would like to give this handsome man, but knew it would complicate things and quickly put the thought to the back of my mind.

'And thanks to you, my adopted family! Cheers!'

I couldn't imagine what I would have done without them.

# Book Tour

The next few weeks were a blur. Luckily most of the writing and pictures were taken straight from the blog. We chased down readers who had sent in content to check we had their permission to print. The women were thrilled to be included, spreading the word to their electronic friends, the audience growing exponentially.

Before we knew it, the first book in the series was ready and just six months after that fateful day in February, 'Chris Brown Stripped Bare - A Guide to Your New Body' was launched.

I had to pinch myself that this was really happening. Work on the rest of the guides had commenced and they would be released over the next few months.

Next we had to start the publicity campaign. We began in Melbourne where I was well known. One story on local radio generated enough interest to see me booked for TV and newspaper interviews throughout the country. With every new interview the traffic to the blog increased and the more sales grew.

As exhausting as the book tour was, I still got a thrill, staying in luxurious hotels, travelling at the front of the plane, being chauffeur driven from one place to the next. It was all such an exciting new adventure.

The tour would culminate in me being a keynote speaker at a health and lifestyle expo. The largest of its kind, it was being held in the capital of hedonism, Surfers Paradise, a kind of beach front Vegas in Queensland, northern Australia.

We would have a stand, selling the books and I would be available to meet, greet and sign.

Who would have thought that this was the way I was going to earn money? A book about my body. The weight loss had been surprisingly easy. Easy because my life was filled with so much more than food. Sometimes too busy to even remember to eat.


I first noticed him endorsing a brand of popular gym equipment. He worked under the stage name of 'The Enforcer'. A closely shaven, muscles rippling G. I. Joe kind of character, tattoos of gun toting sluts adorning his strong arms. He had become famous as a trainer on one of those weight loss shows. A character who got results by demanding a brutal regime of diet and exercise, reinforced with his own unique style of humiliation and bullying. Many women thought he was the sexiest man alive.

I knew him way before this.

I had joined a fitness group with some of the school mums. We had all complained about our lack of success with diets and decided a personal trainer might be the answer. Nic Goodman advertised in the local paper, we decided to give him a go.

We met at the playing field of the school. Some of the women found his brutishness and over-sculpted body primitively alluring. I thought he was a bit of a dumb thug.

He started by making us don boxing gloves, run on the spot and shout, as we punched the air, 'We are warriors!' At his discretion, if we didn't seem enthusiastic enough, he would send us on a lap around the oval. 'Get moving you fat bitches!' was a favourite insult.

Needless to say, I didn't last the distance and, after only a few sessions, snuck out during one of those punishing laps. He probably didn't even notice I had gone. Another failed attempt.

Occasionally I would see some these women, in the park, still trying to stick to his brutal regime. I wondered if it had worked for them?

He had come up to the stand to introduce himself.

'I hear you and I are speakers on the final night. G'day, my name's Nic.'

He didn't recognise me. I had changed.

My editor had insisted that I dress to kill, to show what following the guide could actually do. This had meant sleekly straightened long black hair, tight dress, plunging neckline, vampish make-up and killer heels. More porn star than publisher. This image was juxtaposed against the life-size cardboard cut-out of me before I lost the weight, the very first photo I had taken.

This look, this outfit, was not something I would choose for Fitzroy. However it was entirely appropriate in Surfer's Paradise, where hostess girls wearing gold bikinis, directed hapless tourists to all the big attractions, a hedonists' playground.

I would be lying if I said I wasn't flattered by the attention. Every day he would come up and make small talk, inferring that we were the stars of this show and that maybe we should get together for a drink.

'How about after our presentation on the last night?' I suggested.

'Sure babe. See you on stage,' he said, with a cocky self assuredness.

It was the 'babe' that did it. I had an idea.


The auditorium was packed. The nerves I once felt had long gone. I loved the rush when walking on stage. Equally, tonight I loved the applause when we were done. It had been a long tour and this was the last night.

I was staying at the boutique Hotel Lusso, a welcome oasis of style away from the glitzy crassness of the lifestyle expo. We had been away from home for quite some time, so I let my team fly back early. They didn't have to stay for a talk they'd heard a thousand times before. I would relish a sleep in and breakfast in bed. Some time alone to enjoy the pleasures of this beautiful small hotel.


He was waiting for me in the wings.

'Where to Ma'am? The night is ours,' he said.

'Oh God, I've got no idea.'

'Thought you might say that. I'm staying at 'The King on Broadway'. They have a range of restaurants to choose from, it's just a short walk up the road. You ok in those heels?'

'Sure, lead the way,' I replied and quietly smirked at how appropriate, the name of his hotel, for the walking cliché that was my date for tonight.

The heels were the least of our problems.

It was a Friday night and the streets were packed with revellers. They all seemed to recognise him, stopping for photos, the odd autograph, all pretty manageable, or so we thought.

This was a tourist town full of package deals, theme parks, flashy hotels and on a Friday night, bucks and hens out to party before the big Saturday wedding.

We saw them, women hunting in packs, leading a bride around to the seedier strip joints and clubs, fuelled by cheap booze and party drugs. They needed little encouragement for a member of the bridal party to approach Nic and see just how far they could go. A slurred kiss, bum pinch, crotch grab. Word was getting out, phones spreading the news, 'the Enforcer was on Broadway'.

It was getting annoying, the crowds growing, the attention bordering on harassment. I was being pushed and shoved, the women desperate to get closer. He was trying to be polite until a bus screeched to a halt and a bunch of squealing women clambered out.

'Jeez, I've had enough of this, give me your shoes.'

He grabbed the shoes, took my hand and we started to run, turning down a side street, starting a frenzied chase. I was no fitness freak and was barely keeping up. The race continued, we turned again and found a narrow alleyway filled with dumpsters. He found a doorway and with his body to shield me, pushed us hard up against the recess. We could not be seen.

'I saw him go that way,' yelled one of them, as they ran past.

My heart was pounding, he put his finger to my lips, gesturing me to be still and quiet. He held me there, his muscled body protecting me. We waited for what seemed like ages. I couldn't move and then I felt it, his cock stiffening as he leaned against me. I had scored what they had wanted.

The chase had been exhilarating. The adrenalin pumped through my body, unleashing an animal extinct and a sexual craving that needed satisfying. He grabbed my ass, squeezing my bum, strong muscular arms lifting me up to meet his mouth. We hungrily kissed. The threat of danger heightening my sense of arousal. He reached under my dress, his hands slipping beneath the sheer fabric of my lingerie, feeling the wetness, his fingers entering me. I groaned against his mouth, he ripped off my panties. I wrapped my legs around his waist placing myself over the hard mound in his trousers. He shuffled to reposition me, supporting me with one hand, the door hard against my back, my hands firmly clasped around his neck. With his free hand he stroked me until I thought I would melt with shameless desire. His tongue ploughed roughly into my mouth. I responded with equal ferocity. I felt him move, he unzipped his fly and easily I slid down onto his willing cock.

'Wait,' he groaned, lifting me slightly. Freeing his hand he reached into his pocket, grabbed a condom and frantically ripped the packet open with his mouth. He rolled it on and rammed back into me, his chest rising as he sucked in air. I felt his muscular arms expand and contract as he used his strength to move me rhythmically up and down. I rocked with him, holding tight around his neck, grinding myself hard against his ripped torso, my clitoris throbbing with this friction. The adrenalin racing through us made orgasm swift and we came, violently, together.

'Fuck,' he said, panting. We stood, muscles trembling with exhaustion. I felt him soften, slowly loosening his grip, beginning to relax. He let me down gently, reached for my shoes and steadied me while I put them on.

'This way,' he said, dropping the condom to the ground, taking my hand, leading me out of the alley and back to where he was staying.

The King on Broadway was so unlike the Lusso. Flashy opulence, gushing fountain, gold chandeliered foyer, liveried concierge. So not me.

'Would you like a drink?' he asked.

This was a notorious place where football players showed off after a big match. We walked past noisy, flashing, gaming machines and entered a garish bar decorated with sporting memorabilia. This place was completely alien to me.

There had been a big rugby game at the stadium that night. The local team had won, many of the players were there celebrating.

'Enforcer!' they yelled, followed by grunting sounds.

'Boys!' he responded, with a thin lipped smile.

We sat at a booth. He ordered something with coke, not the drink I would have expected.

I guzzled down a Bloody Mary.

'Thirsty?'

'Thirsty work!' I responded, with a conspiratorial smile.

Before we could even start a conversation, it began again. This time the men coming up to him, demanding more of his attention, asking for a photo, wanting a coaster autographed.

He leaned over and whispered in my ear, 'Let's get out of here.'

I followed. We went to his room. I wasn't sure what this would mean.

'How about room service? At least we won't get hassled.'

'Great idea.'

I looked at the menu. We both ordered the steak. It had been a long day, we were starving.

He opened a bottle of red wine, found two glasses and poured.

'I hate the attention,' he said.

'I understand.'

I told him about the hounding I'd received after the company went broke and the reason I'd started the blog.

'I know. I've been reading your book, checked out your blog. I feel like I know you really well.'

'And you, Nic, what's your story? I know you're on the telly, but how'd you get there?'

'Actually, it was just by chance. I'd set myself up as a personal trainer. One of my clients was a TV producer. She said I'd be perfect as the agro bad guy, the bully who scared people into submission. I was a bit pissed off that she saw me that way, but that's when I realised, it was the person I'd become, how others saw me.'

A knock at the door interrupted us.

'Room service'.

The waiter wheeled the trolley in and set up the dining table. I loved it. Simple, private. We got off the couch and sat at the table.

Between mouthfuls, he told me he had been a UN peacekeeping soldier in East Timor in 2000, long before he started work as a personal trainer. He spoke of the atrocities he'd seen and the powerlessness he'd felt at not being able to do anything. He told me how he'd eventually left the military, pretty fucked up, the issues completely unresolved.

'To my shame, I was a bully, taking out my frustrations on those poor vulnerable women who were only there looking for my help. Once I got more work, I could afford a shrink. He helped by letting me create this fictional character, the guy on TV, packaging up all that shit in 'The Enforcer'. It helped me to let go. It worked, I'm no longer like that guy on TV. I put up with the pitfalls of fame, of celebrity, because it keeps me sane, pays the bills.'

We continued eating, talking about what we do, laughing about how our lives had changed, until we both realised we were really tired and were ready for bed.

'Nic, I've loved meeting you. Tonight was thrilling, but I think I would like to go home, get a good night's sleep. It's been a long day.'

'I understand. Thanks for listening.'

He called the concierge to order a cab.

I kissed him warmly. It would have been tempting to stay.

On the ride home I thought about what had happened and was glad the night had unfolded in that strange way. I did have a plan. I had bought handcuffs from a shabby little sex shop. I was going to shackle him to the bed, leave him there, give him a dose of the humiliation he had meted out to me all those years ago. I had made assumptions about this man. The night could have gone so horribly wrong. I was ashamed at how clever I thought I was.

# On with the Job

The Australian tour was over, there was so much catching up to do.

I had been keeping my followers informed with a travel diary, sharing my experiences and posting pictures of the many readers who had come to hear me speak. I was aware the internet had made big changes to once isolated regional women. I remember how disconnected I'd felt as a kid growing up in the bush.

Cindy had been keeping things going at home. She had become my right hand woman.

When the publishers had said they would pay for an assistant, I immediately rang the careers advisor at a country high school, where I'd recently given a talk, and asked if she could recommend someone for the job. It would have been easy to simply advertise the position, but I knew there were so many country girls, trapped in the cycle of dull job, dull boyfriend and dull life, who needed a little bit of help.

He found me Cindy Winter, an exceptionally mature young woman, who had spent the last few years working in the office at the school. Although good at her job, he thought she was capable of so much more. Her family were happy for her to come to the city and experience a different type of life. She couldn't wait to leave.

She was tech savvy, managing and editing the blog when I was just too busy or away. She coordinated my diary and handled all the bookings for upcoming engagements. She had an almost uncanny ability to read my mind.

On returning home, the tour would be officially over and the financial commitment from the publisher to pay her wages would cease.

It was eight forty five Monday morning. She would be arriving soon, we would have to talk.

'Cindy, you've done a brilliant job managing while I was away.'

'Thanks, Tina, and before you say another thing, I know my time with you has run out. You don't have to feel embarrassed telling me,' she said stoically.

'As usual you've read my mind, but it's not what you think.'

Sales of the book were making bestseller lists and I was starting to see the money come in. The book was about to be released in America, where my followers were getting excited by the upcoming tour there. We had adopted the same strategy and included our American readers' stories, with the same viral response.

We would begin the 'Chris Brown Guide to Escape Money' as soon as the tour finished. The U.S. economy was still in a bad way and our biggest contributors to this page were from the States. There was a ridiculous amount of work to do and I could no longer do it alone.

Things were going to get much, much busier.

'How would you feel about not just working for me, but taking on a much bigger role, sharing in a slice of the action?'

'What have you got in mind?'

I explained to her that I would need a manager. One of the biggest revenue streams had become the public speaking engagements. I had put an enquiry link on the blog and was being inundated with requests. I was aware that there was so much more we could do with the Chris Brown brand and I knew she was up for the challenge.

'But Tina, I'm only twenty one years old. I have no experience in this area.'

'No experience! Bullshit, you've been managing all this while I was away. Not a glitch. Bookings increased, quotes on corporate gigs for ridiculous amounts of money, not a day missed sending out a post.'

'Just tell me, which part are you struggling with?'

'But, I...'

'No buts, Cindy. Six months ago I was this pathetic little woman, no husband, no house, no job, no idea! It's all about bluff, taking a few risks, jumping in at the deep end.'

I paused, the room was silent, she began to grin. She was hungry for more.

'Have you finished your speech?' she said.

'Maybe...?' I replied sheepishly.

'Well, get off your high horse and turn on your computer. We've got a bloody lot of work to do!' she said in a very matter of fact, 'Cindy', kind of way.

Over the next few days we came up with an agreed new wage and a percentage of the profits. She became unstoppable.

What a different twist to a tale. She was the same age as I was when fate intervened. What different paths we'd chosen.

# Japanese Retreat

The publishers had let their American office handle the tour and yes, everything was bigger in the States. Sales were going crazy. In three short weeks we had covered most of that vast country, women queuing for blocks just to get a photo and an autograph. I loved the boundless enthusiasm these people had. It gave me the energy to keep up the gruelling schedule.

On the last night I rang Cindy to have a general whinge about my tiredness.

'Thought you would be. I've been doing some research. You have a stopover in Hawaii, just a couple of gigs. I took it upon myself to give you a few days off and have booked you into a very quiet, very exclusive Japanese spa.'

'Japanese spa?' I said.

'Yes, it's at a remote location. I've organised a driver to pick you up after your last book signing. Gotta look after the talent! Have fun.'


I finished the American tour and just as Cindy said, there was a driver waiting for me. We left Honolulu and headed up into the hills, lush green rainforests and cooling breezes were a welcome relief. We pulled into the drive of a stunning early sixties house. I was greeted by a well built, tall man. Perhaps Japanese?

'Welcome, Tina. I'll show you to your accommodation. My name is Ken,' he said in a deep voice with a broad American accent. Japanese American?

151

I walked into a gorgeous airy lounge room with magnificent views overlooking an infinity pool and the ocean beyond. To one side a glass pavilion intercepted the space, a bedroom.

'This house is beautiful.'

'Yes, it was built for my father in 1962. You should find everything you need here. Please make yourself at home. I've left a copy of the spa program in the bedroom. If you need anything I'm not far away, just call me on this phone. You'll have complete privacy, you're the only guest here.

Please enjoy your stay.'

I could barely contain my enthusiasm. I looked through the house. The bedroom furnished simply with a low bed, a dressing room at the rear. The filmy curtains catching the faint sea breeze, large glass doors opening the entire space to the outdoors. A beautiful pared back Japanese minimalism, a welcome relief from the generic hotel rooms of the last three weeks.

Outside a traditional Japanese bath, an onsen, fed by a hot volcanic spring.

I explored the kitchen next and found platters of Japanese delicacies ready for me to eat, along with some icy cold French wine.

I opened a bottle and delighted in the decadence of drinking alone. It had been an intense time.

It was hot and humid. I peeled off my clothes and slipped into the pool. I luxuriated in the quietness and swam.

The sun was setting, I was hungry. I pulled on a soft cotton robe and took a platter of sashimi from the fridge and read through the house information.

I discovered that the house had been designed by Vladimir Ossipoff for Cameron Mitchell and his Japanese wife Aiko, as a holiday home. Over the years the house had become run-down, seemingly abandoned, until Ken returned to Hawaii, after his parents' death, to oversee its complete restoration. The photos showed the different stages of the life of the house. Two men looking over plans, the tall, handsome American, obviously his father. The new home filled with furniture, a black and white magazine shoot and a mother playing with her son. Then an old couple standing out the front, a derelict house, more building work, the restored shell, and finally the latest shots of the house lovingly brought into this century.

On the coffee table, next to house information, were some beautifully bound books of what I thought were traditional Japanese woodblock prints. That is until I looked more closely. The prints were highly erotic, 'Shunga', graphically depicting men and women, with enhanced sexual organs, fucking in every way possible. I was completely drawn to them, aware of how aroused these graphic illustrations were making me feel. It had been a long time since I'd had sex and here I was at this secluded place, miles from anywhere, not a soul in sight. I slept fitfully, having disturbingly realistic dreams of sex with Japanese men. I got up during the night and had a cooling swim, then went back to bed and slept peacefully.

That morning I looked at the activities on offer. A guided trek sounded interesting. I hadn't been on a decent walk for a long time. I rang Ken, he said we could set off after breakfast, better in the morning before it got too hot.

The trek began along a narrow path, black volcanic soil contrasting with the lush tropical greenery. We chatted as we walked.

'So what brings you to Hawaii? I noticed the booking was made in Australia?'

'I'm an author. My book has just been launched in the States and I've been on a three week tour. My manager thought I needed a few days rest before heading home. She knows I love architecture from this period and I guess that's why she booked me in here. The house, it's marvellous. I loved looking at the photos, you've done a great job.'

'Thanks, it was a labour of love. I felt I owed it to my parents.'

'Why?'

'I felt ashamed that I hadn't been there for them. I had become totally caught up in my own world, working ridiculous hours, always thinking there would be plenty of time to get back home. Until one day there just wasn't.'

'What happened?'

'They were old. I was born after my parents turned forty. I had been a completely indulged child. I rang every week to check up on them. They seemed fine and of course they would never tell me if there was anything wrong. They were happy that their son was a successful plastic surgeon, living in California. In truth they liked their life here. They didn't want to travel and I was always too busy to visit.'

He told me that his father had died first, his mother not long after. An autopsy had shown his mother had poisoned herself. She had been deeply in love and could not bear to be separated.

'It shocked me when I returned to find the empty house in such a state of disrepair. At first I thought I would sell it and get on with my life. Then I found the original plans and a diary my father wrote during its construction. I discovered that he and the architect were friends, who met when they were both living in Japan. My dad was an engineer and they'd worked together on many projects. It made me realise how little I knew about my parents, how I'd been in denial about my Japanese heritage.'

Ken then told me that he had taken a year off, spending time in Japan, becoming immersed in its culture and traditions.

'After that year away I realised I couldn't go back. I'd lost my ambition. I wanted to slow down. I'd turned forty, had enough money to live comfortably and just wanted to fix up the house.'

We continued our walk quietly, the path winding its way down to a small secluded beach with unfamiliar black volcanic sand. It was getting much hotter and we sat in the shade of a palm tree.

'So how long will you remain here?' I asked.

'For now, this is my home. I plan to stay for a while.'

'No one to go back to?'

'Not really. Although there was never a shortage of women. That's the reality of being a plastic surgeon in Los Angeles,' he remarked wryly.

'I was married once. She wanted children, I didn't. I had a vasectomy long before we met and I wasn't prepared to have it reversed. Her need for children was greater than her need for me. When she left, I threw myself into my work.'

We sat staring at the water, with little to say. We were almost complete strangers.

'Feel like a swim?' he asked, breaking the silence.

'I didn't bring my bathers.'

'Bathers?'

'Swimsuit,' I replied, realising he was unfamiliar with the term.

And with that he pulled off his tee shirt and shorts. He was tanned all over, his body lean and muscular. He yelled playfully, as he ran to the water,

'Who needs bathers?'

Last night was the first time I had ever swum naked, that was different, I had been alone.

'What the hell,' I thought to myself, and stripped off too. I was doing a lot of things now that once I had never thought possible. And now I had a body I wasn't ashamed of.

The water was refreshing, cooling after our long walk in the dense tropical heat. The nudity freeing, sensual even. He swam up to me.

'It's good, isn't it?' he said.

'Very good,' I replied.

Eventually we both left the water and sprawled out on the sand, soaking up the sun.

I glanced over at him. Perhaps he was sleeping? He looked calm, his body completely relaxed, his flaccid penis languidly sitting against his thigh. I felt a sudden impulse to reach over, pick it up and gently fondle it, but I dare not touch. It twitched, ever so slightly, the wrinkled velvet skin smoothing, tightening with his faint engorgement. He couldn't see me watching, his eyes were closed. What was he thinking about?

He opened his eyes. I quickly turned away, embarrassed.

It was lunchtime, the walk had made me hungry. We returned to find the house tidied and the bed made.

He left to purchase provisions. Later that afternoon he would be back to give me a lesson in preparing fish.

I ate, swam and still had some time before the cooking lesson. It was hot. I found a movie, 'In the Realm of the Senses'. I drew the curtains and pressed play. I was not prepared for what I saw. This was a sexually explicit, erotic film about a married innkeeper and a young prostitute, set in 1930s Japan. A scene where she places an egg in her vagina, pushes it out, then feeds it to her lover, left me feeling wanton, intensely aroused.

There was a knock at the door. Startled, I quickly stopped the film, covered myself with the robe and went to see who had disrupted my heated meditation.

'Sorry. Were you sleeping?' asked Ken, arms laden with food.

'No, no, come in, I was just chilling out.'

'I found some great food at the market and thought I'd bring it straight to the house.'

He walked to the kitchen, arms laden with produce.

'I have something special for you to try, Namazake Sake. It's unpasteurised, served chilled. I haven't seen it here before. I thought you might like to try it?'

'Sure,' I replied.

He poured from a delicate pottery beaker into two tiny cups.

I had never drunk cold sake before, but its fresh zingy flavour was perfect in this hot tropical climate.

I loved watching him unpack, something very sexy about a man preparing food, each item carefully chosen for this evening's repast.

'I see you found the movie?'

'Ah yeah, I was just watching it when you knocked,' I replied, blushing, as if I'd been caught doing something wrong.

'It seems to capture the Japanese fascination for sex and death, something I observed when I lived there,' he said.

'The Japanese fascination or your fascination?'

'What do you mean?'

'You living here, the movie, the books on Shunga.'

'Ah, you saw those, too.'

'When I went to Japan I was shocked to find such eroticism amongst this restrained group of people. There was one strange practice, 'Nyotaimori', where food is eaten directly off the body of a woman. It isn't widely known, but I was keen to see it practised.'

'So did you find it?'

'Yes, I was taken to a secret restaurant in one of the seedier parts of Tokyo. All these suited businessmen were seated around a young woman lying naked, completely still, on a long table, her body delicately covered in small morsels of food.'

'And is there a male equivalent?'

'Yes, 'Nantaimori', but there is little demand for it.'

'And who are these girls? Are they prostitutes? Are they expected to have sex with the businessmen?' I asked, sipping more of the sake.

'No, not usually. It's more about the restrained eroticism. The preparation of the women is quite a ritual.'

'In what way?'

'Well, her body must be completely hairless, then washed, not unlike the rituals followed at a traditional Japanese bathhouse. She is cooled, dried and then the food is artistically placed on her naked body by a male chef, a specialist in this type of food presentation.'

'Very sex and death,' I said.

'And who are these women?'

'I'm not sure really. They're not Geisha, it's not that kind of profession. I didn't investigate, my hosts chose. I'm sure there is no reason why any woman couldn't perform this task.'

'Even someone like me?' I asked, emboldened by the sake.

'Definitely someone like you,' he replied with a wicked grin.


I paused for a while and watched him put away the last of the food. He had finished and I was not ready for him to leave.

'I think I would like to do this.'

'And I think I would like to do this to you,' he responded huskily.

'How do we start?'

He paused, looking at me, giving the question some thought.

'Well, first I will need to see your body.'

He came around to where I was sitting and took my hand as I stood. With one tug he pulled the tie on my robe, it fell open, exposing me. He looked slowly, up and down, surveying my body.

'Wait,' he said and left the room.

He returned with fluffy white towels, a pillow, a box of toiletries and a small wooden tub, filled with water. He placed the pillow at one end of the table, then covered the entire surface with the towels. He had changed out of his shorts and tee shirt and into a simple indigo cotton yukata, a loose robe worn by both men and women. The mood shifted, he looked different, his demeanour had changed. He had taken on the air of a Japanese master.

'Lie down, on your front, I'll give you a massage. It'll help you relax.'

It seemed that we had begun.

He placed a towel over my buttocks and although we had swum naked together, I was glad that he covered me. I felt less exposed.

He dribbled the sandalwood scented oil over my back, his strong hands massaging it all over my body. He removed the towel, rubbing my buttocks, the action of his hands pushing my hips hard against the table, eliciting a delicious, sensuous ache deep in my pelvis. He finished my back and I knew to roll over.

'I have something to ask. You will need to trust me,' he said huskily, almost whispering.

'What?'

'Your body needs to be completely smooth. I would like to shave you.'

I had just been waxed a few days ago and then I realised exactly what he was saying. I hesitated at first. I had always thought the notion of a completely bald pubis strange. But then something shifted, I had wanted the experience of Nyotaimori and so I said he could continue.

I trusted his skilled surgeons hands.

I closed my eyes.

First I felt him tug gently, snipping away the longest hair. He nudged my legs apart to reach the hair hidden between my thighs, the feeling was electric. Next he soaped a wet sea sponge and began to lather the now shortened hair. Soon a razor was scraping me smooth. He eased my legs further apart, picking up my labia, pulling it taut and delicately shaving around the sensitive skin. My entire sex swelled. I had never felt so vulnerable, yet so willing. When he was done he rubbed the skin with a soothing balm. I breathed heavily.

'I will bathe you now. Come with me.'

We walked to the outdoor bath. He pulled out two low stools, asking me to sit down. I watched him fill wooden buckets from the volcanic spring. He sat down in front of me and using a bamboo ladle, poured the warm water over me. He soaped my body, lifting my arm, sponging the delicate skin, every part of my body, leaving nothing unclean. He then washed my hair, his strong hands kneading my scalp. After rinsing away all the soapy residue, he combed, then braided my hair.

'It is traditional to wash the body before bathing. Now that you are clean, you may enter the onsen,' he said.

I sat in the steamy hot water and watched as he took off his robe, washed himself, eventually joining me. We sat there silent, still, in an almost meditative state. What next? The excitement of the unknown, the ritualistic sensuality of his masterful acts. My mind dizzy with carnal expectation. After a while he spoke.

'I should start the food. Would you care to watch?'

'Yes, I'm sure I have a lot to learn.'

We got out of the bath and he handed me a clean yukata with a simple pink cherry blossom pattern. He retrieved his and we headed to the kitchen.

I sat down at the bench and he poured me a large glass of icy mineral water. I guzzled it down, not realising how thirsty I was.

As I crossed my legs I felt the newly smooth skin, strange, but sensual.

He started by making finger thin nori-maki, black dried seaweed rolls filled with sushi rice and pickled vegetables. He made a thin omelette, deftly folding it into a long square shape then cutting it across forming small egg tiles. Next the vegetables were sliced paper thin, cucumber, spring onions, radish and carrot. Daikon grated into long shreds. The fish, tuna, salmon, garfish, cuttlefish and abalone all cut with the same precision. Lastly he took a piece of dried, smoked bonito, katsuobushi, and shaved it till layers of tissue thin flakes filled a small wooden box. The food and condiments were all placed on a large tenmoku glazed platter and put on a bed of ice.

'I think the food is done. Now we must finish your preparation.'

He took me to the shower.

'Your body has become too warm. I need to cool you.'

He turned on the water.

'I will start with warm water and slowly reduce the temperature so that it is more comfortable for you.'

He took my robe. I stood under the shower, pleasant at first, then gradually becoming cooler, a patina of goose bumps covering my skin, nipples erect.

'I think you are ready. Let me dry you.'

He wrapped me in a towel, patting away the droplets.

Following him back to the room I watched as he opened an antique chest and began to remove its contents. A bamboo mat unrolled and laid out in the centre of the room, an exquisitely embroidered silk cloth, unfurled with a shake, covering the mat.

He scattered around some small cushions and finally, a black lacquered tray, with chopsticks, bowls and cups, completing the scene.

He took my hand and led me to this altar. I lay down, hands by my side, legs together. He placed a small embroidered pillow under my head. I felt very calm.

The sun was setting. He lit candles. I smelt incense, and then heard music, the sound of that strangely haunting stringed instrument, the koto, playing quietly in the background. Music from the film, my desire building.

He knelt down putting the laden platter beside me. I felt the morsels being placed around my stomach, the coldness catching me by surprise.

When he was satisfied with the beauty of their arrangement he paused, pleased with the result. He poured a tepid liquid, Tamari, carefully into the hollow of my belly. I felt the gentle prod of the chopsticks as he lifted the first piece, dipping it into my body's bowl and eating, taking the first bite. He repeated this action, feeding me, then himself.

He took a sip of sake, leaned over and kissed me, the warm liquid dribbling into my mouth. I hungrily thanked him with my tongue. I felt my sex begin to swell.

Next he began to adorn my breasts, my chest rising, my breathing quickened. This would be the fish course, the thin, cold slivers wrapped lacily around my nipples. He scattered the katsuobushi over my left breast and I watched, mesmerised as the flakes magically danced with every heartbeat. He used his mouth this time, picking up the fish in his teeth, dipping into the soy pool, feeding me, then himself. When he was finished, he returned to my breasts, licking them clean of every last morsel then taking my nipples and sucking them hard until they stood to attention. He stifled my groans as he kissed me again, this time more aggressively, passionately.

My human table was empty, but he had not finished. Gently he nudged my legs apart, placing more food on my thighs, wafer thin slices of carrot, shavings of daikon. I lay there silently as he continued to eat, my hunger for him growing. I looked as I saw him pick up a small beaker and pour its contents over my nude pubis, I felt the liquid run between my swollen lips. He leant down and began to lick the salty soy. I wanted more and spread my legs, inviting him to continue his exploration. He sucked and licked hungrily, his teeth biting and gently tugging on my labia. I could barely contain my excitement, but instinctively knew to hold back. He leaned toward the platter. I closed my eyes and waited with aroused expectation at what he would do next. I felt a smooth firmness as he dragged something playfully down my stomach, then temptingly circling my cunt, teasing me until I felt him push it against the entrance, causing my lips to throb with the lusty sensation its thick fullness created. He twisted it, then withdrew, bringing it to my mouth. I tasted, an intermingling of soy and my own salty juices.

'Bite,' he whispered hoarsely.

My teeth bit the end and I relished the fresh taste of cucumber. I dragged his mouth to mine and fed it back to him. Still in his hand, he again held it to my sex and then forcefully pushed it deep inside until it completely disappeared. He watched me as my hips rose in pleasurable response. I squeezed the muscles, then pushed, its rounded green tip reappeared. His mouth went down, sucking, then grabbing the cucumber with his teeth, moving it in and out slowly, before gradually eating, until there was nothing left.

I could take it no longer. I pulled open his robe and saw that his dark veined cock, was stiff, proud, glistening at its tip, ready. I pushed him onto his back, and crawled to his pelvis, sliding my tongue down the engorged ridge protruding on the underside of his penis, then took his silken balls into my mouth, sucking, feeling the hard orbs beneath the skin. He held my head still, briefly, holding me back. He was on the brink. Neither he nor I were ready for this to end. I pulled away, letting him calm slightly. I kissed his face, bit his lips teasingly, a faint taste of this wicked feast lingering. His breathing relaxed, he reached for a condom, rolling it slowly down. I straddled him, lifting my hips, then lowered myself, devouring him until I felt the slight ache of his cock pushing hard into me. Savagely we writhed together, increasing the force with which he drove, until we both erupted into blissful, delicious orgasm. Shock waves pulsated over my entire body.

We lay there, for what seemed an eternity. The candles had all flickered out.

He got up, returning with the wooden bucket, filled with the hot spring water. Gently he bathed me, soaping the folds between my legs, my nipples, before squeezing the sponge, allowing the water to trickle over my body. With all traces of our feast gone we returned to the bath and sat back, fully immersed in the warm tub.

That night we ventured to the bedroom where we fucked once, twice, three times before being completely sated.

My driver arrived early the next morning. I thanked Ken for this memorable retreat and, satisfied, waved goodbye.

# Little Black Dress

The book was now making the best seller lists in America and the next book, 'Escape Money', was in its final stages of production.

I had discovered some of our followers were brilliant writers and was slowly introducing them as regular columnists. Cindy managed them like a seasoned professional. I wanted to make the blog less reliant on me, but understood I could not afford to sever this link, as future projects would be dependent on the publicity the site offered. When I was away I posted a travel diary, so as to stay connected with my readers, keeping in touch so they wouldn't feel abandoned.

For a long time I had been frustrated with shopping for clothes. Thinking that when I lost the weight, entire stores would be at my disposal, spoilt for choice. Not so.

There were many options for teens and young women, a reasonable choice for the oldies, plenty of special occasion dresses. What there wasn't much of were simple, stylish classics for women my age. I didn't want to dress like my daughter and I wasn't ready for sensible elastic waisted leisure wear.

I wondered what the readers thought and asked for their feedback.

The replies came by the hundreds, all agreeing that there was nothing just right for this age group, or any age group. The perfect dress eluded women across the board. They commented that often they would find the 'almost perfect' dress, if it wasn't for just one thing. A colour, a hem, a sleeve length, a neckline. I had an idea.

Lola was back in Australia after a long trip overseas. We hadn't seen each other for ages, so we arranged to meet for lunch.

In typical Lola fashion she arrived looking magnificent, superbly dressed. Charming all those around her.

'Christina, darling, how are you? It seems like ages.'

'I'm great, and you?' I replied.

'Great! That's an understatement. I see that you are now a bestselling author. Everyone is talking. You look radiant. I can't believe you are the same person I whisked away from the press six months ago.'

'I know. So much has happened. Where do I start?'

I told her about the tours and, after a few wines, revealed to her some of the other adventures I'd had along the way. She wanted all the details, her eyes wide with astonishment when I told her about Hawaii.

We talked about her latest trip to Cambodia, where she was getting more furniture made.

'You'd love it. I must take you there one day. During this last trip I took a few days off. Went to Siem Reap, explored the temples. Did a bit of shopping and found this amazing shoe maker.'

She pulled her gorgeous tanned legs out from under the table and showed me her shoes.

'Look at these. They only cost twenty five dollars and were made to fit. I could pick the style and customise it to my specific taste. I picked the upper, the heel, the colour and texture of the leather, they even let me pick the type of sole. They measured my feet and in a few days the shoes were ready.'

That was it! That was exactly what I wanted for the perfect dress. I talked to Lola and she informed me that not only did she have many contacts, but in Cambodia there were many agencies supporting small ethical manufacturing and design businesses.

'I'm going back in a month's time. Do your research and come with me. I can put you in touch with all the right people. Save you a lot of time. It would be fun.'

We discussed the possibilities. Surprisingly she too had trouble finding the perfect dress. We finished lunch. I was keen to get back to Cindy and start making plans.

Over the next few weeks we came up with the idea that we could start an online store. I would design a basic dress and then offer a list of variations. Colour, hem, straps or sleeves, anything I thought could be changed to suit each individual customer. One of my readers had complained that she hated showing her upper arms and wished she could buy dresses with sleeves. I heard this often. It seems we all had bits we wanted to hide. I hated my knees and preferred to wear dresses cut a little longer.

Cindy found a web designer who could create the site we required. All the customer needed to do was enter her measurements, click on her preferred variations and the order would get sent straight to the manufacturer.

It was amazing how the old skills came back. First I designed a basic sheath dress along with all the possible variations. Then I found someone who could make up the patterns and sew up the samples. All the specifications stored on a USB key ready to be shown to potential manufacturers.

I contacted Lola's agent in Cambodia and he put me in touch with a woman, Chenda, who specialised in clothing. She had found a number of philanthropic organisations employing rescued sex workers, street kids and landmine victims. I had decided that if I were to go offshore, I would find a manufacturer who gave something back.

This project was hard work, took up long hours, cost a fortune and I loved every minute of it. Thankfully the book sales, advertising revenue on the site and the growing number of speaking engagements made this all possible.

Finally I was ready to leave. Cindy would keep things going in Melbourne with her usual efficiency. We would keep in contact via the phone and internet.

I looked over at Lola as we were being settled into our first class seats. The attendant poured us a champagne.

'You ready?'

'You bet!'

'Cheers, Lola,' I said, as we clinked glasses, excited by the prospect of a new adventure.

# Cambodia

It had been a mad week, Chenda taking me to lots of different factories till eventually we found the right one. 'Beautiful Sisters' was the name of the charitable organisation. It provided housing for former sex workers and their children. It specialised in training the women in all aspects of clothing manufacture and had developed a niche market making custom made gowns for brides and debutantes in the west. They had just the expertise I needed and the capacity to cope with demand. It was run by an English woman, who had made her fortune with a chain of very successful cosmetics stores. After selling the company, she decided to give something back and put her efforts into this charity, that had once struggled to survive. She used her extensive business skills to turn it into a competitive, yet compassionate organisation. The women were paid good wages and all profits were spent on housing, education and schools for the children.

We had agreed to do a test run with a few close friends and business associates. I would dress them all for my upcoming birthday party. This would be a good trial before I committed to any major financial investment.

Phnom Penh was a dynamic, bustling city, the traffic organised chaos, the weather very hot and humid. I was staying at the Hotel Paris, a small boutique hotel built in a beautiful old part of town near the Royal Palace. It was a French colonial mansion, restored tastefully in an 'Indochine Chic' style. Modern touches mixed with antiques made it very evocative of times past. And although not Vietnamese, it felt like I had stepped into the world of Graham Greene's 'Quiet American'. The hotel was completely surrounded by a high wall, creating a sanctuary from the hustle and bustle outside. The main courtyard contained a pool surrounded by a lush tropical garden, tables arranged under the trees next to the outdoor kitchen and bar. My room was accessed through a breezy arched colonnade, at the quiet rear of the property. A large canopied bed, hung with a mosquito net, dominated the room. It was decorated with Chinese antiques, original mosaic floor. A modern couch and computer, concessions to a more recent time. Through double French doors a small private courtyard, complete with table and chairs, a luxury rarely found in an hotel.

Every morning, Lola and I would begin our day with breakfast in the garden, then venture out separately to attend to our various business meetings. At night we would often head to the Press Club for a cocktail, dinner at one of the nearby restaurants, then back to the hotel for a casual swim. Drinking, chatting with other guests, finding out about their reasons for being in this extraordinary country. In the mornings we would see many of them, looking unfamiliar dressed in their suits, most of them in town for the ASEAN summit. Casual and relaxed at night, professional and distant in the morning.

This clubby, small hotel began to feel like home. So relaxed I often forgot to lock my door. A gentle knock, as one of the staff politely returned the keys I'd absent-mindedly left at our table, completely oblivious to the fact I had not used a key to enter the room.

It was Lola's last night and we were enjoying a drink together, familiar faces were becoming friends. It was comforting to return to the hotel each evening, picking up on the unfinished conversations of the night before.

I had seen him every morning dressed in a dark suit, poring over paperwork, taking notes.

Tonight the suit had gone. He was dressed casually in worn jeans hanging loosely from his hips, tight white tee shirt, bare feet, the dark shadow of stubble appearing on his face. We had been swimming and I couldn't help but notice his lean sculpted body.

His name was Philippe, a scientist who specialised in malaria research. He told us about the talk he had given at the summit on the problems with malaria resistant drugs. The complexities of dealing with this killer disease in such an impoverished country. I was interested in what he had to say.

'Drug resistance is always going to be a problem. It really needs to be a multi-pronged approach,' he said, his French accent provocative, sexy.

'Where would you start?'

'Well, in Italy where malaria was once a huge problem, the swamps were drained. Here it would not be possible as most of the water is intrinsically linked to agriculture. We have to deal with the ongoing problem of living with the mosquitoes.'

'One charity started by providing mosquito nets, only to discover that the nets were being used to catch fish. They realised they had to supply fishing nets as well. A small local net producing factory was set up, funded by the charity, with spectacular results. Jobs for the people, nets for food and fishing and mosquito nets for everyone.'

Although he was at the cutting edge of drug research, he spoke about how he now volunteered, coordinating projects like these where real change could be seen, quickly.

We agreed that it was a big job. Philippe broke the sombre mood of the conversation by offering to buy a round of gin and tonics. He joked that this might be just what a few of us well intentioned Westerners could use, to deal with a localised attack from these all pervasive creatures.

He was sitting next to me, I moved a little closer to afford a more intimate conversation.

'So why Cambodia?'

'My grandparents, or my grandfather, was a diplomat here during the fifties, staying on after Cambodia gained independence from the French in 1953. He'd tell us stories of living in this city, showing us the photos of a time before the civil war, before the dark days of Pol Pot. I'd always had a fascination for this place, remembered so fondly by my grandfather. He had pictures of the grand houses, just like this hotel. I stay here because I fantasised that he might have visited when it was still a residence. Partying and hanging out with the cosmopolitan jet set of Cambodian society,' he said, gesturing towards the grand old building.

'And what about you?'

I told him of my project and he told me of the many other charitable organisations, based around this area doing similar things.

'Beautiful small shops and boutiques. I should take you for a walk, many of these places are located just around the corner on 240 Street.'

I looked over at Lola and asked her if she wanted to come.

'No, no, I've settled in for the night. You go, I'm sure Philippe will be a suitable chaperone.'

He grabbed my hand, and we ventured back out onto the noisy streets, a cicada chorus adding to the cacophony.

Trees lined this vibrant avenue composed of old French colonial buildings, Chinese tea houses and, strangely, a great number of modernist buildings, signifying a building boom in the fifties and sixties. I was amazed at what I saw. Restored shops, gorgeous boutiques, chic little restaurants and wine bars. Many with a focus on rehabilitating lost skills, helping to pick up the pieces of this fractured city and its gentle inhabitants.

I would investigate this more thoroughly tomorrow, but for now we just wandered, window shopping, soaking up the atmosphere of hope and regeneration that this place exuded.

Before coming here I remembered seeing Anthony Bourdain's cooking show, filmed over ten years ago. It depicted the place as a lawless hell hole. Much had changed. People talk about the magic of Cambodia. I understood what they meant and was falling under its spell.

We returned to the hotel to find our little group still gathered around the tables in the garden. Lola greeted me, dangling my room key in front of her.

'You seem to be fond of leaving these lying around. People will get the wrong impression,' she said grinning, pretending to scold me.

'I can just imagine the house parties held in these grand places where the keys were most intentionally left out!' she flirtatiously added.

I shook my head in mock disgust and grabbed the keys, placing them firmly back on the table. The huge decorative tassel attached, meant that I could not fit the keys into my purse. This was the reason why I so often accidentally left them out.

We continued to talk and drink well into the night until Lola stood up. She was off to bed as she had an early flight to catch.

Saying our 'goodnights', I followed her, it had been a tiring day.

After a quick, refreshing shower I crawled into bed and contentedly fell asleep.

I was woken abruptly by a knock at the door. I grabbed a robe, thinking, that once again, it would be one of the staff politely returning my keys. I was surprised to see Philippe.

'Christina, I think these might be yours?'

'Oops, thanks!' I replied.

'De rien. My room is next door and I thought you may not want to have just anyone paying you a visit in the middle of the night.'

'Good thinking, aah... goodnight,' I said, clumsily, as he backed away from the door.

'Bonne nuit, ma cherie.'

I closed the door. 'Ma cherie' he'd said. Did I detect a slight flirtation? What if a complete stranger was to come into my room in the middle of the night? Well, not a complete stranger, one of the guests, Philippe perhaps?

The thought of it sent an intense feeling of desire, the thrill of being woken from sleep and quietly fucked by a stranger in the middle of the night. He was just there, in the room next to mine. I sensed a connection, but lacked the audacity to knock.

I slept fitfully, dreaming of sex, waking aroused.


Lola had left early that morning. I was sitting alone, in the garden waiting for breakfast. It was my last day in Phnom Penh. I was glad of her help when we first arrived, but was surprised how easily I'd managed to assert myself, conduct business and venture out alone in a completely foreign country. Today I would take a more thorough look at some of the shops I had seen on 240 Street, in particular some bags and jewellery that had caught my eye last night. I also wanted to purchase a bikini to take to the seaside town of Kep. Cindy had booked me into a resort there for two nights. She was getting me into the habit of taking some time off after any long trip. When I asked her, 'Why Kep?', she just said, 'You'll see.'

'Excusez- moi Madame, may I join you?'

I looked up, startled from my daydream by Philippe.

'Yes, yes, of course. Please sit down.'

It was daytime Philippe, formally attired, clean shaven, the faint smell of soap, ready for business before the heat of the day took its toll. It had become an unwritten rule that we only socialised at night, when everyone was more relaxed. In the mornings we kept apart, as if we were strangers, a discreet nod the only acknowledgement of our acquaintance. I couldn't understand why seeing him this close in that attire felt so forbidden, yet so intimate?

I had noticed many of the guests had left and a whole new group of unfamiliar faces were around us. I had come to feel very proprietorial about this clubby small hotel and was just a bit uncomfortable about letting the intruders in.

'Are you on your own?' I asked.

'Yes, most of the delegates flew out on an early flight. I don't leave until tomorrow. I have a meeting with the benefactors of the aid program this morning and I'm expecting my driver any minute,' he said.

'My last night, too,' I replied.

His phone rang, his driver had arrived. No time for coffee, just a brief 'A ce soir', and he was gone.

The woman sitting next to me saw the confusion on my face and smiled, happy to translate. He'd said 'until this evening'.

What did 'until this evening' mean? Or what did I want it to mean? Did he have something planned?

It had been a very productive day, new products, new contacts and the potential for a beautiful range of accessories to increase my business. A violent tropical storm in the afternoon gave me an excuse to head back to the hotel.

I had assumed I would run into Philippe at some time this evening, in fact I had hoped we might go somewhere nice for dinner. It seemed like an almost sad farewell. I was surprised at how reluctant I was to say goodbye to a man I barely knew. Like travellers anywhere, we had bonded quickly. I looked forward to what the night might hold.

A massage was a relaxing end to a busy day, then I treated myself to a late afternoon nap.

When I woke, feeling refreshed, the rain had stopped and the sun had set. I decided to put on one of the little black dresses we had been working on this week, convinced that it would be appreciated by my French friend. Dressed and feeling good I went to the garden and ordered a drink. Although we hadn't made any formal arrangement, I just assumed Philippe would be there. Seven seemed to be the usual time.

I sat for another hour, reading the Phnom Penh Post, pretending to be interested, but feeling the growing disappointment of my companion's failure to arrive.

'Excuse me, would you mind if I joined you?' a distinguished looking, elderly gentleman with a strong southern accent, asked.

'Sure,' I replied.

'I hope you don't mind, but I'm here on my own and you looked to be flying solo as well. Calvin Butler, pleased to meet you.' I shook his hand.

'Christina Maxwell.'

'And what's a pretty little lady like you doing sitting here on your own?'

'My friend left this morning. I had no other plans, thought I'd have a quiet night tonight,' I responded, somewhat defensively.

'Well, would you let me buy you dinner? I have no plans either and the menu here looks mighty fine.'

'Calvin, that would be lovely,' I responded more effusively, delighted by his charm, grateful for the company.

I discovered that Calvin had travelled extensively since the death of his wife. We talked about our love for Cambodia. He told me he had been a journalist with the Washington Post and had first come here while covering the Vietnam war. He spoke of the horror at seeing the bombing by his fellow Americans of this neutral country in 1969. Of the savagery inflicted by Pol Pot, the ongoing civil disruption by the Khmer Rouge even after liberation by the Vietnamese in 1979. The famine, the poverty, the corruption. He said how he marvelled at the resilience and the gentleness of a people who had been 'fucked over' for so long. We both spoke about the spell Cambodia casts, Calvin being called back many times by its siren song.

By 9 o'clock I had all but forgotten my original plans. It had been such a wonderfully unexpected night, then suddenly he walked in. My heart skipped a beat. He looked worn out, tired, his suit jacket crumpled, his stubble back.

'Hi Philippe, long day? Would you care to join us?'

In true Southern style Calvin stood, introduced himself and shook his hand. Next Philippe greeted me with two kisses and said, 'Vous êtes très belle.'

I couldn't be mad. We had no plans and he'd said I looked beautiful.

He took off his jacket, unbuttoned his shirt, rolled up his sleeves and began to relax. Casual, rugged Philippe returned.

We drank and swapped stories of our various adventures until the bar closed. Calvin and Philippe had much to talk about and I was tired. I thanked Calvin for the lovely dinner, said goodnight and went to my room.

It seemed empty, I felt alone. I realised I may never see Philippe again.

'Hi, you return?' said Philippe, smiling.

'Yes, I remembered it was your last night, I wanted to say goodbye, and what a pleasure it's been meeting you. Will you be leaving early?'

'Six in the morning.'

He got up.

'I have enjoyed your company very much as well. Maybe we will run into each other again someday?'

He embraced me tenderly and I felt a sudden sadness. Rashly I slipped my keys into his pocket.

'Yes, I hope we do.'


I felt hot with desire, this action had aroused a deep primitive sensuality.

It was a steamy night. I lay in bed, lightning still flickering in the distance, faintly illuminating the room. Eventually the lullaby of the night creatures sang me to sleep.

A rough nuzzling, someone in my bed, I thought I had been dreaming. I felt the full length of his body against my back.

'Ma cherie,' he faintly whispered.

He wrapped his arm around me, pulling me close, my buttocks settling into him, his penis soft.

His kisses caressing me, across my shoulders, the nape of my neck, slowly awakening my body.

His hand wandered along my torso stopping at my breasts, delicately cocooning them, circling a nipple, taking it between his fingers, tugging it till stiffened, sending signals to my sex.

I felt his response, his cock firming, searching between my moistening lips.

In the darkness my senses heightened. I felt his heartbeat, his breathing, his heat.

I remained silent, barely moving, allowing a more primal response.

His hand travelled across my belly, he spread his fingers across my pubis pulling me more firmly toward him, my cleft encasing his now rigid manhood. Deftly the heel of his hand rubbed my clitoris, bringing me into a deep state of arousal. My labia throbbed with fullness. He knew I was ready and slowly entered me. I was aware of the pleasurable sensation of his cock, engorging even more, filling me. We lay there still.

He withdrew, rolled on a condom and in the dark, I reached behind, guiding him back into me. My back arched as he thrust more deeply and quietly, whispering words of adoration in French. We began to rock, rhythmically, together until gradually we were swamped by waves of pleasure as our mutual orgasm quietly engulfed us.

He held me tight. I felt him soften inside me and in this position we fell asleep.


I woke to the sound of monks chanting from a nearby temple, the clock said 6.30. The bed was empty, he had gone. I felt bereft.

I wanted more, I wanted to be loved.

# Part 3

## Kep

The hotel had organised a driver. I sat listlessly, tuned out, during the two hour trip south to Kep.

I knew very little about this destination, other than it had been the seaside playground of the French elite and wealthy Cambodians before Pol Pot. It was once called the more romantic 'Kep-sur-Mer'.

The resort was at the top of a very steep drive, built into the side of a mountain.

My suite was beautiful in a rustic kind of way, a bit 'Swiss Family Robinson' tree house meets 5 star luxury. It was built amongst the treetops, with a massive veranda overlooking the dense jungle and distant sea.

I looked in the bedroom only to be confronted by the sight of a lonely king sized bed and burst into tears. I sobbed from the loneliness, the wasted years, and from the sheer exhaustion of maintaining my protective stoicism. Perhaps a big cry was needed, ugly, indulgent tears. Just give in and let out the frustrations. No one here to watch.

I could've stayed like this indefinitely, wallowing in self-pity, cursing Cindy for not letting me fly straight home. I had been going at a ridiculous pace over the past few months. Driven by a desire for independence, to prove to myself that I could pick up again after such a compromised life.

Instead, I took a deep breath, looked out at the magnificent view and decided that a couple of days winding down was just what my exhausted body and mind needed. A good book, a cocktail, a wander around the resort, a swim, would be a very nice way to spend my last days in Cambodia.

I was woken early the next morning by a loud knocking. I splashed my face with cold water, threw on a dress and opened the door.

'Excusez moi, Madame, your driver has arrived.'

'Driver? I don't understand.'

'It was with your booking, a tour of the houses.'

I still didn't understand, but realising I had nothing better to do, told him I would meet him in the foyer in fifteen minutes. I showered, grabbed a piece of fruit, my bag and headed out.

It was well after ten, I'd overslept. At least I was beginning to relax.

As we walked through the lobby the concierge explained that scattered throughout Kep were many abandoned houses. They were built by wealthy Cambodians who were driven out or murdered during the Khmer Rouge reign of terror.

I climbed into the tuk-tuk still puzzled at why Cindy had bothered. We headed down the hill and followed the coastal road, still not quite sure exactly what I was meant to be looking at. The driver slowed and turned onto a dirt road, eventually pulling up to an overgrown wall and a steep set of stone stairs.

'Come, house this way,' he said in broken English.

I followed him up the stairs till we reached a landing and there I saw it. Standing across from me were the ruins of an elegant modernist mansion. Sweeping curved walls, big open rooms, stone and cement construction, all slowly being taken over by the jungle.

It was the first of many light filled fifties and sixties modern houses. Metal posts holding up expansive verandas, crazy pave facades, external stairways leading to roof decks with views out over the bay. Eerily not a soul in sight, none of them restored, inhabited by ghosts. He pointed out the bullet holes and the grenade damage and I realised that Pol Pot must have meted out a particularly savage form of punishment on this place and its people.

Our communication was limited and I was unable to find out why they lay empty, why none had been restored. He gestured in the distance and said, 'Please, I take you.'

We got back into the tuk-tuk and headed to the seafront. Through large gates we approached what looked like a building site. As we got closer I could see men working on different aspects of what looked like the restoration of a grand seaside villa. My driver ushered me to where the men were congregated around a table of drawings. A tall, hard hatted man, speaking their language, was giving them instruction.

He looked up.

It was Adam Darcy.

I felt sick. My heart started beating rapidly. What was he doing here? I wanted to turn and run. Too late, he saw me and began walking towards us.

My mind was whirring, I had to calm down.

I shouldn't have been surprised. Of course it was a Darcy. His father had made a fortune in this country. His idiot brother had gambled away Paul's money here. Why wouldn't Adam Darcy be at the centre of some property deal in a third world development hot spot?


'Chris Brown?' he said, puzzled.

She had changed. She looked so different from the last time he'd seen her at his friend's funeral.

She was beautiful. Her spirit seemed to be back. She reminded him of the woman he had known when they were much younger. What on earth was she doing here? Surely this was the last place he would expect to see her? Especially after the shameful way his brother had destroyed her husband's business with his idiotic investments in Cambodia.


'Adam?'

'What on earth are you doing here?' he said.

'I've been in Phnom Penh on business. A friend thought I might like to see the abandoned houses of Kep,' she answered coolly.

How did she know about the houses? She was as intriguing now as she had been that day he'd walked into her flat in Brunswick.

'And you? Are you renovating this house?'

'Yes. It's a project I've been involved with for some time. Would you like to have a look?'

'Sure,' she replied nonchalantly.


He took me to the table and showed me the sketches of the finished building.

'This is the grand plan. We're only guessing at how the house once looked. All the records were destroyed by the Khmer Rouge.'

It looked wonderful, like an architect's vision of the perfect sixties house. Two storey, huge glass windows facing the sea, a sweeping curved veranda above the terrace.

We strolled around the grounds till eventually we stood on the vast lawn at the front of the property, facing the water, bounded by a sea wall. We kept being interrupted by his workmen, keen to get instructions for the next step of the project.

I remembered him as a cold man of few words, but here he seemed to show an enthusiasm, engaging the men around him with real interest and warmth. I was impressed by his ability to speak fluently with them, embarrassed at my own complete ignorance of the language. We walked passed a young man struggling under the weight of a load of wooden boards. I watched as Adam tossed away his clipboard and effortlessly helped to carry the timber, patting him on the back when they had finished, the man smiling.

'Sorry, I don't get here very often and the workers are keen to get the job finished. Are you staying for long?'

'No, just a quick trip. I fly out tomorrow.'

'Are you free tonight? Have you been to the crab shacks?' he asked, pointing to the ramshackle wooden buildings lining the shore just a little way along the water's edge.

'Would you like to join me for dinner at sunset? The restaurant at the far end has the best crab in Kep.'

He was inviting me out. Did I really want to spend time with this man whose family I loathed? The alternative was another lonely night in my hotel room. Adam Darcy won.

'Ok, what time?' I responded casually.

'How about five? Your driver will know how to get there, see you then.' And with that he was off.


I returned to my room and contemplated what had just happened. Was I stupid?

I had created a whole new life for myself. Broken free of the shackles of Melbourne's upper class conservatism. Then, with barely a thought, had agreed to spend my last night in this country with a man whose brother treated me with such contempt. Who, for all I knew, was also funding Justin's never ending legal battles against me. Feelings of that insecure student began to return. Did I subconsciously still feel the need to prove myself?

I considered the man I'd just bumped into. He seemed changed. I saw a spark, a humanity that shone above the arrogance I usually associated with Adam Darcy. Had he too been affected by Cambodia? Spellbound by its magic, bewitched by the grace of its people?

I would ask him tonight.

In the meantime, I had an afternoon to kill.

The resort had a massive pool. It was blisteringly hot. A swim would be good and after all I had bought myself a new bikini.

The place was most busy at weekends when hundreds of people would arrive to escape the heat and mayhem of Phnom Penh. I had seen them checking out as I was arriving. Many rich Cambodians, complete with their entourages of wives, children, nannies and thuggish body guards. They drove big black luxury cars and expensive four wheel drives. Their guards carried guns. Up until now my only contact with the people had been the staff at the hotel and the workers at the clothing factory. I had heard about this new elite. Reaping the benefits of Cambodia's rapid economic growth. A ruling class that operated lucratively within a system plagued by endemic corruption. Developers with deep pockets, keen to fast track their projects, bureaucrats rewarded for turning a blind eye.

I wondered how much it was costing Adam Darcy to operate here?

The pool was almost empty, just a few couples lounging around on daybeds. I heard them speaking French. I couldn't tune into their conversations and felt like an observer of some exotic species.

The water was tepid, strange at first to dive in and not be shocked by the cold. I paddled meditatively, loving the freedom the water allowed me to feel. Remembering how I'd stopped swimming when I had become so fat, ashamed to show my body.

I ordered a drink, something with an umbrella in it. I'd regained my composure. I could easily deal with Adam Darcy.

The annoying thing was that he was so handsome. He was a man who wore his age well, in fact I thought he looked better now than when he was a young student. The alcohol made my mind wander. I considered the temptation of seducing him, taking him back to my bed. I stopped, remembering how I had felt after Philippe had left early yesterday morning. I would not succumb to another soulless one night stand. And I would not succumb to a Darcy.

After a short afternoon nap, I showered and thought about what to wear. A white linen shift, something simple and modest, flat, natural leather sandals, a long strand of turquoise beads I'd picked up at the markets on the way home. I kept my hair loosely tied in a bun and applied a brush of mascara. I was pleased with the effect, neutral, cool. Practical in this heat.

The driver was waiting, I had paid him generously to be available during my stay in Kep.

On our way to the restaurant I noticed more of the houses emerging from the jungle. They were still a bit of a mystery. I could only assume they were built after independence in the fifties. A celebration of a new Cambodia, shaking off the shackles of colonialism. A Google search provided no clear answers as to who had built them or why they still remained abandoned. I hoped they would be saved from being devoured by the jungle. Perhaps Adam might know?

We pulled up in front of a row of ramshackle wooden huts built on stilts, hovering precariously over the water. Small shops at the front, restaurants at the back. To the right an open air seaside market where I had bought the beads earlier on. My driver pointed me in the right direction, proudly proclaiming the best pepper crab in Kep. The gracious hostess showed me to a table right against the large open windows, facing the sea. Boys and girls, like kids anywhere, were giggling and frolicking in the water. I sat down and was delighted to see fishermen in long turquoise boats bringing in their catch. Old women were wading to the crab pots to collect the creatures, fresh and alive. Ready to be sold, ready to be eaten.

An army of polite young men were ready to serve me, keen to practise their English. I was quizzed as to why I was alone and tried to convey that I was waiting for a friend. I'm sure they could see a decent tip at the end of the night if they looked after me well.

I guzzled down a glass of the cold local beer. The menu looked interesting, but I delayed ordering, waiting for Adam. He would know the best dishes. And I waited some more. The sun set had been spectacular, the sea now an inky black, but still no Adam. I was embarrassed to be sitting alone, feeling like some sad old spinster, Miss Havisham on her grand tour of Asia.

My appetite had waned, but I was here now and I still wanted to try the crab. The waiters recommended the Kampot pepper crab. Within minutes out came a plate of bright orange crustaceans coated in a thick coconut sauce studded with fresh green peppercorns. I copied the other diners, cracking open the claws, slurping out the meat, covering the inappropriate white dress with flecks of turmeric yellow sauce. I finished, leaving a big tip and a table trashed with scrunched up napkins, empty beer cans and a mountain of denuded shells.

So what if that bastard had not turned up? The food was great, staff friendly and my loyal driver was waiting outside.

I spent my last night in Cambodia on the large balcony outside my room, checking emails and watching the faint flickerings of a storm way out to sea. I loved Kep, but would be reluctant to return, Adam Darcy had claimed it first.

# Life model

'What is wrong with you?' Cindy said, half annoyed, half concerned, observing my strange mood.

I had returned to Melbourne. Cindy had managed brilliantly. Great speaking engagements booked, new projects and many more advertisers. Business was good, no reason to be pissed off.

It was me. Deep inside I knew it was the appearance of Adam Darcy that had brought all the same old insecurities crashing back. I just couldn't get enthused about anything.

The house was still in dispute, it meant I couldn't close that chapter in my life. Adam Darcy was just another annoying reminder, probably financing the legal battle his brother delighted in taunting me with. When would I finally be rid of this family?

'Nothing, it's not you or the business. Sorry for being so grumpy. Guess I'm just a bit jet lagged.' I couldn't be bothered explaining.

She got us both a coffee and returned to her desk.

'We had heaps of strange requests while you were away, but this one sounds interesting. What do you think?' said Cindy.

She showed me a request by Tim Nolan, the painter, who wanted me to pose for him.

He exhibited at Gabriella's gallery. I gave her a call.

'Christina, darling, lovely to hear from you. How was Cambodia? Lola said you had a ball.'

'Good, Gabriella good, it was amazing. Hey, listen, it's actually Tim Nolan I wanted to talk to you about.'

'Ah, he contacted you, yes?' she said.

'He wants me to sit for him. What do you think?'

Gabriella told me she had been talking about the transformation I had made to my life and that he might be interested in the images I had been posting on the blog. He was having an exhibition at the gallery and needed a few more paintings to make the show complete.  It was Gabriella who told him to contact me.

'The show is about the body and perceptions of beauty. He may want you to pose naked. Would you consider it?'

'What a joke! It really would be Chris Brown stripped bare!' I laughed.

She urged me to contact him and gave me his cell number.

I told Cindy. She dared me to call.

I was surprised by the quiet, almost timid voice at the end of the line. We arranged to meet at his studio just around the corner in Peel Street.

I knocked at the old warehouse door. The buildings faded sign told me this had once been a piano factory, at a time when Fitzroy was an industrial working man's suburb.

A small man with disfiguring scars on his face answered the door.

'Tim? Hi, I'm Christina.'

'Chris..tina, welcome, thanks for coming,' he said, gently shaking my hand and gesturing for me to enter.

We walked into a huge white room. Wooden floors showing evidence of the building's previous life, polished but with the scars of heavy use deeply ingrained into the timber.

I was pleasantly surprised by what I saw. Huge canvases of naked figures were mounted in the room, not dissimilar to the work of Lucien Freud. It was not what I'd expected. This small man with the timid voice produced magnificent paintings, bursting with life and colourful exuberance. I was hooked and could barely contain my enthusiasm for the work.

He showed me around the studio, telling me he'd bought it, not long after his first successful show.

Why would he want to paint me?

He said he had been intrigued by my ability to take control of my life and bare my soul.

He only had two weeks to produce the painting, but had already done some sketches based on what he had seen on the blog. What he needed was to see the real me in order to give the painting life. I agreed. This project was just what I needed to get me out of the fug that had been crippling me. We would start tomorrow.

'I thought we'd work in the small studio. It's easier to heat the space. Have you ever sat for a painter before?' he asked.

'No, Tim, this is a first.'

'You can change over there,' he said, pointing to a doorway, 'I've left a robe for you to put on while we decide what pose works best.'

I returned to see that he had brought two pieces of furniture into the centre of the room. A red Grant Featherston chaise and a lime green Contour chair.

'Your assistant, Cindy, told me you have a thing about this era. I'm not sure whether I want you sitting or reclining. What do you think?'

'A thing! I can't believe you have these. The chair, it's so similar to one I had when I was a student,' I responded, quite taken aback by the memories the furniture provoked.

'They're beautiful, aren't they. I have an extensive collection. These two pieces seemed just right for you. I've got many more if you want to take a look.'

'No, no, they're fine. I was just surprised. You must be quite insightful, your intuition was unbelievably right.'

I lay down on the couch, a simple curve with a bolster. I felt exposed, vulnerable. I tried the chair and felt very Christine Keeler, sitting up, in control. And of course I loved this chair. It was almost identical to the one I had in my flat all those years ago. I smiled with the familiarity, the comfort.

'That's it. That's you.'

And so we began this new intimate relationship. I was completely relaxed, we chatted as he sketched. Comfortable, with the nudity, it seemed the most natural thing in the world.

'Christina, I love the way you took control, used your blog to silence the bullies. I can imagine how overwhelming it must have been.'

He came toward me and moved my arm, stepped back, nodded, and continued to draw.

'I went to a very prestigious boarding school. It was hell.'

I learned that Tim had been there with Paul, Justin and Adam. All these poor kids forced to live away from home, when their mothers were just around the corner. A boarding school, not miles away in the country, but right in the heart of the leafy, affluent suburbs. No real need for them to be away from their families.

He told me that he had been hounded mercilessly. At boarding school there was no escape, no sanctuary from the torment of the bullies His acne scarred face, his sexuality and artistic ways an easy target. Justin Darcy had been the ringleader.

'You poor bastard, it must have been horrible.'

'People can be very cruel. My father had gone to that school. It was where his family had always educated their sons. I had no choice,' he revealed.

'I gather from your blog that you grew up in the bush. What I don't understand is how you ended up with Paul?'

I told him the story. My parent's death, the pregnancy, my need to belong, to prove that I was as a good as any of them.

'Also, I didn't want my daughter to have the life of financial struggle that I grew up with. I wanted her to have the opportunities that wealth gave. It just seemed like the easiest option at the time.'

'And if you really want me to be honest, it was perhaps because I wanted to be like those rich girls. The ones who lived on the big old properties around where I grew up. I envied them, wanted the sophisticated lifestyle I thought they had. We all went to primary school together. But when it was time for high school, they left for boarding college, leaving me stuck in a place that held so little hope.'

'So now you seem to be free. Are you happy?'

'I am happy, but I'm not free.'

I told him of the ongoing legal battles I was having and how I still had to deal with Justin Darcy.

'In fact I was in Cambodia recently when I had the misfortune of running into Justin's brother, Adam. It had been a great trip up until then. The bastard didn't even bother to turn up to the restaurant where we had arranged to meet. Did you know Adam?'

'Yes. We try and catch up when he's in town. He's a nice guy. Done well for himself,' said Tim.

'Are we talking about the same man?' I scoffed.

'Adam was never involved in the bullying and, although we weren't close, I always sensed he disapproved of his brother's behaviour.'

He stepped back to study what he had just drawn, then resumed our conversation.

'You know there were always rumours going around about them, that they weren't actually twins. It started when they were very young. They looked so different, were nothing alike. Justin was the stupid fat kid, Adam was good looking, clever. They teased Justin mercilessly, Adam always stood up for his brother. The fact that their father was a sleazebag with heaps of kids all over the place didn't help. There was no truth in the rumours, but the shit seemed to stick. Kids can be very cruel. The harassment was pretty bad. As they got older Justin got bigger, a smarter mouth, clever with his fists. He intimidated people, fought back. Kids became scared of him. He ruled the school yard like a petulant warlord. Always had an army of sycophantic underlings to do most of his dirty work. Justin had gone from being bullied to becoming an even nastier bully.'

'None of that surprises me. My husband was in business with him for many years. I saw that sort of behaviour all the time. But Adam, you say, was different?'

'As they got older, Adam didn't need to defend his brother any more. He became more of an outsider, a deep thinker, didn't really fit in with the other kids. He had a shyness that was often misinterpreted as arrogance.'

'Wow, I had no idea. But come to think of it, he never really had much to say. I too, thought it was arrogance. Adam was a bit of a hero amongst my husband's friends. I think they envied him. Loved that he had followed in his father's footsteps, building his empire, doing spectacularly well. They were probably a bit envious, wished they also had a father like that. Someone to give them support, the knowledge, expertise, financial backing.'

'Actually, you've got it quite wrong. Adam had nothing to do with his father. They had quite a big falling out, not exactly sure why. Adam's wealth is all his own. He distanced himself from all of that. He started from scratch.'

I was surprised. Paul had never mentioned any of this. Maybe he didn't know either?

I was curious. Adam had seemed different in Kep.

Tim continued to draw.

'Well, I think I have all I need for now. Thanks, Christina. You can get dressed.'

The nudity hadn't been a problem. I felt so relaxed I didn't even bother to put on the robe when I got up to see at what Tim had done. I looked at the sketches, large sheets of paper strewn across the floor. It was strange to see how someone else interpreted how I looked. Eventually I got dressed and returned to the studio.

He told me the next stage would be getting the image down on canvass.

'I think I need one more sitting. Are you free next Wednesday?'

'Sure, what time?'

'I intend to have the painting almost finished, but I would like you back later, just to see I'm on the right track. How about six?'

'Sounds good. Maybe we could have a bite to eat when you're done?'

'Great. See you then.'


I returned a few days later. He greeted me like an old friend. This time he was working at a large easel upon which the huge canvas was mounted.

I remembered how much I had resisted having my photo taken over the last ten years. Hating the truth of the images I saw, so different from the me I had in my head. I had raised this issue with my readers and many women told me they also hated their photo being taken. It made me aware that a whole generation of women were choosing to disappear. Family albums devoid of mothers.

I stripped off and headed for the chair. He positioned me in the correct pose and continued to paint.

We both talked about our favourite haunts.

'Do you know much about Mister Smith, that gay bar up the road?' I quizzed.

'What do you want to know?' he replied.

'Well, I see the men going in and out and have often wondered exactly what goes on in a place like that. I have this secret fantasy about having an affair with a gay man. Perfect cook, beautifully groomed, erudite, with the ability to tell me how fabulous I look.'

He laughed, saying that we were all looking for that man.

'I'll let you in on a secret. I own Mister Smith. We could go tonight after we finish here.'

'I'd love to, but wouldn't it be a bit tricky? Wouldn't they be hostile toward a woman encroaching on their turf?'

'Leave it to me. You'd be my guest. '

The time passed quickly. Tim finally put his brush down.

'Well, I think it's perfect. Gabriella will be pleased. She has hung all the paintings and has been hounding me for this last one.'

'Are you coming to the opening on Friday night?' he asked.

'I dare not miss it. Gabriella has been trying to drag me along to openings for years.'

'What! You've never been to one of her openings before?' said Tim, slightly bemused.

'Until recently there were a lot of things I hadn't done before. I rarely ventured to this side of town. I'd been leading a very sheltered life.'

'People think they know me through the blog, but my readers would be quite shocked if they knew some of the things I've been getting up to since being kicked out of home!'

'So, it's not entirely Chris Brown Stripped Bare? You still have some secrets?' he responded.

'I'm not so narcissistic that I feel the need to reveal everything. I have a private life and a daughter to consider!'

I told him of a few of my adventures and how I sometimes introduced myself with different names.

'My parents called me Christina, my mother thought the final 'a' was more exotic than the typical Christine. Paul started to call me Chris pretty much from the moment we met. All his mates had nicknames and

I thought this was just him showing I had one too, was part of the group, a kind of initiation, acceptance.'

'When I married Paul, I took his surname. Not only because it was expected of me, but because I wanted to show I was committed to the marriage and to him, to trick myself into believing it would work. I was shocked at how stateless I felt afterwards. I had gone from Christina Maxwell to Chris Brown. Married into a family that didn't want me, with a name that was not my own.'

'So why don't you change it back?' questioned Tim.

'I have thought a lot about this. Chris Brown is my public profile, my business, my 'Brand'. I don't feel like Christina Maxwell any more. She was the girl who got lost nineteen years ago.'

'So who are you now? What would you like to be called?'

'Well, I think the new me, the real me is Tina, Tina Maxwell.'

'I like it!'

He stood back.


'Do you want to have a look?'

It was interesting to see such a graphic depiction of my body, my face. Tim's interpretation of what he saw. He'd shown me sitting up confidently, the curve of the chair framing my body, dark hair tossed languorously over my left breast, one leg cheekily draped over an arm of the chair. The bold, mainly black and white composition interrupted only with a splash of red for my lips and toenails. And in the background a grey mirror, heavily framed showing a faint image, a copy of that first photo, a barely recognisable me.

'Wow, it's amazing,' I said.

'It will be interesting to see who buys it, maybe one of your fans?'

'Who would want a picture of me?'

'Well, my work is quite collectable and a good nude is usually easy to sell. Speaking of which, you should get dressed. I think we have a date.'

I realised I had been standing there for some time, naked, totally at ease. I got dressed, checked my hair, reapplied some lipstick and followed Tim out the door.

# Gay Night Club

We headed along Smith Street. It was getting late and the bars were just starting to come alive. We passed the entrance to Mister Smith and walked a little further down an alleyway along the side of the building, till we got to a large back door. Tim took out his keys and unlocked it. We went in.

I saw a dark carpeted room, two black leather swivel chairs at a long desk. Behind the desk a bank of computer monitors. We were in what looked like a viewing room, a kind of nerve centre, the TV screens each showing a different image.

'What's this all about?' I asked curiously.

'Some time ago we had an incident where a guy got severely bashed in the bar. We installed CCTV as a security measure.'

'Don't the patrons find it intrusive?'

'No, quite the opposite. When we first installed the cameras, we told our clients, told them they were being watched and to our surprise the number of patrons grew. It seemed they liked the idea of being observed. So much so, that we now hire out this room. Voyeurs are prepared to pay a premium to sit and stare at the screens.'

'Tonight I have booked the room for you alone. You won't be disturbed. Help yourself to drinks in the fridge. I've got the guys from the restaurant across the road to make you up some food. You must be starving,' he gestured to a small table covered in a white cloth, set for one.

He showed me how to use the control panel, zooming in to get a closer look at the activity in each room, sound on or off.

'I won't be staying, I have some things to do. Feel free to leave whenever you like. Just make sure the door is securely shut when you go.'

He left, I poured myself a drink from the generously stocked bar, a sparkling Riesling, something I'd never tried before, Clare Valley. The food was delicious, some croquettes, oysters, duck liver parfait and crispy five spice quail. I wolfed down each of these little morsels not realising that sitting naked for hours had been such hungry work.

I sat in the chair, spinning around like a kid, glancing at the screens and seeing what looked like a whole lot of men mingling in a crowded bar. Not very interesting, until I looked more closely.

I decided to start with camera one. It showed the front of the building. Men entered dressed innocuously, like anyone going out to a bar.

Camera two showed them in a foyer, signing in, some grabbing a key. So this was a club, members only, now I remember seeing the sign.

Camera three showed a room filled with lockers and men in various stages of undress, some naked, some in just their underwear and others in less familiar garb. I saw men in leather jackets and tight shorts, in chaps with their bare asses exposed. Some wore jockstraps and tee shirts, again with their buttocks displayed.

Camera four saw a crowded bar, some men fully clothed intermingling with the men I had seen in the locker room. It was noisy, men were sitting at the bar drinking. My attention was drawn to a couple, both gorgeous looking and stylishly dressed. There was something strange about their behaviour and I zoomed the camera in. They sat very close, close enough to be mutually masturbating, each holding the others' penis. Not vigorous pulling, just a playful tug every so often, enough to keep a generous erection, not enough to stop drinking. It all looked so normal, so relaxed. I found it very sexy, I was enjoying watching.

Camera five was pointed at the far wall, a padded bench running along its length. Men sitting there rubbing their dicks, waiting, keeping themselves hard. I zoomed in on one man whose cock was gigantic, it's girth so large his hand could not close around it. Other men would approach the bench, kneel down and start to suck on any of the available phalluses, their heads being pulled down hard and fast, almost brutally, to increase the friction. No gentle sucking, one guy slapping his dick against the face and tongue then ramming it into the cheek of the guy on his knees.

I returned to camera four and noticed a guy sitting on a bar stool, dressed only in a jockstrap. His back arched, his naked bum stuck out pertly over the edge of the stool. He was greeted by a man, fully dressed, who proceeded to start massaging the seated man's backside. He then leant down, spread the cheeks apart and began to lick the exposed anus. I could see his crack glistening with spit and when the licking stopped, he continued the massage, easily slipping his thumbs into the well lubricated hole.

Camera six answered some questions. This room was white, tiled from floor to ceiling. A wet room. Along one wall a row of showers, men were washing, sucking cocks, some appeared to be pissing on each other.

A man headed to a white towel covered bench. He lay down on his stomach and a masseur began to rub with his strong oiled hands. After some time a rolled up towel was placed under the man's hips. A more intense massage of the man's backside occurred, squeezing the cheeks, then forcefully spreading them apart, exposing a neat tight anus. The masseur then started to rub the guys inner thighs, slowly coaxing the legs further apart, the rolled towel still in place, leaving the guy's bum high and accessible. From a trolley next to the bench the masseur grabbed a small dildo, rolled a condom onto it and then slowly inserted it into the guy. He continued the process with a series of ever larger dildos and while pumping with one hand, rubbed his own cock with the other. The guy on the table was surrounded by a number of men, observers, who were all vigorously rubbing their own stiff proud penises. Then, one by one, they all started to come, spurting over the man's back. The masseur then rolled the man over and with a few frantic tugs brought the man to his own climax. The man returned to the showers.

All this watching made me hungry. I paused to eat before my new found voyeurism called me, quickly, back to the screens.

Camera seven was the only screen I had not visited. It was positioned in a large room. At first I found it hard to focus. By now the room was crowded, large screens playing porn, some men dancing, loud talking above the pulsating music. Hard, hot, sweaty bodies and lots and lots of sex!

Men being pounded, bent over tables, against walls, faces grimacing with the ferocity of their fucking. I zoomed in to watch as a group men were linked ass to cock, daisy chaining, being watched by the appreciative mob.

A stir in the far corner of the room. I heard the men begin to chant 'Big Bob, Big Bob, Big Bob'. A spotlight lit the small stage. I saw a man, his buffed, gladiatorial body glistening. It was the man with the massively thick penis. He gyrated to the sound of the throbbing dance music, pointing to his huge erect cock and gesturing, playfully, to the audience to come and try. A procession of beautiful young men all jumped up to greet him, bending over while he pretended to enter them, his massive girth proving too difficult for their tight little rings.

The crowd was being worked into a frenzy, when an equally beautiful and well hung male danced onto the stage to the delighted yelps and grunts of an appreciative audience. The tattoo across his chest read 'Adonis'. The crowd wolf whistled and started a new cry, 'Donis, 'Donis, 'Donis. He turned his back and began pouring oil over his broad shoulders, drizzling it down his spine. Not missing a beat, Adonis then began to rotate his ass, spreading his legs, looking back at the crowd with a lusty grin. Big Bob smiled and rubbed his cock with more oil, building it into an even more impossible size. The crowd was going spare with anticipation. Bob moved closer and ran his muscular arm along Adonis's back forcing him to bend over. The audience cheered as Bob grabbed hold of his cock and started to slide it up and down Adonis's crack and ever so tentatively pushed against the tightly closed hole, only to give up in mock frustration.

A barman jumped on stage and gave Adonis a stool to lean over, something to hold onto. Adonis grabbed the legs of the stool to brace himself for the onslaught. The barman, obviously part of the act, called for silence, building tension in the audience. He looked at Bob as if to say 'Are you ready?' Only to have Bob shake his head and laugh. More oil was poured until Bob gave him the thumbs up.

The barman handed Bob a box of condoms and, like a true showman, he rejected all the small rubbers until, what looked like the biggest condom I had ever seen was slowly rolled on. Bob edged closer, a cameraman started filming and a close up for all to see was projected onto the big screen.

Slowly but surely Bob's huge cock began to tease Adonis open, first the shiny red tip disappeared, a pause while Adonis gasped, then further until his sphincter closed tight, gripping the entire head. Another pause and then Bob grabbed Adonis and with all his might rammed, with brutal force, his monster phallus deep inside.

The audience erupted into wild shouts, the dance music exploded and holding him like a captured lover, Bob pounded Adonis, pumping to the beat of the throbbing dance music until he rapidly withdrew, ripping off the rubber, showering the crowd with his spurting cum.

I lifted my leg onto the arm of the chair and reached between my thighs, my lips swollen and wet. I needed to find relief.

I was interrupted, startled by my beeping phone. A diary reminder that I had a conference call at 2 am with the publishers in America. The downside of living in the Southern Hemisphere!

It was 1.30 am.

I had been at the screens for hours.

I was breathless and highly aroused, but quietly laughing at my naivety. After seeing these men in homoerotic, testosterone fuelled action, my fantasy of the perfect gay husband was shattered. These men knew what they wanted and it was most definitely not a woman.

The short walk home in the cold night air would be necessary to clear my head.

# Opening Night

Life was moving very quickly, lots was happening. The call from America was to give me an update on the new book, 'Escape Money'. It was being adapted for the U.S. market and was finally ready for me to have a look at. I had spent the last few days proofreading, more time in front of a screen and was ready for a break.

I was dying to talk about what I had seen at Mister Smith, but felt that even telling Cindy would be a breach of the trust Tim had given me. I was still having dreams about anal sex with big cocked men. It was most definitely time for me to get out a bit more.

What I loved most about living in this part of town was just how close I was to everything. Tim's opening tonight was just around the corner at Gabriella's gallery on Gertrude Street. Close enough to wear heels.

I wished I was getting ready for a romantic date, but once again I was heading out on my own. At least Gabriella's gallery would have some familiar faces and maybe even some less familiar who might be interested in going out after the opening. Perhaps coming home with me?

I decided to wear one of the new little black dresses. A simple sheath with a sheer black, subtly patterned silk layer over the top, covering the arms and forming a loose cowl around the neck. Good for the unpredictable spring weather. I had been sent a big box of fabric swatches. Sheer black silks with raised velvet circles, cheques and wavy stripes. The patterns barely discernible, a textural change picked up by the light. I had used the stripe.

I looked in the mirror, the dress needed a lift. I had found the work of a young artist at the Rose Street markets. She made rings. The bright colours had caught my eye, chunky porcelain squares inspired by the bright geometric paintings of Josef Albers. I had shown the rings on my blog and the demand for her work went through the roof. She gave me a selection of rings as thanks. A bright orange and hot pink would give the outfit the splash of colour it needed.

The gallery was full of people. Men in tailored suits and women wearing black. It was a preview, a private showing before the exhibition was opened to the public. I grabbed a glass of champagne, a calming prop, and headed straight for Lola, a familiar face in a sea of strangers.

'Hey, how are you?' I said with a sense of relief.

'Really good. Have you seen the painting?' asked Lola.

'Not yet. I'm a bit too scared to look.'

'Come with me.'

Lola took me by the hand and led me through the first room. White walls hung with Tim's beautiful, voluptuous paintings. I noticed red stickers next to most of the paintings. I was thrilled for Tim. Gabriella would be pleased, too. We squeezed our way past the admiring crowd to the next room.

It hit me.

The only painting on the entire back wall was the one Tim had painted of me. He had made some changes. Along with the red of the nails and lips, he had painted my sex, pink and exposed. This painting looked more like the work of Egon Schiele, famous for his explicit depictions of women.

God, had there been a camera in the viewing room?

This was so confronting. I didn't know where to look, nowhere to hide.

To make it worse, the painting had a red sticker next to it. Someone had bought it and I would be on display to a stranger forever.

Gabriella came over.

'Christina, look at this painting. You look magnificent.'

'God Gabriella, this is not what I saw when we finished up the other night! Who the hell has bought it? Please can I buy it back?' I pleaded.

'Darling, don't be embarrassed. This will become an iconic work. The National Gallery has bought a piece. They wanted this one, but it was sold before they had the chance.

'Well, who bought it?'

'I can't tell you, it would be breaking the rules.'


Adam had come to the gallery early, determined to buy that painting.

Tim had rung him the night before. They met for a drink at Tim's studio. That is when Adam had spied the canvas. Tim had said she was the famous blogger, Chris Brown, known amongst her friends as Tina Maxwell. Adam knew her, Paul's widow. He'd been surprised by how much she'd changed, how beautiful she looked when they bumped into each other in Kep. But this, the painting, was spectacular, the most erotic thing he'd ever seen. His cock responded, he had to have the painting, he had to have her.

He told Tim about how they'd met. When he got that first glimpse of who she truly was, that night he'd dropped off Paul at her Brunswick flat. He also remembered the frosty reception he'd received. He knew they weren't friends, but wondered what had made her so hostile toward him, all those years ago, when they were barely out of university?

He saw her enter the room. She had done it again, she looked exquisite. He wondered how he could approach her, how to overcome his almost crippling shyness. She was talking to the gallery owner. This could be his opportunity, they could talk about the paintings.

I noticed him coming towards me, Adam Darcy. Fuck! Why did he keep turning up? I thought I had escaped that world. I felt resentful that he had invaded my space, this was my territory, the Finestras were my friends.

'Adam, you must meet my friend, Christina,' said Gabriella.

'Yes, Adam, we've already met.'

Of course Gabriella knew him. I felt slightly betrayed. He was a well known patron of the arts.

Almost instantly Gabriella was called away and, uncomfortably, we were alone.


Adam stood right next to her, what could he say? She wore a simple black dress, her body perfectly outlined, a flash of colour on her hand. He wished he had the courage to take her in his arms and tell her how much he wanted her. She had changed so much since Paul's funeral, when she had looked so forlorn, so lost, so hidden. And now there was this picture, giving him the chance to see her more intimately. He could barely contain his desire.

'The show seems to be a success,' he ventured clumsily.

'Yes, Tim should be pleased,' she responded coolly.

This was not going well.

'Do you know Gabriella?'

'Yes, we have been friends for a very long time. They have been like family to me.'

He sensed this was a kind of proprietorial statement. 'Back off' she seemed to be saying. He would change the subject.

'I wonder who buys this work?' he said, trying to maintain some kind of conversation, keep her engaged, near him.

Was he really asking me or was he about to make one of his sneering statements. My blood was boiling. I paused for a while, then began my rant.

'I have no idea really. I guess the odd Arts bureaucrat, sucking off the government tit. Women like her,' I pointed to the androgynously dressed woman in the corner of the room.

'Out for the night with her friends, her playthings, before she returns to her cuckolded husband. A man left at home to look after the kids, let out only occasionally to tend his community garden,' I fumed, proud of my little speech.

He looked bewildered. I turned my back on him and walked away.

That was his answer. He remembered that conversation all those years back in the uni bar. She must have been there, heard it all. No wonder she had been so cold. He needed her to know that he had been wrong, needed to make it up to her. He'd fallen for her the day he walked into her place, but out of respect his friend, Paul, had backed away. In all these years, he had never formed a single enduring relationship. Business and the thought of her had always gotten in the way.

# The House Problem goes Away

A strange thing happened. I got a call from Ruth, my lawyer, telling me the receivers had accepted that the house was not the property of Brown and Sons. That any contestation of the will was over and the house was now officially the property of Kathryn Mary Brown. All claims against me had been dropped.

I breathed a great sigh of relief and was quite shocked that this whole messy business had come to such an abrupt end. Ruth was surprised too, telling me she knew very little about why it had ended, but could shed some light after ringing Justin's lawyers.

She told me that the company was no longer in receivership. A buyer had been found and all debts had been cleared, including the costs of the receivers. She had no idea who the buyer was. Under the terms of the purchase contract their identity was to remain confidential. All that my lawyer could ascertain was that it was bought by an extremely large company and that Browns was just another addition to its expansion program.

Another mystery, why would anyone want this worthless entity? At least the staff would get to keep their jobs, get paid what was owing. I guess someone saw there was still value in the collective experience of all the people who'd worked there. Employees whose connections spanned generations. And without Justin and Fiona around, there was maybe the possibility that the company could regain the trust of its original clients.

I didn't really care. All I knew was that at least I had achieved a win for my daughter. I was proud that I stood up to their bullying. Didn't get railroaded into settling early in the proceedings. The old me would have rolled over instantly and conceded defeat.

'And so that's it? '

'Yeah, the will still stands. Your husband had it drawn up long before he went into partnership with Justin. Seems like he always wanted to make sure the house would go to his daughter.'

'And the company? Is there anything I have to do about that?'

'No, not a thing. You were never a director, have no legal connection to it whatsoever. Paul kept his business quite separate. Sorting out the company is somebody else's problem. Christina, it's over, you're free of them!'

I felt a great weight lift from my shoulders. I had finally extricated myself from those loathsome creeps who had so insidiously become a part of Paul's and my life. It felt so strange.

Just before Paul died I had become increasingly aware that he had become almost obsessed with Justin and Fiona. He spent all day at work with them and then it wasn't unusual for him to be off doing something with them on weekends, bike rides, work functions, business travel. Perhaps it wasn't so much an obsession with them, but an excuse to be away from me?

It was strange how I still mulled these things over in my head. The self doubt lingering just below the surface. I would have to learn to let these things go. At least now, with the case over, I could cut the last of the ties that had seen us so frustratingly bound together. Being able to rid myself of that bastard Justin and his bitch of a wife Fiona was certainly something to celebrate.

I rang Kate. She was pleased.

'So mum, when will you move back in?'

I knew this was coming, I had to let her know what I really wanted.

'How about I come up to Canberra this weekend? There are some papers to sign. We can talk a bit more about it then.'


It was great seeing Kate. She showed me where she lived, introduced me to her friends, took me for a tour around campus. She seemed to love Canberra, her course, university life. She had settled in nicely, she was thriving.

We found a nice restaurant and I enjoyed talking to her, woman to woman, sharing a glass of wine. Proud that she had grown up, had found meaning in her life and was becoming her own person.

I gently told her I didn't want to go back to the house, telling her it was far too big for one person.

It was only partly true. I didn't have the heart to tell her I didn't want to waste another minute inside the place that had been part of my ridiculously compromised life.

I suggested we rent it out. She would not be returning to Melbourne until her course finished and the income would more than cover her living expenses, while she was still a student. And selfishly it would be one less financial pressure on me.

She wondered what I would do. I told her not to worry. That I preferred my flat, it was closer to work. There would always be a spare bedroom there, a place for her to come home to.

It was sad to say goodbye, but I left knowing she was safe and happy. I was keen to return to Melbourne to get the house sorted and finally close that chapter of my life.

The garden had become overgrown, I would pay someone to fix it up. The house smelled musty, I would pay someone to clean it. It was laughable how much time I had once spent on its upkeep.

I had arranged for the place to be let fully furnished through an executive placement agency. They would rent it to a family coming from overseas, needing accommodation in the leafy suburbs, near the good schools.

All I had to do was remove our personal effects.

It was a huge job, but I slowly managed to sort out what was to be trashed or donated. I would rent storage space to house the things I wanted to keep or more importantly the priceless family heirlooms that were part of my daughter's history.

I had spent days on it and was nearly finished when I opened the drawer in Paul's desk. Pulling it out to check that it was empty, I felt a key taped to the underside.

I surveyed the desk looking for the lock and found a keyhole in a compartment, hidden behind the part of the desk facing the wall. I opened it. Inside was a disc. I put it into the computer and was horrified by what I saw.

I could see two people in a bedroom. The back of a woman in a black corset. On all fours a skinny, weedy looking man, facing the wall, hands cable tied, wearing a full faced latex mask, his mouth gagged. It looked like home-made porn.

Is this how Paul spent his time shut away in the office, masturbating to these amateur movies? Is this why he stopped having sex with me?

I had a voyeuristic curiosity and continued to watch.

The woman walked toward the man and took a small riding crop from the bed and stroked it over the man's torso, running it down his backside and tickling his balls. He groaned.

'Silence,' she hissed and thwacked the whip in her hand. She circled him. I couldn't judge her reaction, as her face was covered by an elaborate Venetian mask. The circling continued, broken only by the occasional whip, lashed at full force, on his back, gradually covering it in red welts. With every blow his dick twinged, rising. I watched transfixed as she repeated this until he was fully erect. She climbed on top of him. Leaning forward rubbing her breasts over his back, over the welts, seeming to find pleasure in his pain. She wrapped one arm around his stomach holding him firmly, then with her free hand, reached for his penis and rapidly pulled it. He came, quickly, spurting all over her hand. The screen faded to black.

The picture came back, the skinny man was still on all fours. The woman entered, naked. Now I could see her body more distinctly. She was no nubile porn star, quite the contrary in fact. Her skin looked leathery, old, a rather unattractive tan line suggested too much time under a sun lamp. Her tits, flat white flaps of empty skin. She was unappealingly thin, almost skeletal, her hip bones and spine protruding through her skin.

She wore only the mask and carried a pair of long black, leather boots with stiletto heels.

She sat on him, using him as a stool and pulled on the boots. The camera zoomed in as she zipped them up to her thighs, continuing until her completely bald sex and brown withered labia where in full view. She approached the man with a tube of lubricant, squeezed the contents onto his back, then mounted him, like she was riding a horse, and began deliberately rubbing her cunt along his ridged spine.

He groaned, she told him to shut up, then slapped him firmly on his white pimpled backside.

She got off and walked around to stand behind his haunches. She placed her black stiletto heel onto the centre of his calf muscle and stood heavily, the pain causing his back to arch, she repeated this on the other leg, his penis snaking back to life. Pain, it appeared, was his thing.

Then she kicked the inside of his legs, signalling him to spread them apart and he willingly complied. She picked up the tube and squirted more gel onto the crack of his ass, then spread his cheeks to expose his anus and balls, rubbing the heel of her hand heavily against his perineum.

She leaves the picture briefly to return with a giant black dildo. She is not alone.

Another fully masked man enters the scene, naked, but unlike the man on the floor, he is fat and flabby. He seems to be the new dominant player. He wrenches the dildo from her hand and commands her to lie, back to back on top on the skinny man still on all fours. She reclines and spreads her legs. The masked man then shoves the dildo into her fully exposed cunt and slowly moves its full length in and out of her, she groans. Before she gets too excited he withdraws the big black phallus. Both men are now fully erect.

The masked man then grabs her hand and pulls her to her feet. He fiddles around with a leather harness, securing the dildo and straps the entire apparatus onto the woman. She stands behind the skinny man, still on all fours, and places the tip of the dildo against his hole, applies more lube and then abruptly rams the strap-on into him. He bucks with pain.

As she leans into him, the fat masked man pushes her face down flat onto the skinny man's back. He grabs her legs and pulls them apart, as wide as they will go without affecting her ability to ass fuck the skinny man mounted on her dildo. She is completely exposed, her tight puckered ring sitting just above her now flaming pink folds, swollen, glistening engorged. He grabs the lubricant, rubs it over his now thick purple cock, then smears the gel up his forearm, down through his fingers and forms his hand into a fist. He runs the knuckle along her sex, then nudges her anus, pushing, slowly twisting stretching, encouraging her tight little hole to expand. Slowly, forcefully he thrusts deeper until his entire hand is completely submerged. With his free hand he rubs his cock, keeping it hard.

The more violently he pounds into her, the harder she rams the dildo into the kneeling man. The jolt of every thrust rocking the three of them, frantically in bestial unison until the fat guy tugging his own cock, ejaculates all over the floor.

Spent, he kicks the skinny man to the ground, cuts the cable ties and then snickers, 'Finish yourself off, you lazy dog'. The skinny man eagerly grabs his own tiny little penis and wanks himself, while the woman is seen whipping him brutally. Finally, he too is done and he spurts. A pathetic finale to this ugly, brutal scene.

With his hands now free, the skinny man removes the gag and the mask, weakly grinning at the woman who also takes off her disguise.

It is Paul sitting there, staring at Fiona. I could only presume the masked man was Justin, I recognised his voice.

I felt shocked, ill, horrified by what I'd just witnessed.

I looked back into the folder and saw a white envelope, addressed to Paul. I read the note inside.

*'We know you want more and there is plenty for all of us, as long you continue to cooperate. You fuck up the Cambodia deal and all of this stops. Don't forget, we can always send a copy to your wife.'*

It was becoming clearer now. This was the hold they had on him. No wonder we had stopped having sex. I wondered when the promise of their sordid little trysts had graduated to blackmail?

When I got the call from Justin to say that Paul had been taken to hospital, I had just assumed they had been on one of their regular rides together. Is this what they had been doing all along? The ambulance had been called from Justin's house. Was it Paul's addiction to this brutal activity that had caused the heart attack that killed him?

I was relieved to be back in Fitzroy and glad to be rid of that place. The agents would handle it from now on and Kate would reap the benefits. It would be difficult to ever go back there.

The shower was scorching hot. I felt filthy and stayed under the water trying to wash away the vile images imprinted on my brain. Perhaps it would take a little longer to completely erase these people from my mind.

# The Real Adam Darcy

Lola and I were attending the annual Cambodia-Australia friendship dinner. It was a fund-raiser organised by Cambodian business people living in Australia. The money raised would help pay for schools in the most impoverished regional areas. Lola had booked a table to help support this worthy cause.

Tonight was special. It was the awards night where people were honoured for their contribution to the community both here and in Cambodia. Mrs Pung, the charismatic chairwoman, got on stage and in perfect English began to speak.

'Tonight we have a very special presentation to make. This man has worked tirelessly to make real changes in the land of our birth. His education and training programs have changed the lives of many people. I would like to introduce the recipient of our highest honour, Mr. Adam Darcy.'

From the wings walked Adam, the guests quietly clapping. He commanded the stage. His sophisticated good looks screaming wealth, confidence and... fuckability? My heart raced, I felt a warmth growing in my belly, my thighs. What was happening? Why this response?

He greeted Mrs Pung and graciously accepted a framed certificate, honouring him for his work.

'Thank you, thank you.'

I watched as he walked to the lectern, adjusted the microphone, then started to tell his story. Restrained at first, he told us of his introduction to Cambodia. He'd discovered he had a half sister, Nary, living in Kep. Apparently his father had a liaison with the child's mother Dara. His father had denied paternity and washed his hands of them both. Dara had contacted Adam. Adam went to Cambodia curious about the claim. What he found was a teacher, struggling to run a school and raise a child, on a wage of forty dollars a month. His father had abandoned them. With the threat of the school's closure, she had Googled Adam and asked for his help. That was eight years ago.

He told of how the initial project to save the school had grown to offer employment and training for the students once they left. His face lit up, his conversation became more animated as he continued to speak. He showed slides of the building projects he was supervising and the young men who were learning the trades. I recognised the villa on the waterfront. He praised Dara and her tireless efforts to improve the lives of the people around her.

He told of a new project to build a simple clinic in the area. And of his frustration at having to make the long drive himself to the hospital in Phnom Penh, because no ambulance was available. He showed a slide. I recognised the face. It was the young man who Adam had helped carry the load of timber. Samlain had a cut that turned septic and Adam had rushed him to the hospital in Phnom Penh. A clinic nearby would have saved the need for the long drive.

He told of the joy of discovering his Cambodian family and urged the people in the audience to continue to give generously to their own school funding program. The guests rose to their feet and broke into spontaneous applause.

Mrs Pung took the microphone and told us she was sorry Adam had to leave so soon. He was catching a flight, that very night, to Cambodia.

Adam thanked her and left the stage. The applause followed his exit.

Who was this man? He wasn't the opinionated, arrogant student I once knew. He wasn't anything like his brother. He didn't fit the profile his friends had spoken about. I had got him so wrong. I didn't know him at all. I wanted to find out more.

# Adam Stripped Bare

The dinner had been held at the consulate on King Street. Lola had taken a taxi, I opted to walk home. I needed some time to think. A walk up Flinders Lane would be interesting.

I strolled along this narrow street full of designer boutiques and 'hot' restaurants, past 'The Imperial', a boutique hotel. An hotel built by Adam Darcy.

I was curious, turned around and walked inside. It was a Tuesday night and the small bar off the foyer was empty. No glitzy brass, piped music or water features here. This space was decorated more like a stylish club. White walls, dark timber bar. Yellow and aqua upholstered, sleek designer furniture like the pieces I'd seen in Raphael's showroom. A spectacular black glass chandelier gently lighting the space. I sat down and ordered a drink, a dark syrupy Pedro Ximenez sherry. An indulgent raisiny rich liquid dessert. The manager was doing the night shift and running the bar. He was immaculately dressed, beautifully groomed. He introduced himself, Sam, we started to talk.

I quizzed him about Adam, his boss. He told me he was easy to work for.

'Do you know him?' asked Sam.

'Well, I thought I did,' I replied.

Like any good barman he indulged me in polite conversation. He let me tell him of the dinner I had just attended and how stupid I felt about the judgements I'd passed on this man I barely knew.

'I knew him when we were students. I thought he was an arrogant bastard back then. His brother was my husband's business partner.'

'Justin?' enquired Sam.

'Yeah, the slimy little prick sent the company broke. The last of the legal battles has only just finished. Tried to take our home away. I always thought the whole family was a bunch of arrogant assholes with an over inflated sense of entitlement.'

'No way. Adam's nothing like Justin, always bailing him out of trouble,' interrupted Sam, rallying to his bosses defence.

'And as for his father, Adam has absolutely nothing to do with him.'

'Even so, the business section of the papers always mentions what a difficult operator Adam is. Notorious for his hostile takeovers. A driven man with no friends. A man who also fucks any willing bimbo, then dumps them when they are no longer of any use.'

'Sure, he's a very shrewd operator. He didn't get rich by being 'Mr Nice Guy'. But as for the women, they are just as predatory as he is.'

'So, he's charmed you, too?' I said.

'Don't believe all you read in the papers. He's a good man, but he's no fool. Knows what he wants. Goes out and gets it. As for the women, he's no monk. He's a normal red blooded male. Just doesn't have time for full blown relationships.'

'Here, on the house,' said Sam, as he poured another drink and poured one for himself as well.

'Anyway, he's saving himself for me,' said Sam jokingly, lightening the mood.

Sam was being slightly flirtatious and told me that he'd always had a crush on his ridiculously handsome boss. Had a fantasy about chatting him up, hoping Adam would see the error of his ways and fall for the gorgeous gay man he was. I laughed and told him about a similar fantasy I once had myself.

'Who, Adam?'

'No, no! Just that perfect gay man we straight women all dream about!'

We both laughed.

'You know Adam has a penthouse on the top floor of the hotel?' said Sam.

'No, I didn't. He lives here?' I replied slightly curious about what that space might look like.

'He's not in, flew out tonight. Want to have a look?' said Sam.

'What? His place, here, now?'

'Yeah, there's a separate entrance. I have access. He left tonight. I need to send someone up to clean it. Follow me.'

We walked to a private lift. Sam punched in the code and the door opened. We got in. He gave me a conspiratorial wink.

A quick ride up and we were there. The doors opened into a stark brutalist concrete foyer. A hard space softened with a row of pale woven birch pendant lights, looking more like the entrance to a sleek gallery, than a home. Sam pushed open a pair of heavy black doors. We entered a library like corridor, walls lined with shelves of neatly arranged books, interrupted by doors to somewhere. At the end of the corridor a vast galleria, floor to ceiling glass. Beyond the room, an expansive courtyard, a swimming pool and a spectacular view of the lights and skyscrapers of Melbourne.

A polished concrete bench divided the room. A large Mark Rothko painting dominated one wall, a cavernous fireplace the other. Two long black leather sofas, a Barcelona chair and a large rug the only furniture.

I felt dwarfed by the space.

An empty wine glass, with a few residual drops of red, the only evidence of human habitation.

The room was as I had imagined the residence of Adam Darcy to be, restrained, bold, masculine.

'Where to next?'

'I just need to check a few things, feel free to wander around,' said Sam, as he exited into the corridor.

I opened the door opposite.

Same windows, doors open to the outside, a faint breeze, same amazing view. A bedroom with a provocatively sexy unmade bed, as if the occupant had only just stepped out. I sat down, rubbing my hand over the crisp white sheets and thought about the man who slept between them. I lay back and imagined what it would be like to wake up to this view every morning. I could see trees planted along the periphery, softening the harsh city skyline. I wondered how it was possible to have a pool up here, this high? It was dark, the reflected light from the city the only illumination, the water an inky black.

My moment of contemplation was rudely interrupted. A wave and a splash and suddenly a man, naked, emerged from the pool. The water rushed off.  His body became more defined, he was beautiful. It was Adam Darcy. I didn't know where to look, embarrassed at being caught intruding on his private space. I hoped he hadn't seen me. I needed to get out. I jumped up quickly and ran to the door. Raced along the corridor, into the lift, across the hotel lobby and onto the street.

'Taxi!' I called, heart racing. I dived in and was driven home.


Adam got out of the pool and realised he wasn't alone. Sam was walking towards him, carrying a towel.

'Boss, what are you doing here?' said Sam

'Flight got cancelled. I rang the guys in Kep and it seems they don't need me over there right now anyway. I'll probably go in a few days time.'

'I was just checking what needed doing. Do you want me to send someone up? At least make your bed?'

'Oh, isn't Jeanie in there doing that now? I thought I saw someone in my room?' queried Adam.

'Actually, I have a confession to make. I brought someone up here. She said she knew you, Chris Brown. She flew out the door a minute ago, like a startled rabbit. She must have seen you getting out of the pool,' said Sam sheepishly.

'She was here, in my place? How come?'

Sam was very apologetic about this breach of trust. Adam dismissed it, he didn't care. Sam always had his back. Adam was more curious about why she had been here, in his hotel, in his bedroom.

'She said you were a friend of her husband's, and that she'd been at the dinner. Surprised at what she'd learnt.'

'What? She was at the dinner?'

'Yeah. Said she thought she knew you, but was completely surprised to find out about what you were doing in Cambodia. In fact, she said something about running into you in Kep. Apparently you stood her up.'

'Shit, of course! We were supposed to have dinner, but one of the guys on the work site got sick. I had to take him to hospital. Didn't know how to contact her.'

She had been in here, in his place, curious about him, and now she was gone. Why was she so intimidated? Why had she so abruptly fled?

He'd read about her business success. He thought she had more balls than that.

And then it occurred to him that she had come here willingly, searching him out. She had come here by choice, curious. Did that mean there was some chance for him?

Adam realised that he was going to have to try a lot harder if he was going to have even the slightest chance of becoming her friend, let alone anything more.

# Happy Birthday Green Goddess

I needed to talk to someone and as usual, Cindy was the first on the scene the following morning. I dumped so much on her. She was still so young. I talked to her because she always managed to say the right thing. She was mature beyond her years.

I told her about the dinner, what I'd learnt about Adam. Why I was curious about where he lived and about getting caught.

'Something's happening. He keeps cropping up.'

'Well, is that a problem?' asked Cindy.

'It's confusing. The man I knew when we were young was an arrogant prick. And then I find out all this stuff about him, good stuff, and I just get more confused. I like the man people tell me about. It's as if he's two completely different people,' I said.

'And what's more, I got to see quite a bit of him last night. He got out of the pool and was stark naked. He was gorgeous.'

'Sounds like you're a bit keen?' said Cindy, with a cheeky grin.

'Not so much keen, but a little bit curious perhaps?' I replied.


We went through the workload for the remainder of the week. The content of the blog was no longer solely dependent on me. We'd broadened the range of things the site focused on. Our contributors, many former journalists and media commentators, supplying us with great, thought provoking articles. I still wrote an editorial piece each week, just to let the readers know what I was up to. This week I would write about the schools in Cambodia and asked Cindy to add the links so the readers could donate.

I looked around the messy, crowded room where we worked. It was no longer the stylish minimalist apartment I'd originally moved into. Our desks took up much of the lounge room. Boxes of samples and office equipment were piled high in Kate's room. It was completely inadequate and I knew we really should be thinking about getting a larger, separate office space.

The doorbell rang, the first of what would be many deliveries or enquiries on any given working day. I'm sure the other tenants were getting pissed off at the constant traffic to my door. Cindy answered.

She returned with a large bunch of green goddess lilies, my favourite. Attached was a card. Inside was a disc. I put the disc in the player. We waited with baited breath. It was Tex Perkins singing the haunting ballad, 'You're thirty nine, you're beautiful, you're mine.'

I loved his music, hard to describe, cow punk, sexy, raw. I had seen his band, The Cruel Sea, when I was a student.

This was such an adoring anthem of love. Who had sent it?

My birthday was coming up. I guess it was just a reader. Lots of people knew I was turning forty. Pity it wasn't someone I loved.

'What's the diary looking like this week?'

'All the usual, but you might be interested in this. There's a book launch about iconic Australian houses on Saturday night. I thought you might like to take a look.'

'Sounds interesting. Where is it?'

'At the Architectural Society, King Street.'

'Yeah, sounds good, like that, pencil it in.'

I don't know why I committed to the book launch. This week was looking crazy. I guess I just liked being busy? Kate would be home for my birthday party Friday night, but had informed me she was catching up with old school friends on the Saturday evening. Perhaps it was just that I didn't want to spend the night alone.

Adding to the demands of the week was finalising the soft launch of the dress business. We had arranged for the female guests attending my party to be the first to trial the new site, 'U-Dress-U'. I was interested to see what problems we would encounter and pleased the trial had gone pretty smoothly. All the dresses arrived within three weeks of them being ordered. I marvelled at the precise bespoke tailoring. Only a few adjustments were needed as some women gave incorrect measurements. I would have to think of a way to communicate to the customer the importance of being honest about size. Perhaps a video demonstrating how to take your measurements exactly would help? A team of seamstresses had made the necessary alterations and I now looked forward to seeing the finished ensembles on Friday evening. Curious about the way each woman would put together her look.

The big day finally arrived, my birthday. The celebration was at 'Moonlight', on Gertrude Street, a new restaurant owned by one of the rising stars of the Melbourne food scene. I had booked out the entire space, surprised at the need for so many seats. I thought about what a lonely event this would have been if my life had continued down the bleak path of just nine months ago.

The room was mainly white, except for the inclusion of my favourite green lilies. I arrived to find the guests already seated and was quite overwhelmed to see so many people.

Cindy gave a brilliant speech, ' Forty Things Tina Maxwell Has Taught Us'. She had obviously done her research, contacted many of the people in the room, giving a speech that had us all laughing. She was using my new name, or should I say my real name. All of my friends had happily adopted it. I liked the way it gave me some distance from my public persona, some privacy, my own secret little club.

Lola got up and told the story of when she first took me to meet her parents. Describing that simple transformation from young punk to elegant woman, how she had been given a glimpse of what the future might hold for a talented young dress designer.

My gorgeous Katie brought the room to a hushed silence, as she spoke of the enormous pride she had in her mum and of the huge changes of the past year.

The night was brought to a fitting end when Massimo proposed a toast to the birthday girl, Prosecco of course, and they all sang 'Happy Birthday'.

'Mum, I can't imagine you ever living in that big old place. It seems like you've lived here forever,' said Kate, as we walked along the vibrant street back home to the flat.

'I know what you mean,' I replied, taking her hand and giving it a squeeze.

It really had been an extraordinary nine months. My life had completely changed and it felt oh so good to be here.

# The Dress Goes Viral

The first thing I did on Saturday morning was update my readers with news and photos of the birthday party. I asked them to tell me of their own big birthday experiences. Aware of the need to make them feel included.

I also thought it was a great opportunity for the 'soft' launch of the dress site. I posted links under the photos of the women at the party. Surprised at how each woman's interpretations made that same basic little black dress look so different.

A thump at the door signalled the arrival of the Saturday paper. I fumbled with the plastic wrap, more annoying than usual, as I was particularly eager to see Jane Smith's column.   She was the journalist who wrote about me when the Paul Brown scandal first broke. She was keen for an updated story and I was happy to give it to her. The article would be in this morning's paper.

I was halfway through the story when the phone rang. It was Chenda, ringing from Cambodia. I guess she knew about my birthday.

'Tina, is that you? What is going on there? The computers are going crazy. The printers are spilling out orders. It's madness, we can barely keep up,' said Chenda, a mild hint of panic in her normally calm voice.

I warned her that it was probably going to get worse, telling her of the article in today's paper.

'Will you be ok? Do you have enough staff?'

'Yes, yes. We will call in all the workers. You understand we are not unhappy, we are all very pleased. The more orders, the more money for the foundation. We just didn't expect so much so soon.'

Chenda told me she would arrange to have some of the processes outsourced to cope with the initial demand and emphasised that they were all reputable companies that followed strict ethical guidelines. I told her I was worried the dresses would not be of the same high standard and she reassured me that all the finishing would be done at her site. She would personally check all the dresses before they were shipped.

I told Chenda I would get online and ask the readers to be patient. To wait a few days before placing their orders.

'One more thing, Tina, happy birthday!'


After a frantic call to the I.T. guy, who made sure the system could cope, I was finally able to finish reading. Luckily Jane had not said too much about the dress.

The article was about what had happened since last we met and surprisingly about something more poignant. She had written about the demise of newspapers and the rise of a new breed of communicators. People like me. She ended her article with a tongue in cheek job application. The irony not lost on anyone.

# They Meet

Kate was catching up with school friends, chuffed at arranging to meet them here at our place. The girls cooed with excitement at being in the heart of this cool district. Miles from the predictable confines of their own leafy, but humdrum, suburbs.

I farewelled them to the sound of my taxi beeping impatiently in the street below.

It had been a long day and I was far too weary to make the thirty minute walk. The taxi crawled slowly through the busy Saturday night streets of the city. It seemed more crowded than usual.

'What's on tonight? It's worse than peak hour?' I asked.

'Special international football game between two of the biggest teams. It was a draw. Lot of energy left in the fans. Not a good night to be in here.'

The game had been held in the national sports stadium on Spencer street. It had been a sell out, all 55,000 seats full. The spectators now pouring onto the streets.

The taxi had come to a standstill. I paid the driver, got out. It would be quicker to walk.

Mobs of young men were beginning to gather in King Street, waiting for the nightclubs and strip joints to open. They were walking around in gangs. Loyalties defined by the club colours they wore, blowing off steam, frustrated by the lack of a conclusive result.

What a stupid night to be back in the city. I was starting to doubt the sanity of coming out. It really was an effort, but I didn't want to hang around the flat cramping Kate's style.

And truth be known, I thought it would be good to get out, get amongst the scene. It had been ages since I'd been with anyone, however I couldn't be too adventurous knowing Kate would be home when I returned.

The room at the Architectural Society was packed. I knew no one. A street full of strangers, a room full of strangers, at least inside it was a lot less hostile.

The only familiarity was the stunning photographs of the houses, hung around the periphery of the room. These images were like comfortable old friends. Open, light filled houses, modern furniture, built in the fifties and sixties. At the time, precocious young architects bucking the traditions of Mother England, designing for Australia, its light and its climate. A new post war generation, looking for change. I longed for one of these homes and for the first time I started to think about the very real possibility of having enough money to buy something for myself. Not one of these exactly, but a new version, one that would be a contemporary interpretation of what these architects saw.

Adam had seen her arrive just before the first of the speeches. Perhaps tonight would not be as boring as he'd first thought. He had decided to come to the launch as the cancellation of his flight meant he had a rare free night. Tonight he would not be so shy. He knew she had been up to his place. Sam had told him she was curious, wanted to find out more about him.

He could not reach her, the room was too crowded and the speaker had just begun to tap the microphone. He would try to make contact when the formalities were over, talk to her, invite her out for a drink.

My eyes started to glaze over as some tedious academic began his long winded speech. It really was idiotic of me being here. I could wander into this exhibition any time, buy the book online. I began to fidget, looking around the room and observed a similar bored response from the other guests. Adam Darcy was there. I could just see him leaning against the wall on the opposite side of the room, staring into his glass, as uninterested as me. Perhaps tonight I would talk to him?

Embarrassingly, halfway through the speech my phone began ringing. The room was quiet enough for all to hear. I flicked the mute switch, it was Chenda. I had to take the call and went outside.

'Hi, Chenda,' I screamed above the noise of the mob who were now filling the street.

I could barely understand what she was trying to say. The reception was weak and unwittingly I walked onto the road holding out my phone looking for those elusive extra bars. I turned my back to the men gathering in increasing numbers in the middle of the street and was completely oblivious to the furore that was building. We spoke for about ten minutes. I could vaguely hear Chenda telling me the orders were under control and I need not worry. I thanked her and said goodbye.

In my rush to take the call, I had failed to notice the change in mood around me. As I turned toward the crowd I was shocked by what I saw. Hundreds of men, young and old, bursting onto the road, interrupting the traffic, blocking my path. Chanting like they were possessed, waving flags above their heads, guzzling bottles of spirits.

I began to feel afraid. A lone woman in this volatile horde, being dragged along the street, caught in the chaos of the suffocating pack. No way of crossing the road back into the safety of the hall.

I tried to keep my head down, not make eye contact, but was being aggressively shoved into the middle of the mob as they marched along the street. The odd threatening comment, leering look, groping hand, reminding me of the extreme danger I had inadvertently put myself in.

I watched in horror as a saw a young man stuff a piece of torn cloth into a bottle, light it and toss it into the opposing throng. It smashed onto the tarmac and a blue flash of flames exploded. I heard the sickening screams of burning men. Jostled and bumped, I trembled with fear as the retaliation from the rival gang rained down upon us. Bottles, broken glass, timber, rocks, anything that could be ripped out and thrown.

King Street had erupted into an uncontrolled, testosterone fuelled war zone, more like Beirut than Melbourne. The air was thick with suffocating smoke, the acrid smell of burning tyres causing me to gag. I could barely see in front of me. Nowhere safe, nowhere to hide. I was trapped in the middle of this violent rabble. There was no escape.


Adam saw her leave, it was her phone. The speaker droned on until suddenly he was interrupted by a cop running into the room, slamming the door behind him. He said there was trouble on the street and that for their safety, they were all to remain inside.

She was still out there. Adam hurried to the back of the room and pushed open the fire escape door. From the alley, he could see the riotous activity ahead of him. He couldn't believe it was a Melbourne street. Screaming mobs, thousands of angry men, brutal fighting, cars alight and turned upside down on the road. Shops ablaze, a frenzied, violent crowd out of control.

He scanned the street, desperate to find her, shocked at how dangerous it had become. Just as he was beginning to fear the worst, he saw her there, trapped, pinned against a shop window. Her hands were up against her face, trying to protect herself from the onslaught of violence.

He ran toward her, bludgeoning past anyone who got in his way.

He found her trembling with fear, a bleeding cut above her eye, heat and smoke from a burning building threatening to engulf her. Quickly he wrapped his woollen suit jacket protectively around her, picked her up and, with adrenalin pumping, ran towards Flinders Lane. Breathless he finally reached his hotel.

'Lock the fucking doors and pull down the shutters!' he yelled at Sam, as he tore into the foyer.

He put her down, she blinked, looking like a startled animal and before she could say anything, collapsed to the floor.


I woke up. I was in a bed, the surroundings vaguely familiar. Adam Darcy was sitting looking at me anxiously.

'Are you ok?' he asked quietly.

'I don't know,' I replied, completely bewildered, 'What happened?'

'Here, have a sip,' he said, handing me a glass of water.

My mouth was dry, I gulped the water down.

'You're here with me, Adam. You fainted.'

He told me the story of the riots that had broken out in the streets and slowly I began to recall the events of the night. I remembered the flames and the sheer terror of being caught up in the surge of the mob.

And then my body reacted involuntarily and I threw up. Over my torn and blackened dress, over the sheets and over the man sitting next to me. I burst into tears. He took me into his arms and held me tight.


'It's alright, you're safe, you're with me.'

He could feel her heart still beating madly. He held her until, slowly, she began to calm.

'God, I'm so sorry. Look at this mess.'

'Don't worry, we can get this cleaned up. Would you like to take a shower?'

'Please, but I'm really worried about my daughter, Kate. Do you have a phone?'


Kate had been frantic. She'd been trying to call. She knew I had been in King Street and was relieved to hear my voice. The girls had been out when the riots had started. They went back to the flat as soon as they heard how dangerous the situation had become.

'It's ok darling,' I said.

'Where are you?'

I explained where I was.

'I'll be home soon.'

'Haven't you seen the television, Mum? That part of the city is in lock down. You're not going anywhere.'

I assured her I was fine and that I would stay at a friend's hotel for the night. I gave her Adam's number in case she needed to contact me. We said our goodbyes.

'Love you, darling.'

'Love you, Mum.'


I looked down and was reminded of my bedraggled, filthy state.

'I think I'll take you up on that offer of a shower.'

He showed me to his bathroom.

'There should be a robe behind the door,' he said, the tension in his voice easing.

I let the water stream over me for what seemed like ages, soaped my body and shampooed my hair. Finishing, I grabbed a towel, it was faintly damp, he must have used it before me. This seemed very intimate. I wrapped myself in it protectively, sitting on the floor, trying to comprehend what had just happened.

The sound of sirens could still be heard as I walked into the large main room, swimming in the bathrobe, obviously not made for someone my size.

He too had showered, his hair wet, he wore jeans and a fitted black tee shirt, bare feet.

'Sorry about the robe. I've called Sam, he's bringing up supplies. Are you hungry, can I get you something to drink?'

'I'm not sure. I'm still a bit shell shocked. I can't quite get my head around what just happened.'

'Nor me, I can't believe it either. This isn't the Melbourne I know.'

The doorbell rang and Sam entered followed by a team of housekeepers. One went straight to the bedroom, the other further along the hall. A man in chef's whites started filling the fridge, topping up the cupboards and loading a big glass bowl with fruit.

'Is there anything I can get you boss?'

'No, thanks Sam, looks like you've already taken care of everything. I am concerned about the staff. Are all the guests accounted for?' Adam asked.

'We were lucky that the shift had changed, all the night staff had already arrived long before the trouble started. We have contacted all the guests and those not able to get back to the hotel have been booked into rooms at other places outside the lock-down zone.'

'Did we suffer any damage?'

'Not to my knowledge. Everything appears to be secure inside. I hate to think what the frontage looks like. I guess there'll be plenty of time tomorrow to survey the site,' said Sam, a model of order and efficiency.

'Thanks Sam. I think that will be all.'

Sam left briefly to check on the progress of the cleaners.

'Your rooms are done, all the linen has been replaced and the guest bedroom is ready for Mrs. Brown. I have taken the liberty of gathering up your clothing and organised for it to be washed and mended. Unfortunately we were only able to find one shoe. I hope the house slippers will suffice,' said Sam, looking completely unruffled, responding to the night's chaos with complete composure.


He left us and we were alone, sitting in the vast, dimly lit room, the twinkling lights of the city masking the chaos we had witnessed in the streets below.

'Actually, do you have anything for a headache?'

'Sure.'

He returned with a pack of aspirin, water, and a glass of Scotch.

'This might help you sleep.'

I took the aspirin and washed it down with the whiskey.

I burst into tears again.

He sat next to me and put his arm around my shoulders. I huddled in closer against his chest. I did feel safe, I fell asleep.

Adam sat with her asleep, in his arms. He had wanted this for a very long time, but the moment, the circumstances, were not right. She needed to be taken to bed, not his bed, as he would have liked, but to the guest room. He disengaged himself, got up, leant over and gathered her in his arms. He carried her gently to bed, careful not to wake her. She looked so vulnerable. As he walked, the robe slipped off her shoulder, exposing her breast. He wanted to kiss it, suck the delicate pink nipple in his mouth, feel it harden against his tongue, but he would not.

He pushed the door open with his shoulder, the bed had been turned back, the room was in immaculate condition. He tenderly placed her on the sheets and gingerly removed the robe. She was exquisite, more beautiful than the painting. He wanted to sit and watch her. He wanted to lovingly fuck her, he always had.

His cock was so hard he could not trust himself any longer. He pulled the sheets over her, picked up the robe and left the room.


Bright sunlight was streaming in through the windows. I could see a swimming pool outside. Where was I? I was in a bed, white sheets, white cotton blankets, large room, pale coloured walls. Undressed...

A beautiful bedroom, a tranquil, serene space.

I remembered, Adam's place, the riots.

I needed to pee and headed to the ensuite bathroom. I sat, taking in the room. A large bath looking out onto the roof deck, floor to ceiling windows, a glass shower cubicle. Pure white marble, pristine. I finished and washed my hands. The vanity was well stocked, everything a girl might need. On one side a vase filled with fragrant white flowers smelling of spring, on the other a lidded box. Inside was a beautiful white camisole and pyjama bottoms. They were my size.

I could still smell traces of the acrid smoke in my hair, on my skin. I took another shower, more aware of the need to thoroughly scrub away the last stinking reminder of that horrible night.

This time the towel I grabbed was dry, in fact this was a different bathroom. When I finished I rubbed my skin with the pleasantly scented moisturiser and dressed myself in the pyjamas, more leisurewear than sleepover, stylish and understated. Looking in the mirror I saw someone had placed a bandage on the cut above my eye, now the only visual reminder of the chaos of last night. I was surprised I didn't look worse. I combed my hair and tied it in a loose knot, securing it with a pin.

I ventured out.

Now I could clearly see the main room, a vast gallery like space, polished concrete floor, massive glass doors, pivoted open and pushed back, allowing the fresh air inside. It was a warm, clear Spring morning, the sky a vivid blue. I could smell the aroma of freshly brewed coffee.

'Good morning, did you sleep well?'

I turned to see Adam, standing in the kitchen, wearing a robe and boxer shorts, no top. It was the robe I'd worn after showering last night.

'Coffee?'

'Ah yes, slept like a baby and I would love a coffee,' I responded, slightly taken aback by his presence.

I walked toward him and sat on a stool at the kitchen bench where the Sunday papers were strewn about.

'IS THIS OUR CITY?' screamed the headlines. I pushed the paper away, I wasn't ready to look.

The doorbell rang and a waiter walked in, pushing a trolley.

'Where would you like this, Sir?'

'On the terrace. It's a beautiful morning. We'll eat outside.'

'I took the liberty of ordering breakfast.'

The smell of bacon wafted past. I was starving, things were returning to normal.

I followed Adam and we sat down at the table outside.

The food was delicious. What a luxury, to be served breakfast, to sit outside in the warm sun, to be here in this magnificent place.

To be here with this man.

We didn't have much to say, in truth I barely knew him. His phone rang.

'Everything ok?' I quizzed.

'It's the police. They want to talk to both of us. They found your bag.'

'How did they know to ring you?'

'I called a mate, Steve Madden, a detective, last night. Things were still pretty wild and he was unable to do anything. Sam also reported the incident this morning. He told them what he saw, the damage to the building and the dreadful state you were in last night,' Adam replied.

'When will they arrive? I should get home, check on Kate.'

'No idea, they just said to wait. Apparently the streets are still barricaded. No one can get in or out until the place has been cleared, evidence collected. Why don't you call your daughter.'

Kate was fine. I was disappointed at not being able to spend more time with her, she was flying back to Canberra tomorrow. But in typical teenager fashion she had planned on spending the day with her friends and would sleep at their place tonight. She was over the drama already!

'She ok?' he asked, as I handed back the phone.

'She's fine.'

I poured myself another coffee and tentatively we both reached for the newspapers.

'You know, what I can't understand is how these people, grown men, can behave like this. I don't get why men who live and work together during the day turn into these hate filled thugs, wreaking vengeance on their so called enemies just because of the football team they support.'

'I guess we'll get more details from the cops when they arrive. Sometimes men just explode.'

I read as much as I could before realising the journalists knew very little themselves, the same old stories were being rehashed and repeated. Quotes from onlookers, conspiracy theorists, none with any real insight, I'd had enough.

'Hey look at this, it's you. You're in the gossip pages. A birthday?' said Adam.

I snatched the paper from him and saw the photos with the headline, 'Birthday Party Fashion Launch'. The story talked about what the guests were wearing and the idea behind the 'U-Dress-U' site.

'U-Dress-U?' he said with a curious smirk.

I told him of my new business.

'Actually, that's why I was in Cambodia, remember, Kep. You stood me up!' I said

'Oh man, sorry about that. I didn't know how to contact you. One of the workers got really sick and I had to drive him to Phnom Penh.'

'I know that now. I was at the presentation the other night and heard your story. I had no idea,' I confessed.

'I heard a rumour that you were there,' he said with a wry smile.

'Rumour, what do you mean?'

'A little birdie told me that you also called into the bar afterwards.'

I felt myself turn red. How much did he know?

'This isn't the first time you've been up here. Why did you leave that night?' his conspiratorial grin widened.

'Oh God, I'm so embarrassed. I must seem like some crazed stalker. I heard you talk at the dinner. I was surprised at what you revealed. I was walking home and by chance went past the hotel. I was curious to see what it looked like, what more I would discover.'

'And what did you discover?'

He was playfully teasing her. He already knew the full story.

'Well, Sam told me you'd left and that he was going up to your place to do an inspection. He said he thought you wouldn't mind if I came along.'

Sam knew he was interested in her. Sam had helped organise for the painting of her to be hung in the study.

'I thought it was just Sam and me. When I saw you emerge from the pool, I felt like I'd been caught doing something wrong. I ran off like a naughty schoolgirl. I'm sorry, I feel like such an idiot,' she blurted.

He now knew that she had seen him naked. It made him feel aroused. He checked that the robe was covering the evidence.

'You should have stayed.'


I didn't know what he meant, was he flirting? I had to remind myself that this was the same cold, aloof man who'd made those insulting remarks about me all those years ago. The brother of the man who had been responsible for so much of the angst of the last nine months. A man with a connection to a past I was keenly determined to shed. It was as if there were two different people. I was becoming very fond of this new, friendly, playful Adam.


The awkwardness was broken when the doorbell rang again. Adam got up. He was followed back out to the terrace by Sam.

'Heard you've been confined to quarters. I thought I'd bring up some treats to relieve the boredom. How are you feeling this morning, Mrs Brown?' said Sam, handing me a basket filled with all the latest magazines, handmade chocolates and some books.

'Thanks, Sam, I feel much better. Just sitting out here in the sun seems to make all the difference,' I replied.

'You look much better as well. Is there anything else I can do?'

'Well, actually you can. I don't use the name Chris Brown anymore, well not amongst friends. I would love it if you would call me Tina, Tina Maxwell.'

'Yes, Mrs. Maxwell,' said Sam

'Tina! You cheeky devil,' I said, mockingly chastising him.

Adam and Sam both knew, 'Finding Tina Maxwell' was the title of the painting.

Sam's phone rang, the front desk needed him to deal with a nervous guest. He said his goodbyes and left.


It was a really gorgeous clear blue day, warm, even for late Spring. I left the table and decamped to one of the lounges by the pool. I stretched out, delighting in the feel of the sun on my skin, driving out the cold of winter, the bleakness of last night. After such a frenetic week, it was good to lie back and do absolutely nothing.

Adam took calls, conducted his business, read reports, stopping occasionally to chat, to see if he could get me anything. I read the gossip mags Sam had brought and happily ate the chocolates before they melted.


I woke with a start, no idea of how long I'd drifted off. I felt something cold trickling down my belly.

'Hey sleepyhead, do you feel like some lunch?' said Adam.

He was standing by the edge of the pool, the water had come from the scoop he was dangling over me. The robe had gone, he was just wearing boxer briefs. He had a splendid body, muscular, tanned and strong. He had carried me home last night.

I quickly grabbed the scoop and pushed back, catching him off balance. He fell into the pool. I laughed hysterically at the slapstick stupidity of it all.

I got up and watched as he swam underwater emerging at the far end of the pool. He climbed the steps, my eyes drawn to the outline of his penis, clearly defined under his wet briefs. He was a very big man.

'Watch out! Two can play at that game,' he yelled, as he gave chase.

He had me cornered and I shrieked like a banshee. He picked me up effortlessly in his arms and unceremoniously tossed me into the pool.

The water was wonderful, heated enough to take the edge off. I loved swimming, although it was strange being clothed. Adam dived in and swam up to me.

'The water is pretty good up here, don't you think Ms. Maxwell?'

'Mighty fine, Mr Darcy, mighty fine.'

And mighty fine being here with you, I thought.

I contemplated the strange set of circumstances that saw us together, trapped in a way, being confined here all day in a weird apocalyptic fantasy. Adam and me, the pantry full, kitted out for survival. It was as if we were living a modern day version of the movie the Omega Man.

He let me swim alone for a while. I could see him doing something in the kitchen.

After a short time he came back with a platter, laden with some of the yummy things the chef had left in the fridge. I watched from the water as he cleared the table and reset it with elegant glasses, crockery, cutlery and linen. He returned to the kitchen and after some time came back with an ice bucket and a bottle of champagne.

'Madame, lunch is served,' he gestured toward the table.

Who was this man?

He was funny and charming.

I got out of the pool and to my utter embarrassment the white cotton pyjamas had become completely see through.

'Oops, won't be long,' I said, as I quickly ran across the terrace to my bedroom.

I had seen a robe hanging in the bathroom, same brand as the pyjamas. I peeled the wet clothes off, dried myself and put on the gown. Very fitted, low cut. A fine, dove grey cotton jersey. What good taste Sam had. I felt quite sexy.


Adam had seen her body through the wet clothing, her nipples, her dark pubic hair. He wanted to run his fingers through it, all over her beautiful body. He wanted her. She returned wearing one of the robes Sam had chosen for the hotel's private collection. She looked so elegant and so fuckable.

'This looks delicious, I'm starving,' I said looking at the food on the table. There was a selection of cheeses, terrines, prosciutto, some of the best charcuterie I had seen. Adam sliced a crusty sourdough as I sat down. I do remember reading that this hotel had one of the finest restaurants in Melbourne.

'Some champagne?'

'Yes, please.'

We sat and gobbled the food like hungry beasts. Swimming did that to me. It felt so comfortable being here with him, he had lost that awkwardness I'd witnessed in the gallery. He seemed so relaxed, confident in his own skin, utterly sexy in fact.

Emboldened by the champagne, I spoke first. I was curious about something.

'Adam, last night I was wearing your robe.'

'Yes, it was huge on you,' he responded, quizzically.

'Well, this morning I noticed it was gone. I was naked and I can't remember how I got to bed?' I said, teasingly.

He poured me more champagne.

'What do you remember?' he asked.

'I remember the aspirin, the whisky, me crying and you putting your arm around me, comforting me,' I said.

'And that's all?' he asked.

'That's all' I responded.

'When I put my arm around you, you put your head against my chest. I stroked your back and you fell asleep.'

The thought of that tender intimacy awakened something inside me.

'What did you do next?'

'After some time, when your breathing had relaxed, I picked you up,' he said huskily.

'And then what happened?'

He paused, I wondered what he would say.

'While I was carrying you, the robe slipped from your shoulder and exposed your breast.'

His posture changed, he stretched out, self assured, tilted his head provocatively, a wry smile on his face, challenging for a response.

Two can play at this game.

I got up and stood in front of him and looked intently into his eyes.

'Like this?' I said, as I slowly pulled the gown off my shoulder, my left breast exposed.

'Like that,' he said, his breath quickening.

'And what did you do?' I asked.

'I did nothing, but that's not what I wanted to do,' he answered.

'What did you want to do?' I continued.

'This,' he said and reached for my waist, pulling me closer.

He touched the breast, gently circling the nipple, then pulled down the other sleeve. The robe was left hanging from my hips, my torso naked, exposed. He leaned forward and kissed the nipple then licked it playfully, before taking it in his mouth and sucking, first one then the other. I moved forward, seating myself on his lap, facing him, pulling his mouth toward me, kissing him hungrily.

'I wanted to see what your nipples looked like when they had just been sucked... by me.'

'And what did you want to do next?' I whispered.

'This,' he said and picked me up. I wrapped my legs around his waist, my arms around his neck, close to his face. I held him tight, I felt his erection, I wanted him. I was weak with lust, his arms were strong, I clung to his powerful body.

'I took you to your bedroom, but I wanted to take you to mine. I wanted you in my bed. I didn't want to leave you on your own. I didn't want to be alone.'

'Now I want you to take me there, this is what I want,' I demanded, breathlessly. He carried me toward his bedroom.


He kicked open the door and lay me gently down on the bed, his bed, the ruffled white sheets smelt of him. Masculine, earthy, a familiar scent remembered from last night, when, in his arms, I knew I was safe. He pulled the ties, undressing me, peeling back the fabric, uncovering my body, gazing, mesmerised. He stood and undressed, his erection released, proud, ready, and climbed into bed, next to me, never averting his gaze.

I turned, facing him, looking into his eyes, as if seeing him for the first time. He reached for me and held me close, tracing my mouth with his fingers, brushing the hair away from my face, looking at me with such intensity that again I felt tears. We lay silent.

What was happening?

What was this feeling?

I wanted him deeper inside me and parted my legs, hands against his buttocks, pulling him toward me. I felt his hard cock against me and I reached down, placing it firmly between the lips of my wet swollen sex, luxuriating in the feel of its size, nuzzling me open, deliberately prising me apart until he slipped effortlessly inside. He breathed deeply, chest rising, groaning at the intensity of the moment. Our mouths met, sucking, biting, neither of us wanting to separate, my breasts against his hard chest, my nipples erect, tingling, his hands entwined in my hair.

I had never felt such a deep sense of connection, of intimacy. Every faint movement threatened to send me into irretrievable ecstasy. I didn't want this feeling to end. I wanted to keep him inside me, filling me, connected. Slowly his hips began to move, pushing deeper. I held his ass, pulling him further into me till I felt the exquisite agony of his thick cock, hard against my womb. I moaned in unabashed pleasure at this new sensation. And then he thrust harder, I tilted my hips, my clitoris finding that sweet spot, and we danced this wild, intimate dance, until I felt an overwhelming sensation building, my whole body climbing a sensual peak, then releasing all inhibition and delivering the most perfect, shattering orgasm. Wave after wave engulfing my body, my mind, my soul. His body arched against me, responding to my uncontrolled contractions, his breathing now rapid, his chest pounding, groaning as he came with a ferocity matching mine, his cock pulsating, pumping his seed deep inside me, our love making complete.

We held each other, our breathing synchronised, falling asleep in each other's arms.

I woke and looked at him, secure in his protective embrace. His cock sat silken and soft between my legs. I wanted him and again cocooned him in my warm cunt. I knew he was awake when I felt him stiffen inside me. He opened his eyes, and stroked my face. We fucked silently and I felt the gentle pulsation of his ejaculation as we both climaxed once more.

We remained in bed and watched the sun go down and for once I didn't feel the usual melancholy of a day's ending.

His phone rang.

The police weren't coming tonight.

'They're too busy. They want to speak to you,' said Adam

I spoke to the officer. He said they would interview me at some stage during the week. The city was no longer in lock down and I could go home.

'I'm free to leave,' I said, moving off the bed, looking at him as he lay stretched out perfectly on the white sheets in front of me.

I felt the warm trickle of his sperm running down my leg. We had been in bed for the entire afternoon. I felt sad. I wasn't ready to leave.

I had nothing to wear.

'Could you ask Sam if my clothes are ready?' I said quietly.

'No,' he said sombrely.

'No? Why not?' I asked.

Anna Buckley

'Because I don't want you to go.'

He took my hand and pulled me toward him, back into his bed, gathering me in his arms. I opened my mouth to speak and he kissed me passionately, silencing me.

We remained in bed, waking only to fuck, then sleeping more soundly than I had ever known.

I loved waking up in his arms. I had not woken in the arms of a man for a very long time. And never woken with a man like him.

Hated that tomorrow had arrived.

I didn't want this to stop, but I knew that we both had lives to live.

His plane was leaving soon. He drove me home. We kissed, reluctant to part. I felt grief at having to say goodbye.

# Part 4

## What does this Mean

I ran up the stairs hoping to get there before Cindy arrived. Too late. She had let the police in, she looked confused. I had to stop myself from apologising to everyone. No time for the interview had been set. They had just turned up. The police wanted a full statement. Cindy heard every detail. They handed me my bag and left.

'Jesus, Tina? I've been trying to contact you all weekend. I rang Kate, she was pretty vague, said you were at the Imperial. Tried to get them to put me through to your room, but they said something about not disclosing the names of guests. Are you ok?' said an obviously distressed Cindy.

I wondered if in fact that was the policy of the hotel or whether it was Sam protecting his boss, suspecting that more than just good hospitality was going on in the penthouse above the hotel.

'It was pretty harrowing. I got caught up in the middle of it all, managed to get myself to the Imperial, that's where I've been the whole time. My phone was in my bag, I could only remember Kate's number. Didn't think I'd be stuck there for quite so long.'

I remembered that I had given Kate Adam's number and was quite relieved she had forgotten to pass it on. It would have required me to divulge far more than I was prepared to reveal, knowing only too well how easily Cindy would have tried to find out the truth behind my vague replies.

I could hardly tell her of the real and most surprising events of the last day and a half. Of being fucked beyond my wildest dreams, taken to sensual heights I barely had words for. Discovering emotions, feelings I'd never experienced before. How could I ever explain I'd been sleeping with the enemy. I didn't understand it myself. My sex tingled at the thought, I hungered for more.

I was so not ready to elaborate.

Checking my bag, all seemed to be in order, glad at not having to face the inconvenience of replacing all those cards.

I replied to the messages on my phone and realised I had not given Adam my number. He had handed me his card.

What would I say? I wanted to say that I wished he was still holding me, that I felt empty without him, that I didn't know what this was.

I remembered the clumsy groping in the back seat of country boys' cars, of the loveless couplings with Paul, the sexless years. I smiled at the thought of the fun I'd had over the last few months.

But what I felt now was completely foreign. It was different with him. Is this what love felt like? It shouldn't feel so intense, it had only been one night. I wanted to talk to him, but didn't know what to say. I felt consumed with lust when I thought about him, his body, his touch. Being in his arms, waking up to him, not wanting to leave. Did he feel it too? Or was I just imagining these things, the thoughts of a woman needing to feel love, to be loved. I didn't want to seem too desperate. Adam was a notorious womaniser. I would play it cool.

I texted.

*'Thanks for last night. I feel indebted to you, Tina.'*

Adam was in the first class lounge, waiting for his flight to board when he heard his phone buzz. It was Tina. He read the text, 'indebted'? Had the last thirty six hours meant so little? Her text was so nothing, so non-committal. He didn't know how to reply. What were the appropriate words? He had been waiting for this day, when he would finally have her, fantasised about it for years. Their lovemaking was so passionate. It seemed so charged, so emotionally powerful. He thought she felt it, too. But maybe he was wrong? Was he just willing it to be, because it was what he wanted, longed for? Perhaps he should tread carefully? He had waited so long, he didn't want to lose her now. He was not very romantic, but this would have to change.

He needed to talk to someone. He called Sam. Sam knew Adam's feelings for her and even though Sam was gay, Adam was sure he could help. It had been Sam's idea to send the flowers, although it was Adam who knew exactly what to send.

'Boss, what seems to be the problem?' asked Sam.

Adam explained the situation.

'Now did I get this right. You want me, a gay man, to tell you how to charm a woman?' said Sam, slightly exasperated.

'I know, I know. It's just that I saw what you brought up for her to wear, what you gave her when we were stuck there all day. You seem to have a much better understanding of these things.'

Sam laughed at the irony. He'd been in love with his boss since the day they met. He knew nothing would ever come of it and he liked Tina. He would help. Sam had been following her blog for a while, felt he knew her quite well.

'I think you are too old to beat about the bush, although you don't want to scare her off. You need to be clear about your intentions, but first you have to woo her.'

Sam had an idea. Adam liked it and trusted Sam with the words on a card.

They called his flight, he switched off his phone and thought about what Sam had said. This was so new, this business of pursuit, but so very important to get right.

# New Office

The day had been chaotic. Lots of questions about the riot from readers everywhere, particularly expatriates, shocked that this could happen in their city.

And for those without the personal connection to Melbourne, lots more enquiries about the dress.

The thing about the blog was that it never slept, it was like a hungry baby, always wanting more, always needing attention. On days like today it was even more important to respond personally. It would be inappropriate to fob the readers off with replies from the other contributors.

The trip in the taxi to the airport was the only time Kate and I had an opportunity to have a decent talk. She told me she was not planning on coming home for some time, as she had taken an internship at the Department of Foreign Affairs over the summer holidays. A brief trip home for Christmas would be all.

I loved that she was so independent. Having the income from the house gave her financial freedom. I also realised the flat was hardly a welcoming environment for her to come home to. She had to share her bedroom with computers, desks and office supplies.

I was also aware of the growing problem of working and living in this tiny place and was acutely reminded of my own lack of privacy when I had come home this morning.

'Cindy, we need to do something about our cramped quarters.'

'You're not wrong! I've already been looking into it.'

Sometimes I felt she had the uncanny ability to read my mind.

She showed me a list of properties, many seemed too large for our immediate needs. Obviously Cindy had bigger plans.

There was one place in particular, ironically a 1970s clothing warehouse and factory, just a few streets away in the nearby suburb of Collingwood. It must have been a state of the art building at the time. Chocolate brick facade, huge windows, offices and parking on the ground level. An empty, large open space on the second floor. I could just imagine the whirring of sewing machines and the women who once sat at them, busily churning out garments, in the days before cheap imports.

Fitzroy and Collingwood were full of empty warehouses and factories just like these.

Many of these inner city properties had been snapped up for development, but the housing market in Melbourne was slowing. There had been no mining boom in this city and with the closure of more manufacturers, sites like these were coming up more frequently. What's more, the site was zoned 'commercial'. It would take a change in planning regulations to make this real estate more valuable and with this encumbrance it made the property relatively cheap. I thought about this and realised I had the perfect solution.

'How about we partition off part of the upstairs space?' I said.

'I don't get it?' Cindy said looking at me, puzzled by my suggestion.

I told her I had heard an author speak about the need to leave the house, to go to a specifically allocated space in which to work, away from the distractions and procrastinations of home.

'There must be lots of women who need an office away from home, in the inner city, who can't afford to rent an entire place.'

'And you're saying that we could provide that space at a reasonable rent?' said Cindy.

'Yes, with the possibility that the space could be made available to us if we needed it in the future.'

Not only did this solve our problem of a lack of space, but it made good financial sense. I calculated that we could afford to buy the building, if we had paying tenants to offset the cost of the loan.

I put this question to my readers first. Would they consider renting a small office away from the distractions of home? I was overwhelmed by the almost instant response. We would have no trouble getting tenants.


I rang the real estate agent. I rang the bank. We worked into the night putting together a business proposal ready for my meetings the following day.

The real estate agent told me the space was available for immediate possession. The owners were desperate to sell, said we could move in tomorrow if we got approval from the bank. This would be good as I was heading back to America in three weeks for the next book tour. The eagerness worked in my favour, I was no fool and negotiated a much lower price.

I went to the bank with my plan and they told me I had more than enough for the deposit. The female bank manager could see the clever business strategy and approved the loan. The scheme was quite brilliant. The tenants effectively covered the entire costs of purchasing the building and I could look forward to good capital growth if I chose to sell in a few years time. The risks to me would be minimal. I speculated what the value of the property would be if I could get a zone change to residential. I made a mental note to ring Ruth, my lawyer and ask her to look into it.

By 5 pm that night the deals were done and I had bought my first property. Our little business would be moving out and I would get the flat to myself. Cindy and I opened a bottle of my favourite Prosecco and toasted our new venture.

'No time like the present, cheers Cindy.'

'Couldn't agree more. Cheers Tina.'

Not long after Cindy left, the doorbell rang. It was a delivery. A beautifully wrapped box. I ripped away the paper and took off the somewhat familiar lid. It was the pyjamas, wrapped in tissue, washed and pressed. Inside a note.

'Thought you might like these. Have no need for them here, prefer you naked, Adam.'

'P.S. Will be in Cambodia for the next few weeks. Would love to see you when I return.'

He preferred me naked! That was so sexy. He wanted to see me.

I wanted him. I rang, but to no avail, his phone was turned off. I would wait to hear from him when he returned.

It was probably a good thing that I didn't have the distraction of Adam Darcy right now. The next few weeks were absolutely packed.

We put out word we were moving and called for tenants.

We had many more applicants than spaces.

Cindy would handle the interviews, she was happy to play the role of bad cop. As manager she would be handling the leases anyway. We would arrange for all the rents to be direct debited. We weren't running a charity and could not afford to take on people who were not serious about needing the space.

I took Lola and Raphael over to the new office building. Raphael suggested an office partitioning system for the upper floor. This would be cheap, flexible and easy to install. He rang the company, they could start tomorrow. We now knew exactly how many occupants the space could hold.

Lola made the good suggestion that Cindy and I occupy the entire ground floor, with a separate entrance for the tenants on the floor above. It would be good to have privacy and distance from the other occupants. It also meant that I didn't have to be available, 'on call' all the time and would have the freedom to come and go as I pleased, without constant interruption.

She was a very wise woman. She also suggested that we create something special for ourselves. She and Raphael wanted to design the interior. I thought it was a brilliant idea. I had seen Raphael's apartment, their store and the hotel and knew it would be stunning. I gave them the green light.

There was very little structural work to be done. Raphael used his builder and because he was dealing with all the day to day hassles of the job, the whole project went seamlessly. After just two weeks, the tenants were ready to move in. After three weeks we unpacked our last box, plugged in the computers and were ready to roll.

Lola and Raphael had done a marvellous job. The entire space was gallery like. White walls, polished concrete floor, very stylish, very sexy. Cindy and I had our own separate offices with workstations for any of the team of writers who felt the need to come into the office. To one side a huge cutting table and design space for the dress project.

Paintings from Gabriella's stock room gave the room colour. At the back they had designed a sleek kitchen complete with a vast table that could seat twenty. It was something I had requested. I had wanted to be able to cook for friends. My tiny flat had meant that no more than four could ever be seated.

Cindy had organised a small gathering to celebrate the opening. We were all too tired for anything grand, we had been working round the clock. Raphael filled our glasses.

'Thank you, Cindy, Raphael, Lola. The place is magnificent. I can't believe how much you've done in such a short time.'

'And to you, beautiful Christina. Who would've thought we would be doing this, that you would have achieved such success in so little time,' said Raphael proudly, as if I were his own personal project.

If only they really knew just how far I'd come, I thought wistfully. After that special day with Raphael, he had returned to being the brother like figure I'd always known. There were no awkward moments, no jealousies, it was as if it was all part of some grand plan and he was quite accepting of his part.

No one knew what had really happened during my unexpected stay at the Imperial. The interesting thing was that the interior of the new office was very similar to Adam's hotel, to his penthouse. I was becoming more aware of just how many connections the Finestra family must have had with him. They had every right to do business with Adam. He was one of the richest men in Australia. It must have been awkward for them at times, knowing how I felt about Adam's family, his brother. I didn't want Adam to become the elephant in the room. I wanted them to be able to business with him without feeling they had to keep this a secret from me.

They all knew of the rancour between Justin and myself and I wondered how they would respond if anything were to develop with Adam. I didn't even know how I would handle it. I was quite conflicted. It was easier to push it to the back of my mind, I had no answers. Or did I? Perhaps it was up to me to start the conversation.

'Hey Raphael, did you hear about me being caught up in King Street during the riots?'

'Yeah, it was terrible. Were you hurt, how did you get out of there alive?'

'Horrible, frightening to think something like that could happen in our city. Luckily I ran up Flinders Lane and into the Imperial.'

'Sam, the manager is a really nice guy,' said Raphael.

'Yeah, he gave me a room, gorgeous place. It felt familiar. I noticed the rooms have pieces of your furniture in them, some of the spaces remind me of this, the warehouse,' I said pointing to the room we were in.

'Did you do the interiors?'

'Yes, I'm glad you noticed.'

I sensed his reluctance, I needed to give him permission to explain.

'I hear it's owned by Adam Darcy. You should do more work for him, apparently he owns hotels all over the world.'

'I must confess, I already do, but I was reluctant to talk to you about it, knowing all the trouble that his brother has given you,' he responded, rather sheepishly.

'Oh God, Raphael, you needn't have worried. My problem was with Justin, not Adam. I would hate to think you couldn't talk to me about what you do.'

'I appreciate that and yes, it has been awkward at times. The thing is, Adam is a really easy person to work with.'

'Probably because you and your sister are so good at what you do, and I hear he is nothing like his brother at all,' I said, sneakily bringing Lola into the conversation.

'It's true, nothing at all, in fact you'd probably get on with him quite well. Like you say, he respects people who are good at what they do. He has asked about you from time to time.'

'Really?'

'He's been interested in seeing your business grow, perhaps someday I could arrange for you to meet?'

'Well, that might be pushing it a bit too far. Perhaps some time in the future?'

'Whenever you're ready,' he said flirtatiously, as if he could read my mind.

# First Date

It was the last week of November. The move had gone smoothly. We had employed an office manager to ease the massive workload. The dress business was going crazy. The press was having a field day asking why something this simple had never been done before.

My second book, 'Escape Money' was out and the American publishers were flying me over to the States for a tour in a few days.

I had reclaimed my flat and was looking forward to a quiet night in.

I hadn't heard from Adam. Perhaps it really was just a very long one night stand. I would leave it up to him to get in touch when he returned. That is, if he actually wanted to see me again. I just didn't know how to judge the situation.

Adam had not had a response to the gift he'd sent. He didn't know if she wanted to see him or not. Being away from her had been torture. He had been back for a day and asked Sam if Tina had tried to make contact.

'No, nothing boss.'

'Fuck! I thought she would at least give me a call?' he said, despondently.

'Have you rung her? Does she know you're back? For that matter did she even know what date you were returning?' Sam pleaded.

'Err, no,' he replied sheepishly.

'Jesus! For such a rich, clever genius, you are a complete fuckwit at this!'

Adam knew he had a lot to learn. He had dated many women. He didn't have to chase them, they were always available. He was completely inexperienced in this business of pursuit. He had never felt this way about a woman before.

'Do you have her number?' said Sam.

'Yes.'

'Then ring her, you bloody idiot!'


The phone rang. It was Adam, my heart skipped a beat.

'Hi, you're back. How was the trip?' I said, trying not to sound too keen.

'Good, how've you been?' he responded nervously.

'Busy. We've moved office and I'm off to the States in a couple of days,' I replied.

Sam was just about having a fit as he listened to Adam's less than enticing call. He grabbed a pen and started quickly scribbling on a piece of paper, holding it up for Adam to see. 'ASK HER OUT!!!!!!'

'You're leaving? Ahh, do you want to go somewhere?' he said, whilst reading the note.

'I mean, can I take you out to dinner, now, tonight,' he said clumsily.

'Yeah... I'd love to.'

'I've got a table at Pier, I'll jump in the car now. See you soon.'

He hung up.

'Man, you've got some work to do!' said Sam, as he rolled his eyes at Adam.


It was an unusually hot humid night, typical of the unpredictable weather of late spring. I dived in and out of the shower. A black dress, one of this season's new designs would do, a simple strand of pearls and a suede heel. Pier was where the Brighton set ate. Blonde bobs, cosmetic surgery, rich husbands. A place where Fiona and her friends would feel at home. Seafood and ocean views, ridiculously expensive, not really my kind of place.


He rang the bell. A small sixties flat. Not quite what he expected. Surely she would be living in something better than this? He had heard she was running a very successful business. A few of his venture capital friends were starting to talk about what she was doing.

He had learnt not to make assumptions about her.

He thought that Pier would be good. The owner, Di, had been a tireless fundraiser for his Cambodian charity, and although it was one of the most popular restaurants in town, she always had a table for him. It was a hot night, the sea air would be a welcome break from the turgid heat of the city.

I was only just ready when the doorbell rang. I tried to appear unruffled as I let him in. In truth, my heart was beating wildly, I felt a deep sense of desire in the pit of my belly remembering the brief but passionate time we had spent together. And for the first time in a very long while I thought I might be prepared to let myself be vulnerable, fall for this man who so deeply affected me. He looked more handsome than I remembered, dark suit, dark shirt, designer stubble, lean body.

'Hi.'

'Hi.'

'You ready?'

'Sure,' I grabbed my bag and followed him out.

The thirty minute drive to Saint Kilda beach was broken only by the occasional outburst of road rage. He had a temper. The silence was uncomfortable. It occurred to me that this was probably going to be one of those polite meetings where I would establish that he wasn't interested in anything more than a casual liaison, like the one we had a few weeks ago. He'd been away, had time to think about it. He was a 'Ladies' Man'. Why did I think I would be different from any of the other women he had never formed long term relationships with?

I had enjoyed my various sexual encounters over the last nine months. Perhaps I would just have to resign myself to the fact that Adam Darcy was just another one of those.

The one thing that these rich, properly educated men had going for them was that they at least did the 'right thing'. That was what this dinner was about. The polite let down, the no strings attached speech and, after all, by being polite and honest, it would not close off all the options.


She sat there silently, not a word. He didn't know how to make small talk. He hated his inability to be sociable. She was popular, beautiful and easy to talk to, always had been. He remembered the way she would walk into that bar, confidently, not threatened by his hostile friends, completely oblivious to their subtle bullying.

Adam wished he knew how to tell her what he really thought.


We pulled up near the restaurant and walked the short distance to the front door. It would not budge. He looked puzzled. The menu in the glass case told us that the restaurant was closed.

'Fuck!' he exclaimed.

'I thought they never closed. I'm sorry. I should have realised, nothing's open on a Monday night.'

I looked around. Surely this place, teeming with people, had something to offer?

'Why don't we just get in the car and drive along the esplanade until we see something? I don't mind where we eat. I'm starving, I could eat a horse,' I said, understanding his frustration.

We drove north and the further we went, the fewer people there were, no restaurants, very little sign of life. What I saw was the redevelopment of abandoned industrial wasteland into partly built luxurious seaside apartments. A dimly lit cafe and a pub the only lights on this deserted strip. We went inside and an old man was glumly cleaning the counter top. This would do. I could smell the oil, fish and chips would be fine.

No fancy branded boxes, just two pieces of battered fish and a generous serve of chips wrapped in white paper. I loved that smell. I waited for Adam as he grabbed some beers from the run down pub next door.

We drove up to the construction site. Adam spoke to the security guard and he opened the gate.

I looked across at him as we drove to the far end of the site, past the half built apartment blocks.

'It's one of mine,' he said rather sheepishly as we stopped at a fence separating us from the foreshore.

Adam grabbed an overcoat from the back seat. We crawled through a hole in the fence surrounding the site and walked along a vague path between the sand dunes and on to a deserted beach. He laid out the coat in a chivalrous manner and gestured for me to sit down. I stretched out, opened up the paper parcel and offered him the food.

'I'm really sorry. This is not what I had in mind,' said Adam, looking decidedly pissed off with himself.

'Don't worry about it. It's fine and we've got the whole place to ourselves. It's kind of nice after the hustle and bustle of the city.'

They were completely alone. The roar of the city blocked by the dunes. The only sound, the gentle motion of the waves.

'So how was Cambodia?' I said, kicking off my completely ridiculous heels.

'It was good. We get so much more done now that the guys are becoming more skilled, more confident.'


He followed her lead and slipped off his shoes, took off his suit jacket and tie, undid the top buttons of his shirt and rolled up his sleeves. The uncomfortable silence was back. He had to say something. He didn't care if she didn't feel the same way.

'I missed you.'

There, he'd said it.


I was relieved he had spoken. I liked what he said.

'I missed you, too,' I replied.

He turned towards me, holding my face in his hands and kissed me slowly and passionately. My body leapt to attention. This is what I'd longed for. He licked the salt from my lips.

'You taste good,' he said.

I picked up his hand and licked each of his fingers.

'So do you,' I responded.

He wrapped his arms around me and held me tight.

'I missed holding you,' he whispered in my ear.

He lay back and I put my head on his chest, remembering fondly how we had spent so much of that first night together.

'And I missed this,' I said, snuggling in closer, nuzzling his chest. He smelt wonderful, masculine, clean.

It was if we had been lovers forever. It felt so good, so natural, to be with him. He did really want to be here with me. I felt a sense of contentment. For the first time in many years I felt I could begin to let down the protective emotional barriers fall. We lay like that for ages, watching the stars, just being together. The presence of him, of his body, ignited a slow flickering flame deep in my belly. I needed more. I needed him.

I sat up and straddled his hips. One by one I undid his shirt buttons until his chest was exposed. I licked his nipples and ran my tongue down the middle of his torso. He groaned. I stood and took my dress off, then my underwear. There was no one around for miles. I revelled in the freedom. Uninhibited, I presented my body as a gift to him. His chest rose at the sight of my nakedness. Silently I knelt back down, next to him and removed his shirt, his belt, his trousers and lastly his boxers. We sat there like the biblical Adam and Eve, unclothed, aroused and completely vulnerable.

I took his proud cock in my hand, leant over and started to kiss it's glistening head. I licked away the small orb of moisture forming at the tip and delicately put my tongue into the small slit, then traced around the seam of skin. I ran my lips down his engorged vein and then covered his balls with my mouth and gently sucked. He responded with a guttural moan, his breathing ragged.

I got up and placed one leg over his hips, then knelt down, his cock at the entrance to my damp cunt. Then slowly lowered myself onto him, the thickness of his shaft filling me. He held my buttocks, arched his back and thrust hard. I groaned at this deep sensual penetration. My hips swayed with him. It felt so good. He held me closer and again found that sweet spot, and we fucked with abandon, reconnecting physically till our bodies could hold back no longer. Our shared orgasm intense. I lay back down on his chest, keeping him inside me, not wanting us to part. He enfolded his arms protectively around me.

I felt cherished.

A shock of lightning lit up the night sky, fat drops of rain fell on my back, the cool change was coming. We scrambled to get dressed and ran back to the car. Rain thundered down, obscuring the view. It was too dangerous to drive. He was only wearing his trousers, me my dress, that was all we had time for. His wet torso glistened. I looked over at him and we both smiled.

'Looks like we're stuck here for a while,' I said.

'Yes, we seem to be in the habit of getting stranded together,' he commented.

'I wonder how long this will last?' I said.

'Perhaps long enough to fuck you in the front seat of my car?' he stated, looking at me intently, barely able to hide his desire.

I was shocked by his directness, but thrilled at what was about to happen. My labia tumescent with the thought of his erotic suggestion.

He flicked a switch and her seat reclined. Her dress was wet, her nipples erect, outlined against the cold fabric. He leaned over and placed his warm hand over her breast, feeling the hard nipple as he pressed his palm against her. He wanted her now, immediately. He fought with the damp fabric to slide her dress above her hips. He roughly opened her legs and forcefully pushed his hand up against her wet lips. He slipped his fingers into her and knew she was ready. He unzipped his fly and his cock burst out swollen. He balanced himself over her and thrust hard.

'Deeper,' she pleaded, and he pounded her with an aggressive, lust driven force. She grabbed his ass and pulled him hard onto her clitoris, grinding herself against him. Their fucking was brutal, primal. He was reaching new heights of pleasure and groaned, uncontrolled, as his cock exploded into her, spurting deep. He collapsed on top of her, panting, hot and sweating. He had never felt so satisfied, so complete.

Her eyes opened, he looked at her and kissed her face, her cheeks, her forehead, her lips.

'I can't get enough of you. I want more,' he said.

'I want more of you, too,' she replied breathlessly.

The rain stopped. Adam grabbed his shirt and put it on, I pulled down my dress and he drove home, barefoot. As we headed along the almost deserted St. Kilda road, I put my hand on his leg. He responded by pulling up my dress and slipping his hand between my legs, withdrawing, smelling, then licking his fingers. He turned to me briefly and smiled mischievously.

'Your place or mine?' he asked.

'Whatever is closest... and hurry!' I demanded.


We pulled into the underground car park, the tyres squealing, broadcasting our urgency. He abruptly stopped and we hastily grabbed the rest of our clothes. He punched in his code and the doors to the lift opened straight away. Inside he grabbed me and kissed me lustily as we made our ascent. The doors opened into his private lobby and we tumbled frantically out, trying to undress as we headed for the entrance. We didn't make it any further and fucked madly on the floor. My need for him was insatiable.

'Can anyone see us?' I asked, realising how public this display could have been.

'No, this is private. The security cameras only operate in the hotel and Sam doesn't come up here when I'm in. He always rings first.'

'Not always!' I corrected.

'That was my mistake. He knows I value my privacy.'

'Shall we go inside?' said Adam.

I walked past the mirror.

'God, I look terrible!' I exclaimed, as I saw my bedraggled reflection.

'No, you don't. You look beautiful, beautifully fucked!' said Adam playfully.

'Adam, I have sand everywhere. My clothes are a mess.'

'That's easily fixed. Take your clothes off. Then I can lick you clean. Come here.'

'You are wicked. But I feel disgusting. Could I take a shower?' I pleaded.

My dress was damp and creased. I was embarrassed at the thought of getting my clothes washed by housekeeping.

'And do you by any chance have a laundry?'

'Sure, through that door. But why?' he asked.

'I would like to rinse my clothes. I don't want Sam to have to come up and collect them.'

He said he understood, pointing me in the direction of the laundry. Everything was there that I needed. I shoved my things into the machine, set the cycle to delicate and turned it on. Brazenly, I walked back out to the lounge room naked.

'You are killing me, Tina!'

'I'm sorry, Mr. Darcy, that was not my intention. I just needed to know which shower to use?'

'Follow me.'

We went to his bedroom and through to the bathroom. He turned the water on. I got straight in. Adam stripped off and followed. Two shower heads meant that there was plenty of room and it wasn't long before I felt his soapy hands fondling my breasts.

'Adam, you are incorrigible!'

'I can't help it, you are just so sexy, so fuckable,' he moaned.

He left no part of my body untouched. He delicately soaped the folds between my thighs and then pulled a nozzled hose from the wall. He sat down on the tiled floor and leaned against the glass taking my hand, pulling me down, across his lap. He spread my legs apart and began to rinse, removing all the slippery suds. I was quite sore and the hot water was soothing. I could feel his hardness pressing against my stomach and so I rolled over and mounted him. As we gently fucked he continued to run the hot water over my back, my arms, my belly. We sat and he rocked me into a quiet, but utterly full orgasm. I kissed him tenderly.

I lifted myself off and he saw me wince in pain.

We dried each other.

It was time for bed. No conversation about whose house, we just wanted to be together. He turned off the lights and to my surprise he softly massaged my sex with a soothing balm. It was such an affectionate, caring thing to do. His calming ministration lulled me into a deep sleep.

# The Painting

It was Tuesday morning. I could feel his arms cocooned around me. I had slept soundly. I felt his early morning erection pressing against me. I took him into me and moved enough till I felt the slight pulsation of his ejaculation.

The sun had not risen, but the pre-dawn light softly lit the room. I rolled over and looked at this handsome man. His eyes opened slowly.

'Hi, beautiful,' he whispered.

'Hi,' I said, smiling.

'What are you thinking?' he said.

'I'm thinking that I'm happy being here with you,' I answered.

'Me, too,' he said, smiling back.

We got up and I made us breakfast.

'What are your plans today?' Adam asked.

'Well, I usually like to check with Chenda about the dress orders. See that everything is ok. Then do a bit of editorial work on the blog. Tie up a few loose ends before I leave tomorrow for the States.'

'Fuck! So soon. I can't bear the thought of you going. Do you have to go into the office today? Can't someone handle it?' he pleaded.

'Well, we did go through a lot of stuff yesterday. Do you have a computer here?' I said.

'Yeah, in the office,' he replied.

'I suppose I could login here and do a lot of the work. I'll give Cindy a call once she's in the office.'

I knew that as long as I had the internet and a computer, I could conduct my business from just about anywhere.

'And what about you? Surely you've got work to do?' I asked.

'If it means spending the day with you, I'll ring the office and get them to free up my diary. There'll be plenty of time to work once you're gone. It will help me keep my mind off you. How long will you be away?'

'Just under two weeks. Not quite as long as the first tour. Thank God we have already pre-sold thousands of books or the trip would be much longer. This tour is mainly for TV. Face to face interviews with the big networks. My publicist wants to cast the net wider. Build my brand.'

'Will you be going to New York?' he asked.

'Yeah, last few days. Why do you ask?'

'It's just that I have a place there. You'd love it. It's right in Manhattan. It's yours if you want it.'

'Thanks, but my publishers have already got it sorted. Anyway it'd be no fun without you.'


We finished breakfast and talked about what we might do today. Adam suggested we visit Heide Museum of Modern Art. I'd always wanted to go there, see the gallery built around the modernist house of John and Sunday Reed. I thought it was a great idea.

'Well, I guess I'd better get started. Where's your office?'

'Follow me.'

We walked along the central corridor and he opened a door. I was completely unprepared for what I saw. On one side sat a huge dark timber desk and facing the desk a painting, a painting of a nude woman. Tim's painting of me. Adam was the buyer.

'It was you. You bought that painting. I had no idea, Gabriella wouldn't tell me.'

That was one of the first pieces to sell. He had bought it long before we had become lovers.

'Why did you buy this one?' I asked.

'It was the best in the show. Gabriella rang me and asked if I wanted first look. When I saw it, I knew that I had to have it. I had to have it because it was you.'

'Me? Why would you want a portrait of me? I don't understand?' I said, puzzled.

'It's a long story.'

'I'm listening,' I said and sat on top of the desk, ready for his tale.

'Well, you probably don't recall. It was a long time ago.'


He told her about being thrown by her feisty nature, at how uncomfortable she had made him feel when she spoke out. How he didn't know how to handle her. He'd never met anyone like her, so full of spirit, so alive, so willing to flaunt convention, unrestrained by the rules that he and his friends were required to live by.

'These were things that made you interesting. I'd never met a woman like you before. In fact, I found you a bit intimidating.'

'Me? Intimidating? You were the arrogant asshole,' she responded, defensively.

'Is that right?' he grinned.

'Yes, it was infuriating the way you would just sit there passing judgement, sneering at everything I said.'

'I wasn't passing judgement. I just didn't know what to make of you. Anyway, that's not what I wanted to tell you about.'

'I want to tell you about the time when my feelings for you changed. You probably don't remember it.'


He proceeded to tell me about that night when he dropped Paul at my place. When he saw the room, the furniture. When he saw me in my own place, away from his friends. He remembered that little black dress and how when I turned around my bare back looked so sexy. I'd looked different, I had grown up, so independent, so beautiful.

'I no longer saw you as just interesting, I saw you as desirable. I wanted you then and there,' declared Adam.

I was shocked, I had no idea.

'Why didn't you do anything about it, about your feelings for me?' I pleaded.

'Because Paul was my friend. I knew he was serious about you, I couldn't do that to him.'

It hit me. Had he acted, things might have been so very different.

'And so what then?' I asked.

'As you know, I barely saw either of you. Paul had got what I had wanted. He got you. You were married. You had a baby. It was best for me to not be around. I threw myself into business, lots of things took me away from Melbourne.'

'I was shocked when Paul died, but I was more upset when I saw you. You'd changed. It was as if the life had been taken out of you. You'd lost that verve, that magic and I knew it wasn't only because of Paul's death.'

'Why didn't you try to make contact with me then?'

'Because your husband had just died!' he responded.

Of course. He had no idea of the lie I had been living and I wasn't ready to tell that story yet.

'And then out of the blue you started turning up. I didn't know how to begin. I thought I might try to approach you at Tim's opening, but you hit me with that diatribe about bureaucrats and cuckolded husbands. That was when I knew you'd heard that stuff we'd said about you all those years ago. I realised what an asshole I'd been. I understood your anger.'

'I also had no idea of how to show you my true feelings, so I sent you those flowers and that song. I remembered the flowers on the table that night. I saw them in your flat.'

'They were from you?' I said, touched by the sincerity of the gesture.

He walked towards me and took my face in his hands, staring at me intently, pausing before he spoke,

'I love you, Tina, I always have. These last few weeks have been the best of my life.'

He kissed me with a passion and tenderness I had never felt before.

'I don't want to let you go again,' he whispered.

He'd said it. He loved me, he always had. The tears welled up in my eyes, he wiped them away and then held me close. I did not want to lose him either. I had already wasted so much time. My head was swimming with thoughts of what might have been. I couldn't blame him for behaving as he did. It was the decisions I had made that shaped my life, not his failure to act. I felt sadness at what might have been, at the fickleness of fate, and then I remembered Kate and realised how much I could have missed.

Eventually we let go of each other. I looked at him with a new sense of affection. He radiated a deep sense of calm. He kissed me gently.

'God, I could make love to you all day.'

'I know, me too,' I said, kissing him back.'

I heard the ringing of a phone. It was his phone, in the kitchen.

'I'd better get this, sort out work and then maybe we can have the whole day to ourselves. Here, use my desk.'

He opened up his computer and typed in his password.

'I'll leave you to it.'

He had said those magic words. My head was spinning, I was completely unprepared. It took me a long time to compose myself enough to write.

# A Day Out

It was still early and Cindy wouldn't be at the office yet. I had plenty of time to write the editorial. I knew I wanted to title the piece 'What If?'

Anna Buckley

I emailed the editorial and gave her a call.

'Cindy, I have a favour to ask, could you handle the meeting today?'

'Sure, why?'

'Well, I've decided to check out a few places, do a bit of research on the modernist houses of Melbourne. A friend has been able to get me into some private homes and we thought we might make a day of it.'

'That sounds fine, I can talk to the writers. You don't need to be here. There's only one problem, I need you to sign some stuff from the bank. I'll come over now.'

'Umm, actually, I'm not at home,' I said, sheepishly.

'It's only 8.30 in the morning! Where the hell are you? Did you have a sleepover?' she quizzed cheekily.

'Maybe?' I replied cryptically.

'Last night when I left you were exhausted, the only thing you were curling up with was a good book. Who is he?' she said.

'I can't talk now. I'll call in on the way to Heide and sign those papers.'

'So you're spending the day with him, the mystery man?'

'I'll tell you about it when I drop in. See you at about ten.'

'No problems. You know this is killing me, I want all the details.'

'Thanks Cindy, you're brilliant. See you soon.'

'See ya, Tina, have fun!'

292

Adam was at the kitchen bench on his phone. He looked at me and pointed to the coffee pot.

I poured myself a cup and sidled up to him. I playfully tapped my watch, he looked back shrugging his shoulders, indicating that he didn't know how to get the caller off the phone. I was wearing the grey robe, stood right in front of him and undid the cord. I mimicked his actions, shrugging my shoulders as well.

'Actually Rob, something's come up. I've got to go. If you have anymore problems ring the office. See you mate,' said a completely distracted Adam.

He pulled me towards him and lifted me onto the bench, pushing the robe from my shoulders. He kissed my neck. I arched my back and thrust out my breasts. He greedily sucked each nipple and my cunt warmed with pain and wetness, as his kisses moved down my belly.

His phone rang.

'Fuck!' I heard him groan.

He looked at the caller ID, rolled his eyes and answered.

'Justin, what do you want?'

Adam walked away from the bench and went outside to take the call. I felt uncomfortable knowing who he was speaking with, being reminded of just what a relationship with Adam would really mean. I watched as the conversation became more animated, the expression on Adam's face told me he was not pleased. After quite some time I began to feel a little exposed and pulled the robe back on. Adam eventually returned.

'Everything ok?' I asked.

'Yeah, yeah, family,' said Adam with a look of exasperation.

'Now, where were we?' he asked, his mood lifting.

I grabbed his hand and placed it between my legs.

'Here, I think,' I replied.

'You're wrong. I do believe we weren't quite there yet! This is where we were,' he said, as he removed the robe, and with his two hands grabbed my backside pulling me closer to the edge of the bench.

I leant back and spread my legs in anticipation. The phone rang again.

'Jesus Christ!' he yelled, as he snatched the phone and went outside again.

I could see that the problem was not going to go away. The clock said 10 am, the day was disappearing and I really did need to get in and sign those papers. I would have a shower, the moment was lost.

I took my clothes from the dryer.

He was still on the phone when I returned.

'You've got to sort this shit out for yourself!' I heard him yell, before slamming the phone down.

'God, I'm sorry. My fucking brother is always getting himself into trouble. I'll have a quick shower and we can go,' he said, as he left the room.

The mood was ruined, his fury palpable.


We pulled up in front of my office, his anger still evident during our silent trip to Collingwood.

'Hey, it's ok.' I said, as I squeezed his hand.

'Sorry, it just takes me some time to cool off.'

We sat there for a while until I felt him begin to relax.

'Come with me. I want you to see where I work, meet Cindy. It would be good for you to have her contact details while I'm away. She's got my itinerary, usually knows what I'm up to.'

'Hi, Tina,' said Joan, looking up from the front desk.

'Morning Joan, this is Adam.'

'Pleased to meet you, Sir,' she said, as she stood and shook his hand, looking him up and down, appreciative of what she saw.

'Pleased to meet you too, Joan,' said Adam.

'What time's your flight tomorrow Tina?' asked Joan.

'Early, six am.'

We walked straight through the large open plan studio to Cindy's office and did all the formal introductions.

'God, Tina this is pretty impressive,' he said, looking around the immaculate space.

'She should take you upstairs, that's what I call truly impressive,' said Cindy proudly.

'Want a look?' I asked.

I took him upstairs and showed him the warehouse filled with office cubicles.

'This has been a phenomenal success. We've barely been up and running for a week and we are getting hundreds of enquiries about leasing space. The tenants' fees cover the entire loan repayments. I virtually get the downstairs space for free. Cindy and I are looking for bigger premises where we can offer an even greater level of service. Childcare, food, meeting rooms, workshops. The possibilities are endless.'

As we were heading back to my office, his phone started to ring again.

'Sorry, I'll take this outside,' he said, apologetically.


I signed the papers and knew Cindy was bursting to talk.

'Where is he?' she whispered, conspiratorially.

'He's outside, taking a call.'

'He's gorgeous. You can't seem to wipe the smile off your face,' she said.

'I know, it's happening quite fast,' I replied.

'The only thing I don't understand... isn't he the brother of that dickhead who held you to ransom over the house, Justin Darcy?'

'I know, I know. But Adam's not like them. We've known each other for a very long time. I misunderstood him. He really likes me and I really like him,' I responded defensively, sounding more like a love struck schoolgirl than a forty year old woman.

'Well, I guess you know what you're doing?' she said, somewhat sceptically.

'You just need to get to know him. He doesn't have much to do with his family,' I said, trying to convince myself that this wasn't going to be a problem.

She wasn't buying it. I changed the subject. We discussed last minute details of the trip and I was set to go.

'I've given Adam your contact details and I'm happy for you to keep him informed while I'm away. Here's his number if you need to call him,' I said, trying to unsuccessfully reassert my status as boss.

'Wow, you've got it bad, this is really serious!' she said, still looking perplexed.

'I'll give you a call when I get in to L.A.'

'Sure, thanks. Have a great trip and have a lovely day,' she said, softening her inquisitorial approach.

'Thanks Cindy, I will. See you when I get back,' I said.

Joan and Cindy walked me to the front door and waved goodbye.

'Isn't that the brother of that guy that ripped Tina's late husband off?' asked Joan. She had seen the tabloids.

'No idea,' replied Cindy coldly, always careful to protect Tina.


I met him in his car just as he was finishing the call. He tried to hide his annoyance.

'I should turn this bloody thing off,' he said.

'It's ok. I understand. You can't expect your business to stop just because you want to take a day off,' I said, offering some consolation.

'It's not my business. I've got a great team to deal with that. It's my bloody brother who can't get his shit together!' he yelled, as if chastising me for even commenting.

That hurt. It reminded me of the old Adam. I didn't like it, his short temper, the angry outburst.


He'd raised his voice, he'd hurt her. He couldn't believe what he had just done. Adam turned his phone off and tossed it onto the back seat.

'Jesus Tina, I'm so sorry. I didn't mean to take it out on you. It's just that today is turning into another fuckup.'

'I couldn't manage to get us a table at dinner last night and now my brother is destroying this attempt at lunch. I'm mad at myself for letting this happen. Please forgive me.'


'It's ok,' I said quietly, my head raced at the thoughts playing out in my mind.

We drove out to the gallery, not that far from the Finestras' place. It was on land once used as a dairy farm, set in a magnificent park dotted with many large contemporary sculptures. Down the path and through the gardens there were newer buildings, a restaurant and large exhibition space. To the right, the original, white, stone block, sixties house. It was stunning.

The minute I walked inside I was completely transfixed. The stone block walls remained unpainted. The two storey house comprised of many 'L' shaped spaces, creating indoor and outdoor rooms, secret spaces, human sized alcoves. Large windows lit the space and offered glimpses of the gardens outside. The main body of the house had a large gallery, a mezzanine encircled the double storey interior.

I read that the house had been designed by David McGlashan in 1967 for John and Sunday Reed, art lovers who needed space to hang their collection. It was bequeathed to the government to be used as a gallery to showcase the works of modern Australian artists.

'I love this place,' I whispered reverently.

'This is my dream house.'

It was just the right size. No old money ostentation, no new money McMansion. A pared back simple house, a breathtaking sixties exercise in understatement.

He watched as her eyes lit up, she loved this place. He saw the same look that had so beguiled him when he first met her. He'd noticed that look earlier today, when she was showing him her business, talking about all the possibilities. He'd also noticed the dullness in her demeanour when he'd snapped before. It was the broken look he'd seen at her wedding and at her husband's funeral. He knew he would have to be more careful.

I walked through the place, familiar iconic works adorned the walls, Albert Tucker, Sidney Nolan, Joy Hester. I had read that there had been many amorous love triangles amongst these artists and their benefactors, the Reeds. I could feel the sense of sex in the bedrooms.

When we'd finished, he took my hand and we walked to the restaurant. We were greeted by a smartly dressed waiter.

'Good afternoon, Mr. Darcy, Ms Maxwell, follow me.'

He took us through a side door and along a path lined with a high hedge, through a gate marked 'Private, no entry', into a lush secret garden. I was surprised when we were not seated inside the restaurant. I was utterly delighted to find a picnic rug laid out within the confines of what looked like a beautiful, private garden room.

'Everything you need is here,' said the waiter, as he pointed to the large wicker basket.

'If you wouldn't mind following me to the gate, Mr. Darcy, you can lock it to ensure complete privacy.'

I watched as Adam farewelled the young man and looked excitedly at Adam's smiling face as he walked back towards me.

'This is you, your idea, when did you organise it?' I said, elated by the sweet surprise.

'When you were on the computer this morning. I wanted to make today special,' he said, as he sat down and lovingly kissed me.

I unpacked the hamper grinning like a kid on Christmas morning. He popped the cork and poured me a champagne.

'This is special, thank you. I can't believe you thought to do this.'


As much as I loved this picnic, I was confused about his behaviour. I didn't like the way his anger boiled over, the way he had snapped at me earlier in the day.

After we had eaten, I lay back on the cushions strewn about the rug. Adam lay next to me, but I was reticent in my response to his kisses.

I hated the way I felt my protective wall coming up again.

'What's wrong?' he asked.

'Nothing, it's just that I feel a bit exposed here. I can hear the sounds of people in the park,' I lied.

We finished our lunch and he told me he had another surprise. He drove back into the city, we headed along busy Punt Road and turned into Walsh Street. We pulled up to a nondescript brush fence, walked through a gate and up a flight of stairs to the second storey entrance, a massive brick wall, set with high windows. Adam took out a key and opened the door. My eyes widened as I saw a beautiful mid-century modern house, built around a bright central garden courtyard.

'This was the family home of the architect Robin Boyd. It was built in 1959. I thought you might like it,' he said, smiling at my reaction.

I roamed through every room, it was as if the family had just stepped out. It was filled with furniture perfectly designed for the house. Featherston chairs, just like the one in Tim's painting and in the kitchen, a pair of Clement Meadmore stools, just like the ones I had in my old Brunswick flat.

'I used to have furniture like this. It all feels so familiar. How come you've got keys?' I said excitedly.

'I'm a member of the Robin Boyd Foundation. I can get access if I ask the right people,' he replied, smiling.

'One day I would like a place that uses these elements of light, space, proportion,' I said wistfully.

'You'll have to get to know an architect first,' he said smiling, a sense of humour returning.

'Yes, I will,' I said, as I approached him.

I kissed him passionately, my wall had come down. I reached for his groin and began to rub the cloth separating my hand from his skin. His cock stiffened and I undid the zip.

'This architect would be very handsomely rewarded,' I said, as I kneeled down in front of him.

Before I could open my mouth we were interrupted by the sound of keys in the front door. I hastily stood up, Adam pushed his stiff cock quickly back inside his trousers and pulled me in front of him to conceal his massive erection.

'Oh, sorry, I thought the house was empty. There's a function here tonight,' said a young man in chef's whites.

'It's ok, we were just leaving,' I said, as Adam frog marched me past the surprised man, his hard penis pushing against the small of my back.

We frantically scrambled into the car and giggled like teenagers who'd been caught out. Adam put the keys into the ignition and I sensed his urgency to get home, somewhere private.

'Wait, close your eyes,' I said, looking at him saucily.

He looked at me smiling quizzically and obeyed my command. In broad daylight I leaned over and unzipped him once again. He was still rock hard, I knew this wouldn't take long. I covered his cock with my mouth and began to move my head up and down, sucking hard to increase the sensation.

'Oh God,' he groaned and within minutes came, spurting hot salty blasts onto my tongue and down my throat. I swallowed and kept him in my mouth, sucking tenderly as he softened. I loved his taste, the feel of his flaccid, silken cock in my mouth. I sat up and looked at him, spent, eyes closed, his body relaxed in a post ecstatic state. I kissed him, aware that his cum still lingered in my mouth.

It was late in the afternoon, the sun low on the horizon, as we drove home. He asked me where I wanted to go. I told him I needed to get back to my place and I wanted him to stay. He told me he couldn't bear to leave.

# A Night In

My tiny flat was a stark contrast to his palatial apartment. He seemed big inside the small space, almost uncomfortable, didn't know where to put himself. It was the first time he'd been inside.

'Sit down. Make yourself at home,' I said, as I poured two glasses of Nero D'avola.

'You hungry?' I asked, as I sat next to him, taking the first sip.

'I'm starving,' he said.

'What do you feel like?'

'I feel like this,' he responded, taking the wine from my hand and placing both glasses on the side table.

He unzipped the back of my dress and laid me down on the divan.

'Today I am aware that our sex has been a little one sided. I think it's your turn.'

He removed my dress, then ran his hand up the inside of my thighs, slipping his fingers past the filmy lace, delicately parting my lips and pushing his fingers deep inside me. He removed his hand and I watched as he looked at the gossamer threads forming from my wetness, as he separated his fingers. My chest rose as I breathed deeply, aroused by the carnality of his gesture. He slipped my underwear off then undressed himself, his rigid thick cock taut with readiness. I lifted my knees letting my legs languidly fall apart, inviting him to play. He kissed my open mouth, our tongues briefly touching before he continued his journey down my body. He nuzzled my neck, then let his tongue tease the very tip of my nipples before sucking hard on each one bringing them to pert attention. He kissed my belly and stopped briefly to open my legs further. I felt his tongue on my labia, teasing, biting, pulling the delicate skin. I felt so aroused and wanted more. He used his rigid tongue to prise apart and explore every fold of my throbbing sex till he found my clitoris and began to suck gently as if it were a tiny nipple. He then gathered his fist to form a pointed phallus and pushed inside me until he felt me grip and squeeze the fingers that had entered. He responded by opening out his fingers stretching me wide, and played this game for a while until my breathing quickened and I pushed my pelvis harder against his strong arm, searching for the orgasm I so desperately ached for.

His other hand brushed over me, sensually teasing, spreading the wetness all over my thighs. Then he moved further along, circling my anus and using a single lubricated finger, started to push until the firmly closed muscle began to cede. I had never been entered this way and was shocked at the pleasure the slight pain gave me, awakening a sensitive and virginal part of my body. His mouth and hands worked their magic, my body and mind made that charged connection and I screamed as I convulsed in shear, blissful ecstasy.

When he felt my orgasm subside he edged his way back along the couch to hold me in his arms. He kissed me and I smelled the musky odour of my cunt on his lips. The libidinous me was not sated. I reached for his cock and it easily slipped inside, we fucked hard, frantically, till we both shared another satisfying orgasm. I loved the feel of his weight in and on top of me as his body slackened. His breathing slowed, he opened his eyes.

'Mmm...' he groaned huskily, the sound of a man completely satisfied.

'Thirsty?' he asked, as he got up and reached for our glasses of wine.

'Parched! Have you tried Nero D'avola before?' I asked.

'No. Italian?'

I filled my mouth with the wine and kissed him. He lapped it up as if it was nectar, swallowing, then licking the excess as it dribbled down my chin and right breast.

'Delicious,' he said, sighing contentedly.


'Hungry?' I asked.

'Starving, where would you like to go?'

'How about here? I've got a fridge full of food that should be eaten before I go away.'

'Thrifty and domesticated! Very sexy,' he said, smiling.

We showered. He wore his boxers and I tossed on an old tee shirt.

He sat next to me in the kitchen as I cooked. Some chicken, chorizo, potato, salt, garlic and a tin of tomatoes. While it sizzled away I made a fresh green salad and sliced some ciabatta. A bowl of olives and a chunk of parmesan kept him fed as I worked.

He loved watching her do this. None of the women he had dated could cook. He always ate out or had the hotel bring him his food. He loved this new intimacy. He loved her competency. He loved her. He couldn't help himself. His cock reacted to the innate sexiness of her and what she was doing. He got up and held her from behind, putting his hand under her loose shirt, grasping her breasts, nuzzling her neck. He pulled her hard against his body and she ground her backside into his throbbing cock. She arched her back as he eased her over the bench, exposing her firm bare ass. His hand roughly parted her legs. He saw her wet, glistening, ripe cunt and plunged his cock deep inside her, she moaned and he fucked her hard until she howled with pleasure. His desire for her was insatiable.

When they had finished, she stumbled back to the stove, steadied herself and took a deep breath. He watched as she served the food, he noticed his cum running down her leg. He got down on his knees, embraced her legs and licked her clean.

After dinner they threw on some clothes and wandered along Gertrude Street, just strolling hand in hand, like lovers do. It was a hot night and the street was full of people. It was vibrant, alive, just like her. They walked past Gabriella's gallery and peered through the windows. Called into the Workers Arms Hotel and drank a beer at the tables on the pavement, under the canopy of an ancient cedar tree. People who knew her nodded, she greeted them warmly. This was her territory. He could see why she liked it here and he liked it too. They walked contentedly back to her flat.

'How are you getting to the airport tomorrow?' asked Adam.

'The publishers have organised a driver,' I replied.

'Can I take you?'

'Really, it's not necessary. I'll be fine.'

'But I won't be, I can't bear the thought of you leaving.'

'I feel like it will make it more difficult to say goodbye.'

I saw the hurt in his eyes, it made him look so vulnerable.

'Of course you can take me, I'd love that.'

That night he made love to her with a tenderness and passion he had never known before. He held her against him as she slept. He breathed her in, she was his oxygen.

We woke at three am. He made me a coffee as I showered and got ready for the imminent departure. I didn't see him behind me as I attached a label to some luggage. I bumped him and the tepid cup of coffee spilled onto his trousers.

'Shit, sorry, I didn't see you. Are you ok?'

'All good. The coffee wasn't that hot, just very wet,' he said pulling the fabric away, uncomfortably, from his thighs.

'It's early, would you mind if I called into my place on the way to the airport so I can change?'

'Sure, we've got plenty of time.'

First class passengers got priority service. Gone were the days of long queues and tedious waits.

'Oh, by the way, here is my itinerary and contact details,' I said, handing him a sheet of paper.

The city was still asleep, the streets empty, the trip to his hotel only took a few minutes. We pulled into his private car park, an unfamiliar car occupied one of the spaces.

'Fuck!' groaned Adam, stressfully rubbing his forehead.

As soon as we stopped, the occupant got out of the car and thumped the window menacingly. It was Justin Darcy.

'Where the hell have you been! You turned off your fucking phone, you prick!' screamed a dishevelled Justin.

Adam opened his door and Justin shot me a filthy stare as he realised who was sitting next to his brother.

'WHAT THE FUCK IS THAT CUNT DOING HERE!' he shouted, as he slammed his clenched fist onto the roof of the car.

I flinched in fear and curled up into the corner of the seat, covering my face. Adam quickly got out of the car.

'ARE YOU SCREWING HER, YOU FUCKING TRAITOR! HAS SHE GOT HER GREEDY LITTLE HANDS ON YOU NOW?' saliva spraying, as he spat out the vicious words.

As if this wasn't terrifying enough, what happened next was worse. Instead of berating his almost catatonic brother, Adam firmly put his arm around Justin's shoulders and spoke apologetically, as he tried to calm his brother down, making excuses for having his phone turned off. I watched as Adam punched in his code and they both got into the lift.

I sat there shocked, abandoned, alone. After about twenty minutes I saw the down arrow on the lift light up. Adam must have calmed Justin enough to leave. Sam got out carrying Adam's keys.

'Sorry Tina, I hope you don't mind. The boss has asked me to drive you to the airport.

I felt so humiliated, hot tears stung my eyes. I stared out the window for the entire twenty minute trip. My phone did not ring.

Sam organised for me to be escorted through customs to the first class lounge. Eventually, I robotically boarded the plane.

I vaguely remembered being told I was being upgraded from a first class seat to a private suite. It would be good to hide away and wallow in my own self-pity.

James would be my personal steward for the entire trip. He asked if he could get me anything and I said he could make up the bed.


How could I have so stupidly wandered into such dangerous territory? A place that I loathed. A world where Adam's brother so obviously had control, a world inhabited by people I despised and a place haunted by my dead husband's ghost. All my insecurities returned, I was that other woman again. What a fool I had been to think that this could be ignored, that we could exist in a bubble. There would never be a future in this relationship. Adam's family, his brother would always come first.

My heart ached with the searing pain of what I had experienced and what I had lost. It would be good to get out of Australia, away from the trap I'd nearly walked into.

I took a sleeping tablet, curled up in my protective airline cocoon and let the plane rock me to sleep.

How dangerously close I had come to repeating past mistakes. I would never let anything like that happen again.

Follow Christina on her adventures with the sequels in the trilogy.

# Capturing the lost woman
(book two in the lost woman trilogy)

Christina visits America and sees her business expand beyond her wildest dreams. Amongst the success she receives some pertinent advice;

'Find someone to share the journey with.'
'Find a life away from work.'
'Find a place to escape to.'
'And lastly, have fun... '

Back in Melbourne things don't go to plan. Taking time out, she finds herself unexpectedly in the Tasmanian wilderness.

See who and what she discovers on her adventures.

# Finding the lost woman
(book three in the lost woman trilogy)

Success is not all it seems. Christina needs to look deeply into her soul to begin to understand how she now wants to live her life.

In her search for meaning she finds herself in the most unlikely of places. Discover who she encounters at the end of her quest.

*Available by order from most book shops, buy on-line at Amazon, or as eBook from Amazon, Google Books, Kobo and iBooks.*

*For more information go to* <u>annabuckley.com</u>

www.ingramcontent.com/pod-product-compliance
Lightning Source LLC
Chambersburg PA
CBHW061515020726
47502CB00006B/2086